MacCallister
THE STALKING DEATH

MacCallister
THE STALKING DEATH

William W. Johnstone
with J. A. Johnstone

PINNACLE BOOKS
Kensington Publishing Corp.
www.kensingtonbooks.com

PINNACLE BOOKS are published by

Kensington Publishing Corp.
119 West 40th Street
New York, NY 10018

Copyright © 2018 J. A. Johnstone

All rights reserved. No part of this book may be reproduced in any form or by any means without the prior written consent of the publisher, excepting brief quotes used in reviews.

To the extent that the image or images on the cover of this book depict a person or persons, such person or persons are merely models, and are not intended to portray any character or characters featured in the book.

PUBLISHER'S NOTE
Following the death of William W. Johnstone, the Johnstone family is working with a carefully selected writer to organize and complete Mr. Johnstone's outlines and many unfinished manuscripts to create additional novels in all of his series like The Last Gunfighter, Mountain Man, and Eagles, among others. This novel was inspired by Mr. Johnstone's superb storytelling.

If you purchased this book without a cover, you should be aware that this book is stolen property. It was reported as "unsold and destroyed" to the publisher, and neither the author nor the publisher has received any payment for this "stripped book."

All Kensington titles, imprints, and distributed lines are available at special quantity discounts for bulk purchases for sales promotions, premiums, fund-raising, educational, or institutional use. Special book excerpts or customized printings can also be created to fit specific needs. For details, write or phone the office of the Kensington sales manager: Kensington Publishing Corp., 119 West 40th Street, New York, NY 10018, attn: Sales Department; phone 1-800-221-2647.

PINNACLE BOOKS, the Pinnacle logo, and the WWJ steer head logo are Reg. U.S. Pat. & TM Off.

ISBN-13: 978-0-7860-4006-3
ISBN-10: 0-7860-4006-8

First printing: April 2018

10 9 8 7 6 5 4 3 2 1

Printed in the United States of America

First electronic edition: April 2018

ISBN-13: 978-0-7860-4007-0
ISBN-10: 0-7860-4007-6

Chapter One

Wynton Miller was a fastidious dresser and a man who took pride in his personal appearance. Whereas other men who drifted sought out a saloon as soon as they entered a new town, Miller sought a bath, and if he needed a haircut or a shave, he tended to that as well. His speech was that of an educated man and in every way he presented himself as a professional.

His profession was killing. Wynton Miller was very good with a gun, some said that he was the best there was, and for three years he capitalized on that by putting his skill out for hire. Nobody knew exactly how many men he had killed; some said it was as high as twenty.

Miller made good money by selling his gun because he was seldom hired unless the one who needed killing was, in his own right, a skilled shootist. In many cases his victims were officers of the law who had gotten in the way of whatever evil schemes Miller's employers had in mind.

Then the time came when Miller was no more.

Had he been killed? Had he taken his money and gone east? Had he gone to Europe? Where was he?

The law was after him, but they had always been unsuccessful in their search. Those who lived on the opposite side of the law, men who for one reason or another might have need for Wynton Miller's service, had always been able to find him. But even they had no idea of what had become of him.

Wynton Miller disappeared from sight, but not from legend.

Valley of the Chug, Wyoming

Although men of action who were respected by Duff MacCallister, men such as his cousin Falcon MacCallister and his friends Smoke and Matt Jensen had told him that "making the first shot count" is more important than speed, Duff felt that the time had come for him to increase his skill in the use of the pistol. There was no marksmanship instruction necessary—Duff already had the reputation of being a marksman without peer, having demonstrated that on many previous occasions.

"But it has been an observation o' mine that the rapid extraction of a pistol from its holster is a necessary skill that is nearly equal with the accuracy of shooting," Duff explained to his friend Elmer.

"You may be right," Elmer agreed. "I've seen you drive a nail into a post from a hundred feet away, 'n I ain't never seen no one else who could shoot nowhere as good as you can. But if you could draw faster, why, there wouldn't be nobody who could ever come close to you."

"Would you be for havin' any idea how I might acquire such a skill?"

"I guess you could just practice a lot 'n . . ." Elmer started, then he stopped and smiled. "Wang," he said.

For just a moment, Duff was surprised by the suggestion, then he smiled and nodded.

"Aye, 'tis a good suggestion, Elmer. I believe Wang would be a very good person to teach such a skill."

Some might have thought it strange that Wang Chow, who had never fired a pistol in his life, could be helpful in assisting Duff MacCallister further develop his skills with a pistol, but both Elmer and Duff knew that Wang would be ideal for what Duff needed. That was because they were both aware of Wang's unique background as a Shaolin priest and a man of incredible skill in the martial arts.

Wang revenged the death of his family back in China by killing the fifteen men involved. Upon hearing about the carnage caused by Wang, the Changlin Temple expelled him from their order, and the Empress Dowager Ci'an issued a decree ordering his death. Disguised, Wang left China with a group of laborers who were coming to America to work on the railroad.

It was one year later when Duff MacCallister saw Wang for the first time. Wang was sitting on a horse, his hands were tied behind his back, and a noose was around his neck. He was about to be lynched for driving a surrey with a white woman sitting on the seat beside him.

Believing this to be unjust, Duff pulled his pistol and approached the lynch party.

"Who the hell are you?" one of the men asked.

"I would like to talk to your prisoner."

"What do you mean you want to talk to him? This here ain't none of your business."

Duff pointed his pistol at the men, then he turned to the Chinese man who was sitting quietly in the saddle, awaiting his fate.

"Do you speak English?" Duff asked.

"I speak English."

"What is your name?"

"I am Wang Chow."

"Wang, it seems like every Chinaman I've ever known is a good cook. Are you a good cook?"

"Here! What the hell is all this?" the man holding the rope asked. "We're about to hang this son of a bitch, and you want to know if he is a good cook?"

"Please, don't interrupt my interview with this man."

"Your interview?"

Duff cocked the pistol and pointed it straight at the man's head. "I asked you, nicely, not to interrupt my interview."

The man put both hands up, palms facing out, fingers spread wide. "All right, all right, I ain't a-stoppin' you. Go ahead and talk to him."

"Mr. Wang, I am thinking about hiring a cook. Are you a good cook?"

"I am very sorry, but I am not a good cook," Wang admitted.

"I admire your courage and your honesty. All you would have to say is that you are a good cook, and that would save you from being hanged. So, let me ask you this. If I hired you as my cook, would you be willing to learn?"

"Yes, I will learn to be a very good cook."

"Mr. Wang, my name is MacCallister. Duff MacCallister. And you are hired."

Duff turned to the man who had been the spokesman for the group. "As you can see I do have a vested interest in the fate of this gentleman, since he is now one of my employees. And I would be very disturbed if someone tried to do something such as . . . well, let's just say, hang him. Now untie his hands."

"The hell we will!" one of the three men shouted and, jerking his gun from his holster, he snapped a shot toward Duff and missed. Duff returned fire, and didn't miss.

"You can either untie Mr. Wang now, or I will kill both of you and untie him myself."

"Untie him, Floyd, untie him!" one of the two remaining men shouted in fear.

"That will not be necessary," Wang said, bringing both hands around front to show that they weren't tied.

From that moment on, Wang had been a loyal and valued friend and employee, utilizing his martial arts skills reluctantly, but willingly when needed in defense of Duff or Elmer.

"I do not know how to draw a gun, and I have never shot one," Wang said when Duff approached him with the request that Wang help him learn a fast draw.

"That is nae a problem," Duff said. "I know how to draw a gun, and I know how to shoot it. What I need to know is how to do so quite rapidly. That means I must know how to move my hands very quickly, 'n, Wang, m' friend, never in my life have I seen anyone who could move their hands more quickly than you. That speed of the hand is the skill I wish to learn. Do you think you can teach me?"

"Yes," Wang said. "I can teach you."

For the next several days, Wang devised drills that would increase Duff's hand speed. One such drill, that he had learned while in the Shaolin Temple of Changlin, was to hold a coin in the palm of his hand and have Duff snatch the coin before he could close his hand.

Duff's first several tries were painfully slow.

"Do not think, here," Wang said, putting his finger to Duff's head. "Think here." He put his finger to Duff's hand.

"'N would you be for telling me, lad, how 'tis that the hand, that has no brain, can be thinking, now?"

"If you think in your head first, the head must then tell the hand that it is to move. It is not until then that the hand moves. But if you let the hand move without being told to do so by the head, the hand will move much faster."

"Here now, 'n how can such a thing be?"

Wang put the coin in the palm of Duff's hand.

"I will not reach for the coin until you start to close your hand," Wang said.

"That is nae possible. You dinnae begin to close your hand until after you saw me start to reach, but still I could nae grab the coin. And now you say you will nae try for the coin until *after* you see me start to close my hand?"

"Yes."

Duff smiled. "All right, my friend, I hate to do this to you but 'twill be good for m' soul to see someone else fail after I have failed so many times."

Wang bent his arm at the elbow and held the palm of his hand toward Duff with the fingers extended forward, clawlike.

Duff waited for a couple of seconds, then he snapped his fingers closed around the coin. Wang didn't move until Duff started to close his hand. Wang's hand returned, with his own fist closed.

"Ha!" Duff said. "Dinnae get the coin, did you? Well, don't feel bad about it. You gave yourself an impossible task."

"Return the coin to me," Wang said.

"Aye, 'twill be a pleasure." Triumphantly, Duff opened the hand that had held the coin.

The hand was empty.

"What?" he shouted in shock.

Wang opened his hand to show the coin.

"How did you do that?"

"I let the hand think," Wang replied.

One month later, after going through a series of drills, Duff was able to snatch the coin from Wang's hand, ten times out of ten, not beginning his own move until Wang started to close his fist around the coin he was holding.

It took but a week to apply that newly acquired skill to drawing a pistol, doing it so fast that to the observer the actual draw couldn't even be seen.

"Duff," Elmer said after watching Duff draw with lightning speed and shoot with unerring accuracy, "You are twice as fast as the fastest man I have ever seen. 'N I've seen the best. No," he added with a smile. "I am seeing the best."

Chapter Two

Under a leaden gray sky and swollen clouds, the stagecoach rolled westward, the passengers inside cushioned from the imperfections in the road by the thoroughbraces that absorbed the shocks. They were passing between thickets of brush, mixed with sumac and spruce. Occasionally a deer or a coyote would come to the edge of the road to watch them pass.

Thunder muttered sullenly above the rolling hills, and lightning played across the sky.

"Hope that lightnin' don't get too close," the man riding alongside the driver said.

"Afeared of lightnin', are you?" the driver asked. He had identified himself as G. F. Guy, and the man riding beside him was a passenger who had volunteered to ride up top, because the coach was full.

"Damn right I am," the passenger replied, punctuating his comment with a spit that squirted brown tobacco juice over the spinning front wheel. "Some years ago when I was helpin' to bring a herd up from Texas, I seen a feller that got hit by lightnin' oncet. It knocked 'im right off his horse. Kilt 'im, too."

"Yeah, well, it seems off a ways, so I don't reckon we'll have any problems with it," Guy said, holding the six-horse team to a steady trot.

Duff MacCallister and Wang Chow were two of six people who were inside the coach. Duff was by the window, Wang was in the middle, and a whiskey drummer was on the other side of Wang. Across from Duff was an attractive young mother with two children, a boy of about twelve and a girl of about ten.

Duff and Wang were returning to Chugwater, Wyoming, from Bordeaux, Wyoming, where Duff had bought a new saddle for his horse, and Wang purchased a set of knives for the kitchen at Sky Meadow. The saddle and knives were on top of the coach.

The whiskey drummer had been talking ceaselessly about places he had been and things he had done.

"I saw Wynton Miller once," he said. "Yes, sir, it was in the Long Branch Saloon in Dodge City, Kansas. Chalk Beeson, he owns the Long Branch, you know, is a good customer of mine. Anyhow, I was in the Long Branch when Wynton Miller came in.

"'Angus Quince?' he calls. Angus Quince was a bounty hunter and real good with a gun, so a bunch of outlaws got together and hired Miller to go after him.

"'Yeah, I'm Angus Quince,' a man says from the other end of the bar.

"Miller, now, he was dressed all in black, with a real low-crown black hat that had a silver band around it. I remember that silver band.

"'I'm Wynton Miller,' he says. 'And I have been hired by a group of men who find your profession as a bounty hunter to be abhorrent to them. They have asked me to put an end to it.'

"'Wynton Miller, you say,' Quince says back to him. 'Well, now, there's quite a reward out for you.'

"'You'll never collect one dollar of it,' Miller says.

"And with that, Quince went for his gun, drawing it quick as lightning, but Miller was even faster, 'n when the smoke cleared, Quince was lyin' dead on the floor of the Long Branch."

"Sir, I wish you wouldn't tell such horrible stories in front of the children," the woman passenger said.

"That's all right, Mama," the boy said with a big smile. "I think it was a real excitin' story."

"I beg your pardon, ma'am," the drummer said, lifting his hat briefly.

"Where is Wynton Miller now?" the boy asked.

"Nobody knows," the drummer replied. "He hasn't been heard from in three or four years. Most people think he is dead."

"Is it going to rain, Mama?" the little girl asked.

"It certainly looks like it," the attractive young mother replied, thankful that the subject had been changed.

"We'll get wet."

"No, we won't," the little boy said. "We can close the curtain 'n the rain can't get in."

"What if the other people won't close their curtain?"

"Sure, 'n if it starts to rain, I'll be for closing my curtain, too, so you'll not be getting wet," Duff said.

"You talk funny," the little girl said.

"Emma Lou, that's a terrible thing for you to say!" Emma Lou's mother scolded.

"There is no harm done, ma'am. 'Tis sure I am that the Scottish brogue that rolls off m' tongue, sounds a bit queer to the wee lass."

"I didn't mean bad funny," Emma Lou said, trying to make amends.

"'N it wasn't bad the way I took it," Duff said.

"We're going to see Gramma," the little girl said. "She lives in Chugwater."

"Does she now? Chugwater is a mighty foine place, with many good people. If your nana lives there then she must be a good person, too, especially to have a pretty wee lass like you as a granddaughter."

"Do you like pie?" Emma Lou asked.

"Aye, pie is one of my favorite things."

"What kind do you like best?"

"Oh, cherry, I think. 'N what would be your favorite?"

"I like anything my gramma makes. She has a store in Chugwater where she makes pies."

"Tell me, lass, your nana wouldn't be Mrs. Vi Winslow, now, would she?"

"You know my mother?" the woman asked, surprised by Duff's comment.

"Aye, but then Mrs. Winslow's pies are so good that everyone knows her."

Suddenly there was the sound of gunfire outside, and the coach came to a quick stop.

"Oh! What's happening?" the woman asked.

Someone's head appeared in the window of the coach. The face was covered with a hood. "Everybody out," he ordered, brandishing a pistol. He jerked the door open and Duff and the others had to step outside. In addition to the man who had ordered the coach emptied, there were two more masked men, both of whom were mounted. And like the man on the ground, they held pistols.

"Now, you, driver, throw down the bank pouch," the man on the ground ordered.

"What makes you think we're carrying a bank pouch?" the driver replied.

"I ain't a-tellin' you again. Throw that bank pouch down."

"And I told you, we ain't carryin' a bank pouch," G. F. Guy insisted.

Without so much as another word, the outlaw shot the old cowhand who had been riding beside the driver. Hit in the head, the man tumbled across the wheel, falling to the ground. It took but one glance to know that he was dead.

"Maybe you'll listen to me now."

"Mister, you done kilt a innocent man there for no good reason," the driver replied, the fear in his voice evident. "I told you, we ain't a-carryin' nothin' of any value."

The masked man turned his pistol toward Wang.

"No, don't shoot the Chinaman," one of the mounted robbers said. "There don't nobody give a damn if a Chinaman gets kilt. Grab the little girl. If he don't throw the pouch down, kill her. 'N if that don't work, we'll kill the boy."

"No! Take me instead!" Emma Lou's mother shouted.

As the coach robber on the ground reached toward Emma Lou, neither he, nor either of the riders, noticed the almost imperceptible nod between Duff and Wang. Then, moving so quickly that it was done before any of the three outlaws realized what was happening, Wang brought the knife edge of his hand against the back of the outlaw's neck, and he went down. Even as the outlaw was going down, Duff drew his pistol.

"What the hell? Kill 'em! Kill 'em all!" one of the two mounted outlaws shouted.

The two men raised their guns, but neither of them got so much as a single shot off. Duff fired twice, and the saddles of both horses were emptied.

Emma Lou had rushed to her mother's side and wrapped her arms around her. Her brother, rather than being frightened, clapped his hands in glee.

"You killed both of them!" he said. "They sure made a mistake tryin' to steal from us, didn't they?"

"That they did, sonny, that they did," the drummer said. He looked at Duff. "Mister, I don't know who you are, but I'll tell you true, I believe you're near 'bout as fast as Wynton Miller." He pointed to the man Wang had hit. "I suggest we tie this one up before he comes to."

"He will not wake," Wang said.

"What do you mean he won't wake up? He wasn't shot."

"His neck is broken," Wang said.

"How can you be sure about that?"

"I am the one who broke his neck."

"Just by hittin' 'im like that?"

"Mister, I have seen Wang break boards, one inch thick," Duff said. He pointed to the man on the ground. "'Tis for sure this man will nae be waking up."

"What are we goin' to do with 'em?" the driver asked. "We can't just leave 'em here, on the road."

"Would ye be for knowin' the name of the cowhand?" Duff asked.

"Yeah, we was talkin' quite a bit. I don' know his last name, but he tole me to call 'im Billy. He's a rider for the Pitchfork brand. That is, he was," the driver added.

"We'll put him on top of the coach, for now, 'n when we get back to Chugwater we'll send word to Mr. Allen out at Pitchfork. 'Tis sure, I am, that he'll be wanting to make some arrangements for the burial of his hand."

"What about these here others?" the driver asked. "Think we should throw 'em up there with Billy?"

"Nae, Billy was a good mon," Duff said. "I would nae wish to make him have to enter the hereafter with such brigands. We'll throw their bodies across their horses, then tie the horses onto the back of the coach."

The arrival of a stagecoach always drew attention from the citizens, but this time nearly half the town turned out, their curiosity aroused by the three horses, each horse with a body belly down over the saddle.

Sheriff Sharpie approached the coach as soon as it stopped, and he looked toward the bodies.

"You didn't take the hoods off?" he asked.

"I dinnae want the wee ones to have to see their faces," Duff said.

Sheriff Sharpie nodded. "Yeah, I reckon I can see that. I'll take 'em on down to Mr. Welsh. Looks like the county will be paying for the burials."

"The man on top o' the coach is named Billy 'n rides for the Pitchfork brand," Duff said. "I expect Dale Allen will pay for his burial."

"Billy? Oh, that must be Billy Hughes. A good man, he's been with Mr. Allen for a long time, so I expect he will want to make the arrangements. I'll send Deputy Logan out to the Pitchfork and let them know what happened."

"You said you were going to get some pie," Emma Lou said.

"Aye, lass, that I did. 'N what about you, Johnny? Will you be wanting some pie as well?"

Johnny was Emma Lou's older brother, and Duff had gotten to know the whole family better, for the last few miles of the trip.

"I like pie," Johnny replied with a broad smile.

Fifteen minutes later Duff, Wang, Ethel Mae Joyce and her two children, Johnny and Emma Lou, were seated around a table at Vi's Pies. Mr. Jordan, the drummer, declined the invitation to join them, because he had business to attend to.

"Emma Lou told me that you liked cherry pie the best," Vi said. "But didn't I already know that, the way you go through a piece whenever you and Elmer pay me a visit? And Wang, fried bow ties and honey for you."

Wang smiled and dipped his head. "A thousand thanks, Madam Vi," he said.

"I'm so thankful to the two of you for saving the lives of Ethel Mae and my two grandchildren," Vi said.

"'Tis sorry I am about the violence in front of the wee ones," Duff said.

"Oh, don't be silly, Mr. MacCallister," Ethel Mae said. "I'm just thankful that you and Mr. Wang were on the coach. Why, there's no telling what might have happened if you hadn't been."

As Duff, Wang, and the others enjoyed the dessert provided by Vi Winslow, down at the opposite end of the street, several people were gathered around the three upright coffins, each occupied by the body of the would-be stagecoach robbers.

"I don't know what ever give them the idea that Jim Bob was carryin' a bank pouch," one of the onlookers said.

"I don't know, neither. All I know is, it's a good thing Duff MacCallister 'n that Chinaman that works for him was on the coach, or more 'n likely that little girl woulda been kilt. 'N Mr. Guy, too, I'm a-thinkin'."

"You know who that feller there, in the middle is, don't you?" one of the crowd asked, pointing toward the center of the three coffins. "That there is Zeke Bodine."

"Zeke Bodine? The gunfighter?"

"Yes, 'n he's got 'im a brother, Lucien Bodine, who's even faster."

"If you want to talk about fast, what about MacCallister? The stagecoach driver told me that the two men he shot already had their pistols drawed but that didn't make no nevermind to MacCallister. He drawed his own pistol 'n shot 'em afore it was that they could do anything."

"More 'n likely, Bodine's brother is goin' to raise some hell when he hears about this."

"Yeah, but that's liable to be a while. I hear tell that he's down in Texas now. Or maybe it's New Mexico or Arizona. I ain't quite sure where it is, but I just know for sure that he ain't nowhere close around here."

As Duff and Wang were leaving Vi's Pies, they saw Dale Allen, owner of the Pitchfork Ranch. Though not as large as Sky Meadow, Pitchfork was quite large and employed a dozen full-time hands. Allen was driving by in a buckboard, but he stopped when he saw Duff.

"I heard you were on the stage when Billy got hisself killed," Allen said.

"Aye, I was."

"Nothin' you coulda done to stop it, I don't suppose."

"I'm sorry. 'Twas no way to know that the brigand was about to shoot your mon."

"No, I don't reckon there was," Allen said. "Mr. Guy told me what happened, 'n how you saved the little girl. I'm glad you were able to do that."

"'Twas Wang who saved the lass."

"Yes, well, what's done is done. And I'm damn glad that the son of a bitch who kilt Billy is dead now. I thank you for that."

Allen nodded at Duff, who returned the nod, then Allen slapped the reins on the back of his team, and the buckboard jumped ahead.

* * *

When Duff and Wang returned to Sky Meadow, Duff's ranch, they were met by Elmer Gleason.

"Well, that's a good-lookin' saddle you bought while you was over in Bordeaux," Elmer said, running his hand across the tooled leather. "And what about you, Wang? Did you get the knives you wanted?"

"Very good knives."

"You won't be sneakin' up on me to cut my throat in the middle of the night, will you?"

"You do not need to worry," Wang said.

"Yeah, so you say. But who can trust a heathen?"

"You will not feel a thing."

Duff and Elmer laughed.

"Oh, did you hear about Clifford Potts?" Elmer asked.

"Aye, I heard that he passed."

"Well, it warn't no surprise to no one, bein' as he's been at death's door for two or three months now," Elmer said.

"I'll be attending his funeral," Duff said.

"Yeah, me, too. He was a good man."

Chapter Three

Sulphur Springs, Texas

Brad Houser was quite vain about his appearance. He bathed frequently, he kept his blond hair neatly trimmed, and he was clean-shaven. Most women found him a handsome man when first seeing him, but upon closer observation there was something about him that was off-putting. Though few could put it in words, they believed it was something about his eyes.

His eyes were a very pale blue, but, as a woman once said when describing him, "His eyes don't let you see into his soul. They are like the eyes of a perfect portrait . . . without life."

At the moment, a man named Robert Dempster was in Brad Houser's office. An attorney-at-law, Houser was one of only two lawyers in town, and he represented the Bank of Sulphur Springs, which was owned by Dempster.

"One hundred thousand dollars," Robert Dempster said, a broad smile spreading across his face.

"That's the most money we have ever had, at any one time."

"Bob, have you told anyone else how much money you have on hand?"

"Of course I have. Why, it'll be in the newspaper this afternoon. Something like that is good advertising."

"Yes, I suppose it is," Houser agreed.

Not long after Dempster left, Houser had another visitor to his office. Like Houser, the visitor had blond hair, but unlike Houser, his hair was long and unkempt. He had a purple and disfiguring scar that started just above his left eyebrow, darted down through the eyelid, sparing the eyeball but reappearing in the lower aspect of the socket, and ending just above the cheekbone.

"I was almost unable to locate you," Houser said to the man who was now sitting in the same chair that Robert Dempster had occupied a short time earlier. "I didn't know what name you had taken."

"I wrote you a letter 'n told you I'd changed my name to Shamrock."

"I didn't open the letter and didn't even think about it until the letter I sent you came back undeliverable. Shamrock, like the clover? How did you come by such a name?"

"I seen a saloon that was called the Shamrock Saloon, 'n I just likened the sound of it so I taken it for my own name. Anyhow, I don't know why you're so surprised. After you got me off that last charge, you told me I should change my name."

"Indeed I did tell you that," Houser said. "Your real name had accumulated too much opprobrium."

"What does that mean?"

"It means that people connected your name to the evil things you had done."

"Like the name you used for a while? What do you think people thought when they heard *that* name?"

"That was no more my real name than this one is," Houser said. "I not only shed myself of that name, I have also abandoned the persona of my former self. I take it that you have done the same thing. Is Shamrock your first or last name?"

"It's my last name. Sid is my first name. Sid Shamrock."

Houser nodded.

"What'd you send for me for? I thought you said you didn't want me comin' round no more. You told me to keep away."

"Yes, but I also told you to keep in touch with me, so I could get ahold of you if it became necessary."

"Yeah, well, you done that, 'n here I am. What is it you're a-wantin'?"

"Have you any money?"

"What? No, I ain't got no money. That is, I don't have none to speak of. You're a big rich lawyer, what are you askin' me that for? You wantin' to make the borry of some money? 'Cause if you do, you done come to the wrong person."

"I don't wish to borrow any money. I asked you about the state of your finances to see if you would be interested in a job I have for you."

"A job? You mean a job like goin' to work ever' day?"

"No. I mean a job that will pay you ten thousand dollars."

"Ten thousand dollars?" Shamrock said, fairly shouting the words. "You've got a job for me that pays ten thousand dollars?"

"Why don't you go outside and shout it in the street?" Houser invited.

"Why do you want me to do that?" Shamrock asked, clearly confused by the suggestion.

"Never mind. Actually, I will pay you fifteen thousand," Houser said. "I expect you to find someone to work with, and you can pay him five thousand."

"Who do you want me to kill?"

"I don't want you to kill anyone. As a matter of fact, if you do kill someone in the course of this job, you won't get one . . . red . . . cent."

"All right, all right, I won't kill nobody. What is the job?"

"I want you to rob the Bank of Sulphur Springs."

"Are you kidding? You want me to rob a bank in your own hometown? I thought you was always a-sayin' you didn't want me to be doin' nothin' anywhere close to where it was that you was a-livin'."

"Yes, because neither your skills nor your demeanor are sufficient to the task of keeping my name out of it. But this is a job I have conceived myself, and if you follow my instructions explicitly, you will make yourself a tidy sum of money, and you won't be in danger. But of course you must leave town immediately and never return."

"Yeah, all right, I can do that. Leave town, I mean. But what does expilla . . . explea . . . uh, whatever it is that word you say that I'm supposed to follow?"

"It merely means that you are to do everything I say."

"All right."

Two days later, Brad Houser spent the afternoon with Arnold Stone, a nearby rancher who was a client of his. Houser had helped him draw up a will.

"You've done quite well for yourself, Mr. Stone," Houser said as he examined the figures.

"Yes, well, I came here right after the war, was able to get the land for a song, and then make a gather of cattle that, during the war, had run free 'n started multiplying."

"So ranching can be quite a lucrative profession."

"Well, if you got into it early enough, yes." Stone shook his head. "Not that many opportunities left here in Texas now. If a man really wanted to get a start now, why, he'd have to go someplace like Wyoming, or Utah, or the Dakotas, I would think."

"Interesting observation," Houser replied. He put the papers he had been working on in a small satchel. "You come into town sometime next week, Mr. Stone, and I'll have these papers ready."

"Thanks. And thanks for coming out here to work on this for me. You didn't have to, you know. I would have been glad to come into town."

"I didn't mind at all," Houser said.

In Sulphur Springs, Sid Shamrock and Abe Sobel waited outside the bank.

"It's near to four o'clock now," Shamrock said.

"Brad told me that the teller leaves at four 'n locks up, but Dempster, the banker, stays there until 'bout four-thirty. So when we see the teller leave, we'll go in."

"How are we going to get in, if the bank is locked?"

Shamrock smiled and held up a key. "This'll get us in," he said.

Abe didn't ask how Shamrock came by the key.

"Look there, he's about to come out," Shamrock said, pointing across the street.

They watched as shades were pulled down in each of the two front windows and in the door. A sign, reading CLOSED, was turned around, then a man stepped through the door, locked it, and walked away.

"Wait till he gets around the corner," Shamrock said.

A moment later, when the street was clear, Shamrock and Abe hurried across, unlocked the door, then stepped into the bank.

"What did you forget, Lee?" Dempster called without looking around. He was standing in front of the open vault.

"Put your hands up," Shamrock called out.

Dempster put his hand on the vault door, as if to close it, and Shamrock pulled the hammer back on his pistol.

"You close that door and you are a dead man," Shamrock said menacingly.

Dempster jerked his hand away.

"What do you want?"

"I want you to put all the money into this gunny-sack," Shamrock said, pulling the sack from inside his shirt and tossing it toward him.

It took less than a couple of minutes for the sack to be filled. Shamrock took the bag from him, then hit Dempster over the head with the butt of his pistol. Dempster went down.

"Damn! You didn't kill him, did you?"

"Nah, I didn't hit 'im that hard. Just put 'im to sleep is all."

The two men went out the back door of the bank. One block behind the bank they mounted their horses that had been inconspicuously tied at a hitching rail in front of a saloon.

Houser was returning to town to prepare the document. One mile from town, as had been arranged, he reached the intersection of two roads, one running east and west between Sulphur Springs and Phantom Hill, the other north to Albany and south to Belle Plain. He examined his watch, and if everything had gone as planned, he would be meeting Shamrock here. He saw two riders approaching. They were coming fast, and they reined up when they came even with him. This was as expected, and Houser pulled up on the reins to the horse that was drawing the surrey.

One of the riders was Sid Shamrock, but Houser didn't know the other rider.

"Did you have any trouble?" Houser asked.

Shamrock smiled. "Nah, it was like you said, there warn't no one but the banker, all by hisself when we was there, 'n he didn't give us no trouble at all. Abe Sobel, this here is my brother, Brad Houser. He's the one that set this up for us."

"No!" Houser said, holding up his hand. "Say no more. The less everyone knows, the better it is."

"All right, I won't say nothin' more."

"Where's the money?"

"Here it is," Shamrock said, handing the gunny-sack to Houser.

Houser opened the sack and looked into it. Some of the money was in loose bills, but much of it was in bound stacks of twenty-dollar bills, fifty to a stack. He took out fifteen stacks and gave them to Shamrock.

"Looks to me like there's more 'n fifteen thousand dollars left in that sack," Shamrock said. "How much did we get?"

"You got fifteen thousand dollars, the agreed-upon amount," Houser said. "Whatever remains is none of your concern. Now, I suggest you two divide up your share, then separate here, at this intersection. Oh, and Thomas, uh, I mean Sid, we don't need to meet, ever again."

"Here's the thousand dollars I promised you," Shamrock said, giving one of the bound stacks to Abe.

"Seeing as you got fifteen thousand, one thousand doesn't seem right."

"It's like the feller said," Shamrock said. "One thousand dollars was what I said I'd give you. Hell, what are you bitchin' for? How much money did you have when you woke up this mornin'?"

Abe nodded and reached for the money. "I reckon you have a point," he said.

Houser had intended for the man Shamrock found to get five thousand, not one thousand dollars. But if Abe was satisfied with a thousand, who was he to comment? That would just mean more money for his brother and a greater likelihood that he would never have to see, nor hear, from his brother again. A prospect that he found most agreeable.

"I expect you two had better get going," Houser said. "I'm quite sure there will be a posse along, soon. Oh, and I would suggest that you separate here."

"Yeah," Shamrock said to the other rider. "Come on, let's go."

The two men left, Shamrock going north and the other rider continuing to the west.

No more than five minutes later Houser saw Sheriff Peach and a body of men coming toward him. He stopped the team.

"Mr. Houser, what are you doing out here?" Sheriff Peach asked.

"I had a meeting with Mr. Stone, who is a client of mine. What is it, what is going on? If I didn't know better, I'd say this looks like a posse."

"It is a posse," Sheriff Peach said. "The bank was just robbed."

"The bank? Oh my goodness, that's awful!" Houser said. "Wait, you wouldn't be after two men, would you? I thought they were riding awfully fast."

"Yes! One of them had a scar, here, 'n the other was wearin' a white hat and a red shirt. Is that who you saw?"

Houser shook his head. "That's exactly who I saw." Houser pointed behind him. "I was just approaching the Phantom Hill and Belle Plains intersection. As I said, they were riding very fast, and they took the road south, to Belle Plains."

"Thanks, Mr. Houser, we appreciate it," Sheriff Peach said. "Come on, men!"

Peach and the ten men in the posse swerved around the surrey and continued west, toward the intersection. With a smile, Houser snapped the reins, and the horse pulling the surrey started out again at a comfortable trot.

In his room that night, Houser counted the money. If there was $100,000 as there was supposed to be, he should have $85,000 in the bag. To his pleasant and unexpected surprise, he had $88,297.

He closed the bag and contemplated his next move. He couldn't stay in Sulphur Springs—there would be no way he could justify his sudden influx of cash. He was going to have to leave town . . . but he couldn't just pull up stakes and leave, either, for to do so might arouse suspicion. He needed a reason to leave, and as he sat there, he knew what he was going to do.

Even though the boardinghouse where he stayed furnished a cleaning lady, he was not concerned that anyone would discover the money. He had pulled three boards away from the wall, put the money inside the wall, then replaced the boards. Even a most careful observation couldn't detect any anomaly with the boards.

Chapter Four

The money was safely hidden and Shamrock and Abe had managed to avoid being caught by the posse, so there were was no way to make any connection between Houser and the bank robbery. All Houser had to do now was find some way to leave town without arousing suspicion. Three weeks after the robbery took place he put his plan into operation. Making his move, he waited for the summons. It came, as he expected it would, the very next day after he put it in motion.

"You sent for me, Your Honor?" Houser asked, standing in front of Judge Marshal Craig.

The judge, who was a tall, lean man with a full head of white hair, shook his head and made a clucking sound.

"Brad, Brad, Brad. I am so disappointed in you," the judge said.

"Disappointed in me? Why, what are you talking about, Your Honor? I don't understand."

"This is the affidavit that you gave to George

Gilmore, is it not?" Judge Craig said, pushing a form across the desk.

"Oh," Houser said quietly.

"You did sign this, didn't you?"

Houser sighed. "I . . . I'm not sure."

"Mr. Houser." Judge Craig had dropped the first name. "It is a simple question. Did you sign this affidavit that you presented to another lawyer, knowing even as you signed it, that it was a lie, or didn't you? And I remind you, Mr. Houser, that in the time I have been a judge, I have seen your signature a hundred times or more. So I ask you again. Did you sign this affidavit?"

"What . . . what is going to happen?" Houser asked quietly; the question, and the expression in his voice, admitting the guilt.

Judge Craig pulled the document back across his desk and looked at it for a moment as he shook his head.

"You are a lawyer, Mr. Houser, and you have been a very good one. To be honest with you, I was grooming you to take my place someday. But after this"—he took in the paper on his desk with a casual wave of his hand—"after this, that is no longer possible. Surely you're aware that for committing such an act as falsifying an affidavit, you could go to prison for up to five years," he said.

"What? Your Honor, surely you aren't going to send me to prison!"

"I don't want to. And it was caught so quickly there was no real damage done as a result of the false filing. Why did you do such a thing, Mr. Houser?"

"I thought I was looking out for my client."

"You thought wrong. Don't you see that, by what you have done, you have put your client in even greater jeopardy?"

"Yes, I suppose that is so. But, Your Honor, is there any way I can avoid prison?"

"Yes, there is a way. If you'll sign a confession and repudiate this affidavit, I'll drop the charges."

"Thank you, Your Honor," Houser said. "And I promise you, I'll never do it again."

"Oh, I'm sure you'll never do it again," Judge Craig said. "At least, not as a lawyer in Texas."

"What? What do you mean?"

"I intend to have you disbarred."

"No, Judge Craig, please! Do you have any idea how embarrassing that would be? Why, I would be so humiliated that I could never face anyone in this town again."

"You should have considered that before you knowingly lied."

Houser lowered his head and pinched the bridge of his nose between his thumb and forefinger.

"What . . . what will I do? All I know is the law."

"I'm sorry," Judge Craig said. "But there is nothing I can do. You are an intelligent and well-educated man, Brad. I'm sure that you'll be able to find something to do. It just won't be the practice of law."

"Yes," Houser said, nodding. "Yes, I'll not let this get me down. But whatever I do, I can't do it here. I hope you understand, Your Honor, I'm going to have to leave Sulphur Springs. I'm probably going to have to leave Texas. I . . . I just can't stay here."

"Oh, I fully understand. I'm sorry, Brad, but I'm

sure you realize that you brought this on yourself. I wish you good luck, wherever you go."

The next afternoon a few of Houser's friends came to the depot with him, to see him off. Robert Dempster, the banker, was there. So was Sheriff Peach. Rosemary Woods, who ran the Saddle and Stirrup Saloon, was there as well. Rosemary had always entertained the notion that someday she and Houser would be married.

That was not a notion Houser shared.

"I don't understand why you are leaving," Dempster said. "Since the bank was robbed, we need a lawyer now, more than ever before."

"It was Judge Craig who suggested that I leave," Houser said.

"Why?"

"I . . . I did something wrong. I signed a false document."

"Hell, you mean you lied about somethin'?" Sheriff Peach said. "Who the hell ain't told a tall tale now 'n then? I don't know why that would make you think you have to leave town."

"You don't understand, Sheriff. I am a lawyer, an officer of the court. Falsifying an official document is the same thing as committing perjury. Why, if Judge Craig didn't have such a good heart, I could have wound up in prison."

"But you ain't goin' to prison, are you?" Sheriff Peach asked. "I mean, if you was, wouldn't the judge have said somethin' to me?"

"I'm not going to prison, but it's something almost as bad. I've been disbarred."

"What does that mean?" Rosemary asked.

"It means I can't practice law anymore." He turned his attention to the banker. "So, Bob, even if I were to stay, I would no longer be able to represent you."

"That's all right, honey. I'm sure Mr. Prescott would hire you, and you could run the Saddle and Stirrup Saloon with me," Rosemary offered.

"No, I couldn't. I appreciate the offer, I really do. But you folks have no idea how humiliating a disbarment really is. There is no way I could stay in Sulphur Springs, or even in Texas, and hold my head up."

The sound of a whistle signaled the approaching train.

"Well, we're goin' to miss you around here, Brad, 'n that's for sure," Sheriff Peach said.

"Take me with you!" Rosemary shouted impulsively as the train approached.

"I can't. I don't know where I'm going, and I don't have enough money to support the two of us. But I will get in touch with you as soon as I have settled somewhere."

The train rattled to a stop, the arriving passengers disembarked, and the conductor stepped down from the train. Lifting his hand to cup it around his mouth, he called out, "All aboard!"

With a final wave of good-bye, Houser, who had never loosened his hold on the small valise he clutched to him, stepped onto the train and settled in one of the day coach cars.

As the train pulled away, he took a tighter grip on the valise, drew it closer, and smiled. His plan to leave the town had worked perfectly, and he was leaving with over $88,000 in cash. Though he had shared his destination with no one, he was going to Chugwater, Wyoming. He had chosen Chugwater as his destination by the simple act of closing his eyes over a map of Wyoming, circling his finger, then bringing it down. When he opened his eyes the town closest to his finger was Chugwater.

At the next stop after leaving Sulphur Springs, Houser upgraded his ticket and moved from the day coach to the Wagner Palace Car. Two days later, he was approaching his destination.

Practically the entire town of Chugwater, and many from the valley, turned out for Clifford Prescott's funeral. Prescott, who had been a colonel in the Union army during the war, received the Medal of Honor at the battle of Davenport Bridge, Virginia, where, according to the citation, *"By a gallant charge against a superior force of the enemy, he extricated his command from a perilous position in which it had been ordered."* He was being buried in his uniform, and he lay in an open coffin with the medal, a five-pointed star suspended from a small representation of the flag, pinned to his breast.

After the service in the church the coffin was closed and the pallbearers, Clyde Barnes from the Cross Fire Ranch, Dale Allen of the Pitchfork Ranch, David Lewis of Trail Back Ranch, Merlin Goodman of Mountain Shadows, Webb Dakota of Kensington Place, and Burt Rowe of North Ridge, carried the coffin out to the hearse. The pallbearers were made up of the largest ranch owners in the Valley of the Chug.

Because Duff's ranch was the largest of them all, to him went the honor of offering his arm to Martha Prescott and walking with her as they followed her husband's coffin out of the church.

By the time they reached the cemetery, puffed-up clouds filled the sky like a flock of grazing sheep, while gusts of wind moved leaves around and caused the black mourning ribbons to flutter in the breeze.

The townspeople gathered around the open grave as the Reverend E. D. Sweeny of the Chugwater Church of God's Glory, gave the final prayer.

"Unto Almighty God we commend the soul of our brother Clifford Prescott departed, and we commit his body to the ground, earth to earth, ashes to ashes, dust to dust; in sure and certain hope of the resurrection unto eternal life."

Martha dropped a handful of dirt onto the coffin, as did Harlon, her son.

Duff and the other ranchers went directly from the cemetery to the depot to tell Martha and her son good-bye.

"Mrs. Prescott, are you sure you're doing the right thing by selling the ranch?" Burt Rowe asked.

"It is my son's idea," Martha said.

"Have you given this a lot of thought, young man?" Burt asked.

"I've given it very little thought," Harlon answered. "Mother is perfectly free to remain here in this"— Harlon looked around with an obvious expression of distaste on his face—"godforsaken desert, if she wishes. But, if she wants to live with me, and to see her grandchildren grow up, then she will come to Memphis. I'm sure we can find her someplace to live that is sufficient to her needs."

The whistle of the southbound train interrupted any further conversation.

"Is there anything we can do for you? Look out for your ranch?" David Lewis asked.

"That isn't necessary," Harlon said. "I have made all the arrangements necessary for Twin Peaks to be sold."

"We will miss you, Martha," Mary Beth Lewis said.

"Oh, and I will miss you as well. I will miss all of you," Martha said as tears rolled down her cheeks.

"Get ahold of yourself, Mother," Harlon said. "You will make new friends in Memphis."

On board the approaching train, Brad Houser was sipping a whiskey that had been delivered to him a few minutes earlier by the porter. He was getting special treatment because he was the only one in the car. The train was approaching the town of Chugwater, and he was enjoying the scenery through the window. The most noticeable feature was the Chugwater Foundation, which was a high-rising cliff that was mostly brick red, though the color was periodically interrupted by streaks and spots of a light bluish-gray shade.

Even before he left Texas, Houser had begun growing a well-trimmed Vandyke beard. He was wearing a three-piece suit of the highest quality and a gold chain that formed a loop across his chest. Removing the gold watch that was attached to the chain, he opened it and checked the time. It was three o'clock, almost the exact time that the railroad schedule said they would reach Chugwater.

"Mr. Houser," the conductor said, approaching his chair.

"Yes?"

"We are in Chugwater, sir. Your destination."

"Thank you."

"I do hope that your trip has been satisfactory."

"Oh, most satisfactory," Houser said, reaching for the valise. The valise had not left his side from the time he left Sulphur Springs, Texas, though several times he had been offered the opportunity to "check it through."

The entire trip, including buying new clothes and traveling and dining first class, had cost him less than $250, which meant he still had $88,000 in cash.

Duff watched the train roll into the station and stop with a hiss of steam and a squeal of brakes.

"What about the hands who worked at Twin Peaks?" Dale Allen asked. "Have you made any arrangements for them?"

"I have dismissed them all."

"Harlon, there are cattle there," Burt Rowe said. "Someone has to look after them."

"What is there to look after? Cows eat grass and drink water. Surely they can do that on their own."

As Duff listened passively to the interchange, he saw a passenger step down from the train. The passenger wore a neatly trimmed Vandyke beard and was exceptionally well dressed. He was clutching a valise, holding it with both hands as if frightened that someone might take it from him.

"I have already made arrangements for Mr. Turley and Mr. Cooper to stay on, until the ranch is sold," Martha said. "Mr. Turley has been the foreman for some time, and Clifford always set a great store by him. He also thought that Mr. Cooper was a good hand. I'm sure they will be of big help to whoever buys the ranch."

"Mother, I had no idea you had done that, and there was no need for it. It is an unnecessary expense," Harlon said, his irritation with her action making his voice quite loud.

"I believe it is necessary," Martha replied quietly, but firmly.

"I'll check in on them from time to time," Rowe promised.

"All aboard!" the conductor called.

"Gentlemen, we appreciate your service at father's funeral. And now, we must take leave of you."

Martha took one last look around as if hesitant to leave.

"Come, Mother," Harlon said, taking her by the arm and escorting her onto the train.

Chapter Five

As Houser stepped down from the train, someone approached him.

"Would you like a cab, sir?" the man asked.

"Yes, as soon as I get my luggage, I think I would."

While Houser waited, he saw a small gathering of people around a young man and an older woman, who he took to be mother and son. From what he could observe the gathered men were telling the young man and woman good-bye.

"Mother, I had no idea you had done that, and there was no need for it. It is an unnecessary expense!"

It was the young man who spoke, validating Houser's belief that they were mother and son. As his voice was quite loud, and with a tone of obvious irritation, it was the only line of dialogue that Houser heard from the conversation.

He was somewhat discomfited when he saw that one of the gathered men, a tall man with golden hair, wide shoulders, and muscular arms, seemed to be looking at him. The unblinking gaze made him a little ill at ease, and he clutched the satchel even closer to him.

"This must be your luggage, sir, as you were the only one on the train," someone said. This was the man who, but a moment earlier, had solicited him for a cab.

"Yes, it is, thank you."

"Shall I get it for you?" the cab driver asked.

"Yes, please do."

The cab driver reached for the satchel, but Houser jerked it out of reach. "I'll carry this," Houser said.

"Yes, sir."

Houser had the driver take him to the "nicest hotel in town," where he took a suite of rooms. He wasn't sure how long he would be staying in the hotel, and he wanted to be as comfortable as possible.

From the hotel, Houser, still carrying the satchel, walked two blocks to the Bank of Chugwater, where he asked to meet with the president.

"Yes, sir, what can I do for you, sir?" Joel Marsh asked with a businessman's smile.

"I have a rather sizable sum of money that I would like to deposit with your bank," Houser said. "And I want to know if you can handle an account this large."

Marsh's smile grew broader. "Oh, I think you will find that we are quite capable of handling any amount you might wish to leave with us."

"Do you have a vault?"

"We have a Yale and Towne vault, sir. There is none better. Exactly how much money will you be depositing with us?"

"Eighty-five thousand dollars," Houser said.

"Oh my, that *is* a rather substantial amount. Are you moving to Chugwater?"

"Yes. I shall be looking to buy a ranch while I'm here."

"Twin Peaks," Marsh said.

"I beg your pardon?"

"You are in luck, sir, as I have just been given the authority to sell Twin Peaks, a ranch that once belonged to Clifford Prescott."

"You have repossessed it, have you?" Houser asked.

"Oh no, sir, nothing like that. Clifford Prescott, who owned Twin Peaks Ranch, died earlier this week. In fact I, just a few minutes ago, returned from his funeral. If you just arrived on the train today, you may have seen his widow, Mrs. Prescott. Her son is taking her back to Memphis, and it is he who is selling. He has offered the ranch, and all stock and accouterments, for sale for fifty-five thousand dollars."

"You know the area. Is the ranch worth that much?"

"Oh, dear me, yes, that, and much more," Marsh said. "And I told young Prescott as much. But he wants nothing to do with the ranch, except to get rid of it as quickly as possible."

"How large is this place?"

"One hundred and ten thousand acres. Only Sky Meadow is larger."

"Can you arrange for me to see it?"

"Absolutely. I'll take you there myself."

Elam, Texas

For a while, Sid Shamrock was the wealthiest man in Elam, and he lived like it. Rather than take a room in the hotel, Shamrock took a room in Miss Wanda's House of Accommodating Women. Miss Wanda was a madam, and the six "accommodating" women who lived and worked there were whores.

"Ha!" Shamrock said. "I've always wanted to live in a whorehouse, 'n now I do."

By living there, Shamrock was able to enjoy any of the girls he wanted, anytime he wanted. Such an arrangement cost him a great deal of money, but he had a great deal of money.

Shamrock was very generous with his money, many nights buying drinks for everyone in the saloon until the saloon closed. He also played cards, betting large sums and losing a lot of money. On one occasion, he lost well over $1,000 in one game.

He didn't seem to be bothered by his losses, because the next night he would buy drinks for everyone, lose more money, then return to the whorehouse where, even though he lived there full-time, he paid the going rate for whichever whore he selected for the night. It didn't seem as if he would ever run out of money.

If Wanda and her girls wondered how he came by so much money, they never bothered to question him.

There was, however, one man in town who did wonder where Shamrock got all his money, and a few weeks after Shamrock showed in town, he knew.

T. J. Carmichael, who was sheriff of Swisher County, was also sheriff of Elam, since Elam was the only town in the county. At the moment, he was holding a wanted poster.

WANTED FOR ROBBERY
of the BANK OF SULPHUR SPRINGS
$2,000 REWARD
☞ TWO MEN, *identities unknown*

First man is about 5'10" tall, long blond hair, approximately 165 pounds, with a purple scar running from his left eyebrow, down through his left eye, ending at the top of his cheek.

Second man has brown hair and blue eyes. He is about 5'8", 155 pounds, with no identifiable marks.

Sheriff Carmichael had no idea who the second man might be, but he was certain that the big spender who was calling himself Sid Shamrock was the first man.

Carmichael went over to the Silver Bell Saloon, where Shamrock was playing cards. Carmichael watched until the game broke up, then he called out to him.

"How was your game, Mr. Shamrock?"

Shamrock smiled. "Well, I won a little today, but not enough to make up for all the losin' I been doin'. How 'bout lettin' me buy you a drink?"

"Oh, you could do that, I suppose. Or you could come over to my office and let me give *you* a drink. I have some good Kentucky bourbon, which is much better than anything you'll find in this place."

"Yeah? I don't think I've ever drank me no real Kentucky bourbon."

"Well, my boy, you are in for a treat," the sheriff said.

The two men walked down to the sheriff's office and Carmichael stood back to let Shamrock go in first. Then, as Shamrock stepped in through the door, Carmichael jammed his pistol into Shamrock's back.

"Just keep going on back and step into that open cell," Carmichael said.

"Here, what's this about?" Shamrock asked.

Carmichael slammed the cell door behind him.

"You got no call to do this!"

Carmichael picked up the wanted poster and showed it to Shamrock.

"This is you, isn't it?"

"No, that ain't me."

"You've got the scar, you've got a lot of money that you can't account for. I can take you back to Sulphur Springs and have you identified, or . . ."

There was an implied escape in the sheriff's "or" and Shamrock leaped at it.

"Or what?"

"There is a two-thousand-dollar reward out for you."

"I didn't think the law could collect on rewards," Shamrock said.

"Oh, we can't, unless . . ."

"Unless what?"

"Unless we collect it from the wanted man himself."

"I ain't a-followin' whatever it is that you're a-gettin' at," Shamrock said.

"I'm going to give you a choice, Mr. Shamrock. You can let me take you back to Sulphur Springs, where you will be tried for armed bank robbery and most likely serve from fifteen to twenty years in prison. But of course if I do that, I will be doing it as a matter of civic duty, only, because, as you correctly pointed out, I can't collect the reward. We both lose if I do that."

Sheriff Carmichael smiled and held up a finger. "On the other hand, there is a way where we can both win. You pay me the two-thousand-dollar reward, and I'll let you go, but with the stipulation that you leave town, and never come back."

"I don't have much over two thousand dollars left," Shamrock said.

"But you do have two thousand dollars?"

"Yeah, I've got it."

"It's your choice, Mr. Shamrock. You can choose prison or freedom. Which will it be?"

"Let me out. I'll go get the money and bring it to you."

Carmichael chuckled and shook his head. "No, sir, Mr. Shamrock. We will both go get the money, then you'll leave town."

"All right," Shamrock agreed. "Come on, I'll take you to the money."

Sulphur Springs

Shamrock had less than twenty dollars left when he rode into Sulphur Springs. He knew he was taking a chance, not so much that the banker might see and recognize him, but that someone else might identify him from the description. And the description had gotten out, because it was on the wanted poster Sheriff Carmichael had shown him.

Despite the danger, Shamrock had returned to Sulphur Springs because he didn't think he had any other choice. He knew that Brad Houser had gotten a lot more money from the bank robbery than he had, and he knew that if he asked for some more, his brother would give it to him. Actually, his brother had no other choice, because if he didn't give him the money, it could get out that he, too, was involved in the bank robbery.

Shamrock laughed at the prospect. His brother always lorded everything over him—he was smarter, richer, and better-looking. But this time, Shamrock was holding the ace.

Shamrock rode up to the Saddle and Stirrup Saloon, tied his horse off out front, then went inside. He saw the girl he was looking for leaning against the piano, perusing the girls who were working the saloon. Although he had never actually met her, he knew that this was Rosemary Woods, and he knew that Rosemary had a thing for his brother.

He walked up to her.

"Hello, Miss Woods," he said.

"Do I know you?" she asked.

"No, we ain't never met. I need me a lawyer, so I come here to see Houser, only when I went to his office it was closed. When I went to askin' about 'im, I was told he was sweet on you, so I figured maybe you'd know where he is."

"Wait a minute!" Rosemary said, gasping. "You're the one that robbed the bank."

"No, I ain't robbed no bank. I was in Elam when the bank was robbed, 'n the sheriff there can prove it. But I need a lawyer 'n that's why I come to see Houser."

"Brad isn't here any longer," Rosemary said.

"He ain't? Where is he? Do you know?"

"Yes, I know," she said with a smile. "When he left, he said he would send for me as soon as he was settled in."

"Where is he?"

"He's in Chugwater."

"Chugwater? I've never heard of it."

"I hadn't heard of it, either, but it's up in Wyoming."

"Damn, that's a long way off," Shamrock said.

"Are you going to see him?" Rosemary asked.

Shamrock shook his head. "I'd like to, I truly would. But I don't have enough money to go up there. Fact is, I don't have no money at all. Which ought to prove that I didn't rob the bank, on account of 'cause if I did, I wouldn't be broke now, would I?"

"I'll give you some money if you'll go up there and remind him that he said he was going to send for me."

"How much money will you give me?"

"I can give you a hundred dollars," Rosemary said. "That's all I can spare."

Shamrock smiled, then held out his hand. "All right, you give me that money, 'n I'll go up there 'n tell him to send for you."

Trail Back Ranch

Half a pitted steer was being slowly turned over a fire, and a band had been hired to come up from Cheyenne. David Lewis, owner of Trail Back, was hosting a welcome party for Brad Houser, the new owner of Twin Peaks Ranch, and in addition to Duff MacCallister, Clyde Barnes, Dale Allen, Merlin Goodman, Webb Dakota, and Burt Rowe were also present.

"I think Martha's son was right to sell Twin Peaks after Clifford died," Mary Beth Lewis said. "There is no way she would be able to operate that ranch by herself. Why, it's bigger than Trail Back, and I certainly wouldn't try to run Trail Back by myself."

"I know what the boy was asking for the ranch, and believe me, you got a very good deal," Burt Rowe said.

"Yes, except for the cattle," Houser replied.

"The cattle? My good man, are you saying that there is illness among the cattle?" Webb Dakota asked in a precise, British accent. Dakota didn't own Kensington Place outright. He was but one of a consortium of English investors in the cattle industry of the American West. "If there is, we must take care of it straight away, rather than take the danger of it spreading."

"No, no, there is no disease," Houser said. "It's the number of cattle I'm talking about. Why, a ranch the size of Twin Peaks should accommodate from eight to ten thousand head. I've got less than twenty-five hundred head."

"Yes, well, I know for a fact that Clifford sold off most of his cattle there toward the end. He was too ill to look after the ranch himself. He knew the end was coming, and I think he was just turning cattle into cash."

"And, more 'n likely, there was a lot of maverickin' done," Clyde Barnes said.

"Mavericking?"

"Yeah, you know, every spring before roundup,

quite a few of the new calves wander off before they can be branded. Truth is, for the last two or three years, Clifford wasn't none too worried about roundup. He let all his hands go except for Ben Turley and Ty Cooper, so there warn't no brandin' goin' on at his place," Clyde said.

"What happens to the maverick cattle?" Houser asked.

"Well, sir, they belong to whoever happens to round 'em up," Merlin Goodman said.

"And most of the time, that's the small ranchers," Dale Allen added.

"So, what you are saying is, the small ranchers are stealing from the larger ranchers," Houser said.

"Well, no, sir, I wouldn't say that. It ain't stealin', exactly. It's legal, 'n ever' one does it, it's just that the small ranchers do it a lot more 'n anyone else does," Dale said.

David Lewis, who was listening in on the conversation, chuckled. "Hell, half the small ranchers in the entire country owe their whole herds to mavericks they've rounded up."

"Yes, well, they'll get no more cattle from me," Houser declared resolutely.

Chapter Six

Twin Peaks Ranch

When Houser first set foot on the ranch he had just bought, he was met by a tall, lean man with dark tendrils of hair hanging over his forehead from beneath his hat, dark eyes, and prominent cheekbones. He was about six feet one and was thin, though there was more of a rawboned edginess to his physique than actual attenuation.

"The name is Turley, Mr. Houser. Ben Turley. I heard that you bought Twin Peaks. Me 'n Ty Cooper have been lookin' out for the place for Miz Prescott till she could sell it."

"Do I owe you any money?" Houser asked.

"No, sir, Miz Prescott's done paid both of us for what I was doin'."

"How many hands are there now?"

"Besides me they's just three more here now: Ty Cooper, like I said, 'n a couple of weeks ago, we took on Slim Hastings, Dooley Carson. We ain't paid them nothin' but found 'cause I don't have no money, but

I told 'em you'd more 'n likely hire 'em on, as you'll need hands."

"Would you like to stay on as foreman?"

A broad smile spread across Turley's face. "Yes, sir, I would. I was hopin' you might ask me to. What about Slim, Dooley, 'n Cooper? Can we keep them, too?"

"Yes. How many more men do you think would be necessary for optimum efficiency?"

Turley got a confused expression on his face.

"How many more men for what?"

"How many more men do you think we would need to operate the ranch?"

"Oh, about seven more, I reckon."

"Hire them.

"Yes, sir!" Turley replied, the smile returning.

Houser was there less than a month when he received a letter from Rosemary Woods, the woman he had left back in Sulphur Springs. He was both angry and shocked to receive the letter. How did she know where he was? He had told nobody where he was going.

Dear Brad,

   I hope this letter finds you in good health. When I didn't hear from you as you promised, I began to worry that something may have happened to you, so I checked with the railroad and found out that you had gone to Chugwater, Wyoming.

   What a funny name is Chugwater. I hope that you have found a job there and are saving your

*money. I am sure that you will send for me as soon
as you can.*

*After I found out where you went, I met a man
named Shamrock who said you was his lawyer and
he was looking for you. I told him where you was.*

Waiting anxiously to hear from you, I remain,
Your
Rosemary

Angrily, Brad tore up the letter. The last thing he
needed now was any connection with his past in Sulphur Springs, especially if it was a former saloon girl.
And he certainly wasn't happy to hear that she had
told Thomas, or Shamrock, as he was now calling
himself. He wouldn't answer the letter.

Gradually, Brad Houser began to put his mark on
the Valley of the Chug. The owner of Twin Peaks
Ranch was a vain man who eschewed the jeans and
cotton shirts of most ranchers so that he could dress
in accordance to what he considered his "station."

From Ben Turley and the hired hands he demanded servile respect. He very rarely made a personal inspection of the cattle in the field, and when
he did do so, he inspected his domain, not from the
hurricane deck of a horse, but from the leather
padded seat of a surrey.

This morning he was in his ranch office, which was
a small, white building that was halfway between what
the riders called the "Big House" and the bunkhouse.
Houser was going over his books when Ben Turley
knocked on the door.

"Yes, Mr. Turley, come in," Houser called out to him.

"Mr. Houser, we can't move them cows onto the Pine Flats like you wanted."

"And may I ask why not?"

"We can't do it on account of Kenny Prosser's cows is already there."

"I thought you told me that Mr. Prescott always used the Pine Flats for grazing."

"Yes, sir, we've done it all the time since I been workin' here, only the Pine Flats ain't none of our land. It's open range, 'n that means that it belongs to whoever is the first person to put their cows on the grass."

"Not so much as one acre of Twin Peaks is 'our' land, Mr. Turley. It is all 'my' land," Houser said.

"Yes, sir, that's what I meant. Onliest thing is, like I told you, we couldn't put the cows onto the Pine Flats, seein' as Prosser's cows is already there, so what I done is, I put 'em out in the Sweet Grass Pasture."

"Didn't you tell me that the Sweet Grass Pasture has been overgrazed?"

"It ain't entirely over et, but it damn near is."

"Correct me if I'm wrong, but didn't Prosser used to ride for Twin Peaks?"

"Yes, sir, he done for a little while, but whenever Mr. Prescott let ever' body go, well, what Prosser did is, he commenced to homesteadin' some land, bought hisself some cows, 'n started his own ranch."

"Bought cows, or stole them?" Houser asked.

"Well, sir, Mr. Prescott, he give 'im twenty head, 'n Kenny, he bought another thirty head from Mr. Prescott, 'n twenty more head from Mr. Lewis over at Trail Back. After that he rounded up some mavericks, around ten or fifteen of 'em, I reckon. So now he's runnin' somewhat shy of a hundred head."

"And now he is grazing on my land."

"No, sir, it's like I said, he's on the Pine Flats, 'n that ain't nobody's land."

"It is grazing that Twin Peaks has always used, you said. And don't you think Prosser knows that?" Houser asked angrily.

"Yes, sir, I reckon so. 'N 'cause he also knowed it was good grazin' 'n open range is why I figure he put his cows there."

"Mr. Turley, I want you to go back out to the Pine Flats and make a thorough perusal of all of Mr. Prosser's cattle."

"I beg your pardon, boss? What is it you want me to do to his cattle?" Turley asked, the expression on his face reflecting his confusion at the word *perusal.*

"Take a close look at them," Houser explained. "Make a very thorough examination. I want you to make certain that none of Prosser's cows are wearing the Twin Peaks brand."

"Well, sir, there's liable to be fifty of 'em that is, on account of like I said."

"Do you not think it strange, Mr. Turley, that Prescott would give some cattle to a common cowboy, but he gave none to you, when you were the foreman?"

"No, sir, it ain't all that strange. He offered me some cows if I wanted to go into ranchin' my ownself, but he told me if I would stay and help 'im look after the ranch till he died, he'd give me money that would be equal to what the cows was worth."

"I see. And so now you are asking me for that money?"

"No, sir, Mr. Houser. Mr. Prescott, he done give me that money. And Miz Prescott, she give me some more money to stay on till the ranch got sold to the next owner, which wasn't very long 'cause you was here within a week."

"Do you know this man who is running his cattle on the Pine Flats?"

"Yes, sir, I know Kenny pretty good, 'n I don't think he'd take any Twin Peaks cows. Most especial since he used to work here, 'n even though he don't work here no more, well, I reckon he's still loyal to the brand. I mean, there really ain't no need to check on 'im 'n maybe embarrass him none."

"Please, just do as I say, Mr. Turley."

"Yes, sir."

Sky Meadow Ranch

Duff Tavish MacCallister and his friend Elmer, a man who was in his late fifties, but looked much older, were working on the gate of his corral. Elmer was more than a ranch hand, and though he was second in charge of the ranch, he was also considerably more than a foreman. Elmer was a partner, his position in the ranch secured by the gold he had taken from a mine he had discovered on land that subsequently became a part of the large Sky Meadow Ranch. But he had more than just a monetary investment. Elmer had often put his life on the line for Duff. Their relationship could be described as symbiotic: Elmer had saved Duff's life more than once, and Duff had returned the favor just as often.

"I seen that feller Houser in town the other day," Elmer said as he lifted up on the gate so Duff could connect the hinge. "He was dressed up all fancy like he owned the world."

"Aye, he does like to dress the dandy, now," Duff replied.

"I tell you the truth, Duff, they's somethin' about that feller that just ain't right. I cain't hardly put m' finger on it, but he just don't sit right with me."

"He is obviously a very well-educated man," Duff said. "And while some men are subdued about their education in a way that is quiet and dignified, some, like Mr. Houser, wear it in a vainglorious way, as if it were a suit of pomposity."

"Yeah, well, I don't know what it is that you just said," Elmer said. "But it sort of sounded to me like you don't take that much of a likin' to the son of a bitch, neither."

Duff chuckled. "That is most astute of you, Elmer."

"Astute. Is that a good thing?"

"Aye, 'tis a very good thing." Duff finished putting in the last screw. "Ye can be for letting it down now, I think it'll swing free."

Elmer released his hold on the gate, and Duff pushed it closed, opened it, and closed it again.

"There, we fixed it."

"You fixed it, you mean," Elmer said. "All I done was hold on to it."

"Hello, someone is coming," Duff said.

Looking down the long road that led toward the arch in which the name of the ranch, Sky Meadow, was worked in wrought iron, they saw a rider approaching. He was clearly coming toward the main compound, and he was pushing five Black Angus cows.

"That's Percy Gaines, ain't it?" Elmer asked.

"Aye, 'tis at that," Duff replied.

At one time Percy had worked full-time on Sky

Meadow, and even now, he often augmented his income by working for Duff. But last year he had started his own ranch.

"Wonder what it is that he's a-doin' with them five cows?"

The two men watched as the young cowboy brought the five cows all the way up to the corral.

"Good morning, Percy," Duff greeted.

"Good morning, Mr. MacCallister, Mr. Gleason," Percy replied. "I been roundin' up m' cattle the last few days, 'n yesterday I found these five critters wearin' your brand, so I brung 'em back to you."

"That was a decent thing for ye to do, lad," Duff replied. "Would you be for enjoying a breakfast with Elmer, Wang, and me?"

"Better be careful afore you say yes," Elmer warned. "On this ranch you're as likely to wind up with haggis or rice 'n weeds as you are with bacon 'n eggs. Nothin' American."

Duff chuckled. "I believe Wang said he would be serving biscuits and gravy this morning. Is that 'American' enough for you?"

"Well, hell, why didn't you say so?" Elmer replied with a wide grin.

When they stepped into the house a moment later, they were greeted with the rich aromas of sausage and baked biscuits.

"Hello, Wang," Percy greeted.

"It is good to see you again, Percy," Wang replied.

"Smells good in here," Percy said.

After being rescued by Duff, Wang had dedicated himself to serving Sky Meadow. And though he had initially been hired as a cook, over the last three years, he had become much more than a cook.

"How's your ranch coming along?" Duff asked Percy after the four men sat down for breakfast.

"It's comin' along just fine," Percy replied with a proud smile. "I'm runnin' a little more 'n a hundred 'n fifty head now. Oh, 'n I've named the ranch. I'm callin' it The Queen."

"The Queen, is it? This is just a guess now, Percy, but I'd be for saying that it would nae be Queen Victoria that the ranch is named for. 'Tis thinking, I am, that it would be for the young lass ye have waiting for you back in Kansas City."

"Ha! You got that right," Percy said. "Only she don't know it yet. After we get married 'n I bring her back out here, I'll tell her then that the ranch is named for her. It'll be a big surprise."

"When are you a-plannin' on gettin' yerself hitched?" Elmer asked.

"Soon as roundup is done. I ain't got all that many cows to round up, 'n that's what I'm doin' now. That's how I found them Sky Meadow cows."

"Aye, 'n 'tis appreciative I am to ye for bringin' them back to me."

"Well, sir, I'm wantin' to grow my herd fast as I can, but I'll not be addin' other folk's beeves to my own."

"You're a good man, Percy," Elmer said. "And don't you pay no nevermind to any o' them bad things Wang says about you. I don't care what this here heathen says, I think you're a good man," Elmer said.

"What?" Percy replied.

"Elmer is teasing you," Duff said. "Wang has made nae derogatory comments about you."

"Elmer would speak without thinking, as he would sleep without resting," Wang said.

"Now, see there?" Elmer said, pointing to Wang. "That heathen Celestial is always saying things like that, things that there don't nobody else know what it is that he's a-talkin' about."

Despite the seemingly contrary interchange between Elmer and Wang Chow, the two men were the best of friends, and because Percy had worked on Sky Meadow, he was well aware that there was genuine cordiality in the barbs.

After breakfast, Percy told the others good-bye, then left for his own ranch.

"I just hope that little ole gal he's got waitin' for 'im back in Kansas City knows what a good man she's goin' to be gettin'," Elmer said as they watched the young rancher ride away. "Damn, I've let m' coffee get a little cold."

"Elmer, I'll be leavin' things in your hands for a while, as I'll be ridin' into town this morning," Duff said.

"Did you hear that, you heathen?" Elmer said to Wang. "It's my hands he's leavin' the ranch in, not yours."

Elmer raised his cup to take another drink, but before it reached his lips, Wang snatched it from his hand. "What the . . . ?" Elmer started to say in a startled voice, but before he finished his comment a new cup was put in his hands. Elmer took a swallow and saw that it was hot.

"Did you not say that your coffee was cold?" Wang asked.

"You ain't human, Wang, you know that? There ain't no way a human man can do all them things you can do."

Wang smiled.

"And why are you grinnin' like that?"

"I believe that, my friend, is what one would call an enigmatic smile," Duff said with a chuckle.

Chapter Seven

Some seven miles distant from Sky Meadow, in an area of open range land known as the Pine Flats, Kenny Prosser was watching over his herd when he saw Turley riding toward him.

"Good morning, Mr. Turley," he said, greeting the man who had once been his boss.

"Good morning, Kenny," Turley replied.

"What can I do for you?"

"If you don't mind, I'm going to take a close look at your cows."

"Why? I mean, I don't mind, but what are you looking for?"

"Houser wants me to make certain . . ."

"Oh, I see. He wants to make sure that I don't have any of his cows," Prosser said. "Go ahead, take a good look. I ain't got nothin' to hide."

As Turley began riding through the small herd, Prosser rode with him.

"He ain't really worried none that I've got any of

his cows, is he? What he's pissed off about is that I got my cows to the Pine Flats before he did."

"You know Twin Peaks has always been usin' the Pine Flats," Turley said.

Prosser laughed. "Yeah, I know it. It serves the new guy right that I got here first."

"All right," Turley said when he had examined every cow in the herd. "I didn't see none o' our cows there. But, Kenny, if I was you, I'd get your cows away from here."

"Why? This is public land, 'n you know it."

"Yeah, but they's somethin' about Houser that's kind of troublesome."

"What do you mean?"

"Well, I don't like to carry tales 'bout someone I'm ridin' for, 'n truth to tell I don't really know him all that good, I mean, bein' as he ain't been here all that long. But I've kind of got it in mind that he ain't the kind of person you want to make mad."

"Yeah, well, I don't know nothin' about 'im, 'n I don't care to know," Prosser said. "But I've got as much right here as anyone does, 'n you know that, Mr. Turley. This here is open range, for anyone as wants to use it."

"I know you do, Kenny, 'n I ain't never goin' to do nothin' to make you leave. But like I say, Mr. Houser, well, he ain't like Mr. Prescott was, who, if you 'member, was just the same nice to ever' one, whether he be an ordinary rider or one o' the other big ranchers. This feller, well, I can't promise you what he'll do."

"All right," Prosser said. "I'll get m' cows back to my own grass today."

"I ain't rushin' you or nothin', but if you want, I'll help you drive 'em back."

"Yeah, thanks, I'll appreciate that."

"Kenny ain't got none of our . . . uh, that is, Prosser ain't got none of your cows mixed in with his'n, 'n besides that, he's moved his cows back to his own place," Turley said, reporting on his visit with Prosser.

"He may not have had any of my cows mixed in with the cows you examined," Houser replied. "But I've no doubt but that he and all the other small ranchers are increasing their herd at my expense."

"I don't know. It could be, I suppose. But to be honest, Mr. Houser, you ain't been here all that long, 'n you ain't lost no cows at all since you come. I know, 'cause I been keepin' a pretty good track on it."

"We are losing grazing range and watering holes, though, are we not?"

"Well, yes, sir, some of what used to be free range for us has been took up by homesteadin', that's true, and even what is still free range is bein' used, not only by Kenny, but by all the small ranchers. But I reckon, bein' as it is free range, that they got a right to use it. 'N anyhow, I don't see that it hurts none, I mean, seein' as they ain't none of 'em got enough cows to really graze the range out, 'n right now you ain't got enough cows to overgraze your own land."

"Perhaps, individually, that may be so," Houser said. "But I am told that there may be as many as fifteen or twenty small ranchers, and if you take into consideration all the cattle they are running, then they certainly can make an impact on the supply of grass and water."

"Yes, sir, I reckon if you put it that way, they could," Turley agreed.

"If you look at the big picture, and as a rancher that is exactly what I must do, then the threat to the well-being of any of the larger ranchers can easily be seen."

Turley didn't answer, because he had no idea what the answer should be.

"I shall consider all my options," Houser said, though he was speaking more to himself than he was to his foreman.

Santa Fe, New Mexico

The man standing at the far end of the bar was, perhaps, the most unprepossessing figure in the saloon. He was smaller than the average man, his trousers, shirt, and low-crown hat were all faded and indistinct, not broken by any color. He had very dark eyes, set rather deeply under shaggy eyebrows. His face was narrow, and his nose resembled the beak of a hawk. He was standing by himself, staring into a mug of beer that had sat before him, undisturbed for over a minute.

At the opposite end of the bar stood two cowboys wearing blue denim trousers and wide-brimmed hats. They differed in appearance only in their shirts. Tanner wore yellow, Cole wore white.

"Hey, you!" Cole called to the man who was staring into his beer mug. "What you expectin' to find in that glass you're a-starin' at? Maybe a catfish, swimmin' around?"

Tanner laughed. "No, he ain't lookin' for no catfish. He's lookin' for one o' them mermaids."

"What's a mermaid?"

"It's half woman 'n half fish. The top half is a naked woman, 'n the bottom half is a fish."

"If the bottom half is a fish, how do you . . . uh . . . I mean if you was wantin' to . . . uh." Cole was unable to form his question.

"Well, it don't make no nevermind for that ole fool standin' down at the other end of the bar," Tanner said. "He's so ugly he can't get no woman whether she be half-fish or not. Hell, he likely can't even get a woman if he pays her for it. He's the kind we wouldn't want hangin' around no calves, if you know what I mean."

"Ha!" Cole laughed. "Hey, mister, is that true? When you cain't get no women, do you go out lookin' for calves?"

During all the provocation put forth by Tanner and Cole, the man at the end of the bar had not moved, but after the latest taunt, he lifted his glass and drained the rest of his beer.

"You have hurt my feelings," he said without turning toward them. His voice was low, almost like a whisper.

Tanner laughed. "You hear that, Cole? You hurt his feelin's."

"I would appreciate an apology," the man said.

"You want me to apologize?" Cole asked incredulously. "I tell you what, why don't I just wipe the floor up with your scrawny little ass?"

The man turned, for the first time. "I have a better

idea," he said. He smiled, though there was more evil than humor in his smile. "Why don't I just kill you?"

"Kill me?" Cole asked. The bravado had faded somewhat, because of the way the man had made the remark. It wasn't challenging, and he hadn't raised his voice. It was the low-key, matter-of-fact way he said the words that Cole found disconcerting.

"Mr. Bodine, I'm sure if these boys knowed who you was, why, they would be glad to apologize," the bartender said. "There's no need to carry this any further."

"I done give 'em the chance to apologize," Bodine said. "Now I'm goin' to give 'em a chance to back up their words."

"Bodine?" Cole said, his voice cracking a little. "Did you call him Bodine?"

"I tried to warn you boys," the bartender said. "This is Lucien Bodine."

"Cole, back off," Tanner said. "Back off. My God, you don't want to go bracing the likes of Lucien Bodine!"

A weak smile spread across Cole's face, and he stopped, then opened his fists and held his hands, palm out in front of him.

"My friend is right," he said. "We was just a-funnin' with you, is all. We didn't neither one of us mean nothin' by it. I mean, it ain't worth either one of us dying over."

"You don't understand, do you, cowboy? It ain't goin' to be either of us. It'll just be you," Bodine said. He looked over at Tanner. "You, too, if you decide to take a hand in this."

Tanner shook his head. "No, it ain't goin' to be

Cole, 'n it ain't goin' to be me, neither, on account of there ain't neither one of us going to draw on you," he said. "I don't reckon you'll be a-wantin' to shoot us in front of these here witnesses. Unless you kill ever' body so's they ain't no witnesses."

"Look here, cowboy!" one of saloon customers said, suddenly frightened by Tanner's suggestion that everyone might be killed. "You 'n your friend here is the ones what opened the ball. Don't you go gettin' none of us mixed up in it."

"You'll draw, all right. You'll draw first, and these witnesses will say that."

"They ain't goin' to be able to say it, 'cause we ain't goin' to draw on you," Cole said. He looked over at the customer who had spoken out a moment earlier. "You don't need to worry 'bout us gettin' you into this, on account of there ain't goin' to be nothin' happenin' here for you to get into. There ain't neither one of us goin' to draw on Lucien Bodine."

"Oh, I think you will," Bodine said, calmly, confidently.

"Please, Mr. Bodine, we don't want any trouble," Tanner said. "Why don't you just let us apologize and we'll go on our way?"

Bodine shook his head, the evil grin spreading. "Uh-uh," he said. "Like I said, it's too late for that."

Cole and Tanner looked at each other, then, in a signal understood only by the two of them, developed over a couple of years and many hours of riding together, they made a ragged, desperate, awkward, and ultimately ineffective grab for their pistols.

So bad were they that Bodine had the luxury of waiting for just a moment to see which of the two offered him the most competition. Deciding it was Cole, Bodine pulled his pistol and shot him first. Tanner was next, dying even before he knew that his friend had already been killed.

Bodine stood there for a moment, holding the smoking gun. He put it back in his holster, poured himself another drink, then turned his back to the bar and looked out over the shocked faces of the customers in the saloon. Though they had just witnessed a tragedy, the foremost thought in the minds of many of them was that they had seen Lucien Bodine in action. It was a memory they would retain and share with others for the rest of their lives.

"Is there anyone who didn't see them draw first?" Bodine asked.

"They drew first, I seen it," the customer who had asked to be left out of it, volunteered.

"Yes, sir, I seen it, too," another customer said. "They drawed first, the both of them."

"Bartender, you saw it?"

The bartender was staring down at the two young men who he remembered had been laughing and joking when they pushed in through the batwing doors no more than fifteen minutes ago.

"I asked, did you see that they drawed first?" Bodine repeated.

The bartender looked up at Bodine. His face showed more sorrow than fear.

"You goaded them into that fight, Bodine," he said. "They was just two cowboys, they wasn't gunfighters. They didn't have no idea who you was, 'n they was just jokin' aroun'. They never had no idea of somethin' like this happenin'. You goaded them into it."

"Did they draw first, or didn't they?"

"They drew first," the bartender admitted.

Bodine put some money on the bar. "Give ever' body in here a drink on me, and have one for yourself," he said.

"A drink, yes," one of the customers said. "Damn, do I need a drink."

The twelve customers and the two women who had been hustling drinks all rushed to the bar.

"Phil, I need a real drink," one of the girls said. "Not the tea me 'n Leena drink all day."

"Yeah, me, too," Leena said.

Even as everyone was having their free drink, the sheriff came in.

"You sure got here fast," Phil said from behind the bar. "How did you hear about it?"

The sheriff looked down at the two dead cowboys and shook his head. "I didn't know nothin' about this," he said. "I just come to give Bodine a message."

"Yeah?" Bodine replied. "What message is that?"

"Your brother got hisself kilt."

"Who done it?" Bodine asked.

"I don't know who done it, I don't even know where it was done. All I know is I heard that he got hisself kilt."

Bodine left the saloon, and the other patrons began talking excitedly among themselves, sharing the experience of having seen the infamous Lucien Bodine in a gunfight.

"Well, if you're goin' to be true about it, it really warn't much of a gunfight, 'cause them two boys he kilt wasn't really no gunfighter."

"Yeah, you're right. You think Bodine is goin' to go huntin' for whoever it was that kilt his brother?"

"Looked like he had it in mind."

"Now, there's a gunfight I'd like to see."

"The one I'd like to see would be between him 'n Wynton Miller."

"That ain't goin' to happen, 'cause Wynton Miller is dead."

"Where at did you hear that?"

"There ain't nobody heard nothin' about him for a while, has there?"

"No, but that don't mean he's dead. More 'n likely that just means he's hidin' out somewhere. They's a ten-thousand-dollar reward out on 'im, you know."

"Yeah, well, if he ain't dead, there ain't nobody ever goin' to get that reward without they shoot 'im in the back."

"That could be done, all right. Look at what happened to Jesse James."

Chapter Eight

Valley of the Chug

Biff Johnson had named his saloon Fiddler's Green after the cavalry legend that says all cavalrymen who have ever heard the call "Boots and Saddles" will gather on a cool glen in the afterlife, and there, they will share drinks and tell tall tales.

Biff was sitting next to the piano at a special table reserved only for him or his personal guests. As it was still relatively early in the day, there weren't that many customers in the saloon at the moment. The piano was quiet, but the piano player, anticipating a busy afternoon, was arranging some music.

"Jim, do you know what today is?" Biff asked.

"Why, yes, sir, it's Thursday. . In another hour you won't have to ask, you will be able to tell by the size of the crowd."

"It isn't just Thursday. It's June twenty-fourth. Tomorrow it will be exactly ten years ago since it happened."

"Since what happened?"

Biff nodded toward the recently acquired painting, *Custer's Last Fight*, by Cassilly Adams. The large painting occupied a prominent position on the wall behind the bar.

"Since that happened," Biff said.

"Oh yes, I see."

"Play 'Garry Owen' for me."

One of the first things Jim Siffer had to agree to, upon taking the job in the saloon, was to learn to play the song that belonged to the 7th Cavalry.

As the music came from the piano, Biff found his thoughts slipping back ten years, to the 25th of June, 1876.

Sergeant Major Biff Johnson had come up with Benteen. Biff thought they would be going to relieve Custer, because Custer had sent a note issuing that very order, but Benteen stopped to reinforce Reno.

"Major Reno, Captain Benteen, we must go to relieve General Custer!" Captain Tom Weir pleaded.

"No doubt Custer is covering himself in even more glory now," Benteen replied. "We will maintain a defensive position here."

"Sir, with or without your permission, I am taking my company to join Custer," Weir said.

"Captain, if you will allow me, I'll go with you," Biff said.

"You are welcome to come along, Sergeant Major," Captain Weir said.

But Captain Weir's single company encountered stiff Indian resistance and was unable to rendezvous with Custer. They were forced to withdraw, where they rejoined Reno and Benteen.

The next day, after the Indians withdrew, Sergeant Major Biff Johnson was in charge of the burial detail.

Now, ten years later, he was still haunted by the sight of 206 men, stripped, pale, mutilated, and scattered over the field, an image that filled his mind as Jim Siffer continued to play.

As the last notes of "Garry Owen" echoed through the nearly empty saloon, Biff saw his friend Duff MacCallister coming through the front door.

"Duff," he called, thankful to put the troubling memories aside.

"Biff, m' friend, 'n how does this day find ye?" Duff asked.

"Fit as a fiddle," Biff replied. "I'm surprised you're here with me, when you could be visiting with Miss Meagan," Biff said.

Duff glanced up at the clock. "Aye, 'n in five more minutes of the clock I will be," he said. "The lass 'n I will be taking our lunch at Tacky Mack's Café."

"The lady still has some cattle parked on your ranch, doesn't she?" Biff asked.

"Aye, that she does."

Biff chuckled. "That explains it, then. I can't see any other reason why such a beautiful young woman would have anything to do with an ugly old bum like you."

"Perhaps I should always keep ye at m' side, Biff. 'Tis said that you're so ugly the stork sent a letter of apology to yer mum. Next to you, I'd be an Adonis."

Biff laughed. "You know what they say. Ugly on the outside, handsome on the inside."

"Aye, Biff, ye are a good mon, I'll be the first to say that."

Without being asked to do so, Siffer began playing "Scotland the Brave."

"Ye've my thanks for that, Mr. Siffer," Duff said.

"It can't compare with the way you play it on the pipes," Siffer replied. "But it's a good song, even on the piano."

"Aye, that it is, 'n no matter how it's played, it takes me back to m' Highlands."

"I'm a bit melancholy myself today," Biff said.

"Oh?"

Biff shared his memories of the battle at Little Bighorn with Duff, and though he had told the story a few times before, Duff listened without interruption. He knew that telling the story was Biff's way of dealing with it.

Because of Duff's own troubled past, he knew that such unpleasant memories could never be totally erased; they could only be padded over, like a pearl in an oyster shell. And Biff's telling of the story added another layer onto the oyster.

Chugwater was the closest town to Sky Meadow, and as such it was the town where Duff did most of his business. The little town had been moribund until a railroad, connecting Cheyenne with Fort Laramie, passed through the town, saving it from extinction.

Before the arrival of the railroad, all the ranchers were required to drive their cattle to Cheyenne so they could be shipped to the eastern markets. And though that posed no major problem to the large ranchers who had many hands to make the drive, it was almost impossible for the small ranchers, who couldn't afford drovers to help them. The railroad had been a particular boon to them.

After leaving the saloon, Duff walked down the street to visit with Meagan Parker. Miss Parker owned Meagan's Dress Emporium, which was one of the most successful business operations in all of Chugwater. And, as Biff had pointed out to Duff, she also owned several head of cattle that were intermingled with Duff's herd.

Originally Meagan's participation in the ranch had been the result of a loan she had made to Duff, but when he attempted to pay her back, she said she would rather him consider it an investment.

Meagan and Duff were, as the women of the town explained to anyone who might ask about their relationship, courting. It had been an extended courtship . . . Meagan wasn't ready to give up her dress shop and move out to Sky Meadow, and Duff didn't want to move in to Chugwater. But though they had never finalized their relationship by way of marriage vows . . . the affection they felt for each other was none the weaker for any lack of documentation.

"Would ye be for takin' yer lunch with me at Tacky Mack's?" Duff asked.

"Aye, 'n 'twould be the greatest o' pleasures for ter be seen dinin' with m' mon in such a foine place now," Meagan teased, perfectly mimicking Duff's Scottish brogue.

"Och, lass, 'n ter hear you, 'twould make one think ye be Scottish born, 'n raised in the heather."

"Well, are we going to stand here jawboning all day, or are you going to feed me?" Meagan asked, laughing.

"Mary Ellen, I'm going to lunch. Keep an eye on things for me, would you?"

"Yes, ma'am, Miss Parker," her employee replied.

"How is your new girl working out?" Duff asked after they left the shop.

"Oh, she has been a wonderful help, but I'm not sure how long I'll be able to keep her."

"Is she that expensive for you?"

"No, not at all, and I'll keep her as long as I can. But she's sweet on that cowboy that works for Mr. Prescott . . . I mean Houser. Actually he's more than just a cowboy, he's the foreman, Ben Turley."

"Aye, Turley is a good mon."

"A good man that may wind up taking Mary Ellen away from me."

During the three-block walk to Tacky Mack's, conversation turned to Sky Meadow Ranch, and Duff had Meagan laughing about the barbs Elmer and Wang had exchanged with each other this morning.

"They argue like children, but either one of them would take a bullet for the other one," Duff said.

"Or for you," Meagan added.

"Aye, lass, or for me."

Rudy York owned the café, and he had named it Tacky Mack, after his son, Mack. Tacky Mack's Café used a black-and-white color scheme. The walls were black, halfway up, and white the rest of the way. Even the wooden floor was painted in checkerboard squares of black and white. York was a large man with white hair and a gregarious smile. He greeted all his customers by name if he knew them, and he did so now, as Duff and Meagan stepped into his place of business.

"Duff MacCallister and Miss Meagan Parker," York greeted effusively. "Welcome, welcome, come with me, I'll find a nice table by the window for you."

"Thank you, Rudy," Duff said.

"Duff, I know how much you like lamb," York said. "I got some in fresh today."

"Great! 'Tis lamb chops I'll be havin', then."

"And I, as well," Meagan said.

"Good, two lamb chop dinners it shall be," York said, leaving to see to their orders.

"Lamb chops? Did I hear you say that you want lamb chops? No self-respecting cattleman would ever eat lamb." The speaker was a large man, bald, but with a full, and bushy, black beard. He was sitting at a table very near to the one where Duff and Meagan had been seated.

"Merlin Goodman, sure now, 'n the best o' the mornin' to ye," Duff replied to the loudmouthed gentlemen who had made the derisive comment about lamb chops.

Goodman's Mountain Shadows Ranch was one of the eight very large ranches in the Valley of the Chugwater, but it was considerably smaller than Sky Meadow.

"You can keep your greetin'. I want you to answer me," Goodman said. "Do you, the largest cattleman in the valley, actually intend to sit here, in front of God and ever' body else, 'n eat lamb?"

"I like lamb," Duff said.

Goodman turned to address the other diners in the café. "Now, I ask you folks, what kind of man would eat lamb? Ever' one knows that anybody who would eat lamb ain't fittin' to be around."

"Why, Mr. Goodman," Meagan said sweetly. "Didn't the Lord Himself eat lamb?"

"Ha! She's got you there, Merlin," one of the other diners said.

"Give me m' bill, York," Goodman said in a blustering voice. "Maybe the Scotsman is goin' to eat it, but I sure as hell don't have to stay here 'n watch it. Pardon the language, ma'am," he added quickly to Meagan.

"Merlin, 'n would that be meanin' I'm to take you off the guest list for m' lamb supper next Easter?" Duff called to him as he left the café in a huff. The others in the café laughed.

"I tell you the truth, Duff," Bob Guthrie said. Guthrie owned the lumber and building supply company. "I probably like lamb as much as you do, but I'd never eat it out in public. Why, I'd more 'n likely lose half my customers if I did that."

"We've nae such problems as this back in Scotland," Duff said. "We have sheep and cattle raised right next to each other. Some farmers grow both and turn them out to graze in the same field. 'Tisn't true what the ranchers believe about sheep destroying the grass."

"I doubt we'll ever see anything like that here," Guthrie replied. "You folks enjoy your meal now," he added as he stepped over to the counter to pay for his lunch.

During their lunch, Charley Blanton, editor of the *Chugwater Defender*, came into the café.

"Hello, Rudy," Charley said. He held up a stack of papers. "Here's today's issue."

"I hope you leave me enough today. We were sold out by two o'clock yesterday," York replied as he took money from the cash box to pay for the papers that had been sold the previous day.

"If they're selling that well, you might want to consider increasing your ad space," Charley suggested.

Rudy chuckled. "That's what I like about you, Charley. You're always selling."

Charley saw Duff and Meagan at a nearby table.

"Good morning to you, Duff, and to you, Miss Meagan," Charley greeted.

"Hello, Charley," Duff replied. "Tell me, lad, how goes the continuing fight of the free press for truth, justice, and dare I say it, Scotsman that I am, the American way?"

"It is good that you would make such an inquiry, my friend," Charley replied. "With the newspaper as our mighty shield, we move forth with resolute valor and absolute determination!" Delivering his response in oratory fashion, Charley held up his finger to make a point.

"More honor to ye," Duff said.

"Miss Meagan, if you would like, I can just give you your paper here and tell the boy not to drop one off at your dress shop. That way, you can have a look at your ad."

"Thank you, Mr. Blanton, that would be nice."

Charley took a paper from the stack he had set by the cash box and handed it to her.

Meagan separated the pages of the newspaper then leafed through the pages in search.

"Ah, this is what I was looking for," Meagan said a moment later. She turned the newspaper around so that Duff could see the page she was speaking of. It featured an advertisement for her store.

LADIES' APPAREL

FINEST *garments made according to latest fashion*

MEAGAN'S DRESS EMPORIUM

"I see nae need for ye to be advertising, lass, since you are the only dressmaking store in town," Duff said.

"When you're in business, it never hurts to toot your own horn," Meagan replied with a broad smile. "And it also supports the local paper. You do agree with that, don't you?"

"Aye, lass, that I can agree with."

Chapter Nine

Newman, Texas

The tiny town of Newman, Texas, was on both sides of a single street. It had a general store, a drug-store, a leather goods store, a school, a church, and two saloons.

It had cost Sid Shamrock $2,000 to avoid going to jail in Elam and he had survived the last few weeks on the $100 he had gotten from Rosemary Woods. Now that money was almost gone, and he was here, in Newman, with barely enough money to buy drink and food for himself.

Glancing up toward the bar, Shamrock saw a man about five feet eight inches tall, with a narrow face, sunken cheeks, a nose rather like the beak of a hawk, and deep-set very dark eyes. This was someone who he knew, someone with whom he had once done a job.

Shamrock had very little money left, but what money he did have was worth investing in an idea he just had. This was someone he might be able to do business with.

Shamrock stepped up to the bar alongside the man, just as the bartender was pouring him a whiskey.

"I'm buying," Shamrock said.

The man looked toward him, and though no smile ameliorated his almost skeletal face, he did nod.

"Hello, Bodine," Shamrock said.

"Jefferson," Bodine replied.

"I'm using the name Shamrock now. How 'bout joining me at my table?"

Bodine picked up the glass and followed Shamrock back to his table, which was now occupied by a young cowboy and one of the saloon girls.

"That's my table," Shamrock said.

"You wasn't here, so now it's mine."

"Get up," Shamrock ordered, letting his hand rest on the butt of his pistol.

The cowboy looked at him for no more than a moment, then he stood up and reached for his drink.

"Leave the drink."

"The hell I will. I just . . ."

"I said leave it."

"Come on, honey, we can find another table," the bar girl said with a frightened glance at the two men who were standing there.

"What do you want?" Lucien Bodine asked.

"I want to do something that'll make us a little money," Shamrock replied.

"You got something in mind?"

"No. I was hopin' maybe you would."

"Yeah, I got an idea," Bodine replied.

* * *

Two days later the two men waited behind some rocks that shielded them from the road leading into Wayland, Texas.

"His name is Crites, Garrison J. Crites," Bodine said. "He's goin' into Wayland to buy a prize bull, 'n he'll have the cash money with him."

"How much do you think he'll have?" Shamrock asked.

"I don't figure he'll have any less than a thousand dollars on 'im," Bodine replied. "We'll split the money fifty, fifty."

"Five hundred dollars apiece," Shamrock said. He thought of the $14,000 he had just gone through, and by comparison, $500 was minuscule. On the other hand, compared to the $12 he had now, $500 was a fortune.

"Here he comes," Bodine said. "Wait till he gets close. We don't want him runnin' away. If he's well mounted, he could get away from us."

"What if he starts to ride off soon as we call out to 'im?" Shamrock asked.

"We won't be callin' out to 'im," Bodine replied, pulling his pistol.

Crites was well dressed, and riding a golden palomino with a Mexican saddle liberally decorated with silver. As soon as he drew even with them, both Shamrock and Bodine moved out into the road, right in front of him.

"My word, where did you two . . . ?" That was as far as he got before Bodine shot him.

"Twelve hundred 'n eighteen dollars," Bodine said a bit later, after counting out the money.

"I want his horse and saddle, too, unless you want it."

"You can have the horse, but leave the saddle."

"You're wantin' the saddle? All right, long as I'm gettin' the horse. 'N I don't blame you none, this is a damn fine-lookin' saddle," Shamrock said.

"Yes, 'n that's the problem. It's too fine-lookin'. It's the kind of saddle that people might recognize. We'll leave it here."

"Oh yeah, that's most likely right, ain't it?"

Bodine stuck his $609 down in his pocket, then remounted.

"Where you goin'?" Shamrock asked.

"Not sure," Bodine replied. "But wherever it is, we'll not be goin' together."

"Yeah," Shamrock replied. "Yeah, that's probably right."

Three weeks later, in the little town of Duxbury, Texas, Shamrock found himself in the Trail Dust saloon, sitting across the table from Jeb Jaco. Running into Jaco had been by chance, just as it had been when he had encountered Lucien Bodine a little earlier. And like Lucien Bodine, Jaco was a man Shamrock knew from his past, for the two had once joined together to rob a store.

Although Shamrock was more careful with the $600 than he had been with the $14,000 he had netted from the bank robbery in Sulphur Springs, he had managed to spend most of it, and once more, he was in need of cash. Meeting up with Jaco might just be the opportunity he was looking for.

"What are you doin' now, Jaco? How are you makin' a livin'?" Shamrock asked.

"I'm ridin' for the Duxbury brand," Jaco said.

"Duxbury?"

"J. F. Duxbury. He's a big rancher here in Fisher County, 'n he's the feller this town is named after."

"You like cowboyin', do you?" Shamrock asked.

"Twenty-one dollars a month and found? What the hell is there to like about that? Hell no, I don't like it, but it's three hots 'n a cot."

"How would like to do a job with me?"

"What kind of job? 'Cause to tell you the truth, that last job we done only got us about forty dollars, 'n it warn't hardly worth it."

"That's because we robbed a store," Shamrock said. "This time we'll rob a bank."

"A bank? I don't know, that seems like a pretty big job for just two men. I figure a job like that would call for at least six men," Jaco said.

"Do you know where to get four others?" Shamrock asked.

Jaco smiled. "Yeah, come to think of it, I do," he said.

"Then get 'em."

Twin Peaks Ranch

After supper one evening Brad Houser sent word to Dooley Carson and Slim Hastings, telling them that he wanted to see them in the ranch office. He had a plan in mind, and of all his hands, he believed that these two were best suited to carry it out.

Houser got out a bottle of whiskey, then put three

glasses on his desk as he waited. A moment later, there was a knock on his door.

"Come in!" he called.

It was very unusual for anyone to be summoned to the ranch office for any reason, but it was particularly unusual for someone to be summoned this late in the day. As Dooley and Slim came in, they exchanged nervous glances with each other.

"You . . . uh . . . wanted to see us, Mr. Houser?" Dooley asked, speaking for both of them.

"Yes, I do," Houser said. He poured whiskey into the three glasses, then picked two of them up and handed one to each of the two men.

"Have a drink," he invited.

"Yes, sir!" Dooley and Slim replied, a big smile spreading across their faces. They still didn't know what this about, but if they were about to be fired, they didn't think Houser would offer them a drink first.

"Salute," Houser said, holding his glass out toward them.

"Uh, yes, sir, here's to you," Dooley replied as he and Slim lifted their glasses as well.

"Gentlemen, I have a task I would like the two of you to perform for me."

"Yes, sir, whatever it is you want me 'n Slim to do, why, you can count on us a-doin' it," Dooley said.

"Tonight," Houser added.

"Tonight?"

"At midnight."

"This job you got for us has to be done at midnight?"

"Or shortly thereafter," Houser said. He refilled

the glasses. "It's a very special job that needs to be done in the middle of the night, so that no one sees you. It will require men of courage and intelligence. Do I have the right men for the job?"

"Yes, sir," Dooley said, smiling as his glass was refilled. "You got the right men, all right."

Houser took out two twenty-dollar bills.

"I forgot to tell you that it's worth twenty dollars apiece for you to do it, but you must tell no one else what you are doing."

"What about Turley? I mean, him bein' the foreman 'n all," Slim said. "He might figure out that me 'n Dooley left in the middle of the night. Oughten we to tell him?"

"Absolutely not. When I say I don't want anyone to know, then I mean I don't want anyone to know, and that includes Turley."

"All right, we won't tell 'im nothin', even if he was to ask," Dooley said hesitantly, wondering now what this was all about.

"And, if you handle this job well enough, there will be more jobs exactly like it for you to do, and more money for you."

Dooley and Slim smiled at each other.

"We'll do whatever it is you're a-wantin' us to do," Dooley said, "'N we won't tell nobody nothin' about it."

"Yes, sir, you can count on us," Slim added.

"Good, very good."

Houser began to give his instructions, and as the two men listened, they thought they had never heard anything so bizarre, even though that word wasn't in their vocabulary.

The two men discussed the task that had been given them as they walked back to the bunkhouse.

"Why is it you reckon he's a-wantin' to do somethin' like that?" Dooley asked. "Why, that don't make no sense at all."

"I don't know, but he give us twenty dollars to do it, so what I think we ought to do is, just do it."

Except for taking off their boots, neither Slim nor Dooley undressed for bed that night. Then, when they were sure everyone else was asleep, they left the bunkhouse as quietly as they could, went straight to the barn, and saddled their horses.

"Maybe we should lead them away instead of ridin' them," Dooley suggested. "That way we'll have a better chance of not bein' seen."

"Yeah, good idea," Slim agreed.

Five minutes later, with the horses saddled, Dooley and Slim led them away from the barn on the way to performing the task Houser had set for them.

The next morning Louie Patterson, who was one of the small ranchers recently arrived in the valley, was checking up on his small herd. Louie was a lean, lanky cowboy who seemed overpowered by the ten-gallon hat he wore. As he came to the top of a slight rise, he saw six cows cropping grass on the open range.

"Hello, cows," he said, speaking aloud. "Where did you critters come from?"

Louie was riding alone because his ranch was so small that he couldn't afford any hands. At the moment he didn't really need anyone as he had less than fifty head of cattle and one man could easily tend to a herd that small.

But now he was about to add ten additional cows. These were mavericks, cows that had been born, then wandered away before they were castrated and branded. Because there was no way of knowing who such cattle belonged to, they belonged to anyone who claimed them. Louie was a very active cow hunter, and more than half of his herd consisted of mavericks he had found and branded.

Particularly skilled in being able to approach isolated cattle without alarming them, he rode slowly up to the ten cows who, content with their grazing, paid no attention to the horse and rider who was coming near them.

"Well, now, it looks like you ten are about to get a new home. What do you say we . . ." Louie paused in midsentence. None of the ten cows were actually mavericks; all ten were wearing the Twin Peaks brand.

"Ahh, I see that you aren't mavericks," Louie said. "But since you have gone to all the trouble to come over here, I hate to have to send you back home. Besides, Twin Peaks has so many cattle that they won't be missing ten cows. I think I'll just take all of you."

Louie got the cows moving, and soon they were with the rest of his herd. Using a running iron, he turned the Twin Peaks brand into his own. The adjusted brand could pass a cursory glance, but not a close examination. He was taking a chance that there would be no close examination.

* * *

Ben Turley was beginning to get a little aggravated by the fact that two of his men, Dooley Carson and Slim Hastings, had not yet shown up for work. It wouldn't be so bad if it hadn't happened before, but this was the third time within the last week. When he stepped into the bunkhouse, he was angered, but not surprised, to find them both still in bed.

"What the hell are you two doin' in here, layin' around on your asses?" Turley demanded. "It's after eight o'clock in the morning and you two lazy bastards is still asleep."

Groggily, the two men got up.

"I seen that you didn't neither one of you get back in till near two o'clock this mornin'. 'N this isn't the first time. Are you two layin' out with whores that long? Where at are you gettin' enough money to do that?"

"We're gettin' up," Dooley said, waving his arm as in a motion to stop the haranguing.

Leaving the two men to get dressed, Turley hurried over to the ranch office to knock on the door. He entered when he was invited.

"Yes, Mr. Turley, come in. Coffee?" Houser offered. A bluesteel pot sat on a small stove, the aroma of the coffee perfuming the office.

"Yes, sir, I don't mind if I do."

Houser poured two cups and handed one to Turley. "Now, what can I do for you?"

"First thing is, Kenny, that is, Prosser, he's pulled all his cows off the Pine Flats, so if you want I'll move some of ours onto it."

"Whose cows would we be moving?" Houser asked pointedly.

"Your cows," Turley corrected hastily. "It would be your cows."

"Very good, Mr. Turley. All right, have some of the men divert a portion of the herd to the new grazing."

"Yes, sir. And now the second thing is, it looks like maybe somebody has been rustlin' Twin Peaks cows after all. I been keepin' a pretty good count of the young ones, most especial the ones that's less than a year old. Damn if they ain't been nigh on to fifteen or twenty of them been took, just in the last few days."

"I have suspected as much," Houser said.

"Yes, sir, well, it might be some of our own people."

"Why do you say such a thing?"

"I don't know. They's somethin' goin' on with Carson 'n Hastings, somethin' that don't seem quite right. They laid out, real late last night, 'n just a couple o' nights ago, they was out real late, too. So, it's got me to wonderin'. I mean, how is it that they've got enough money to do that ever' night? I'm thinkin' 'bout firin' 'em, if you want to know the truth."

"No, don't fire them now. Later, perhaps, if they give you any more trouble beyond their nocturnal habits. But they have been here more than most of the other hands, and they know the ranch intimately. I think there is something to be said for experience."

"Yes, sir, if you say so."

When Ben Turley went back outside, he saw three men come riding up toward the house. He stepped over to meet them.

"Can I help you men?"

"Yeah, we come to work."

"All right, dismount, and we'll talk."

"Talk about what?" one of the men asked.

"Why, talk about you workin' here, of course. I'm the foreman."

"No need to talk to you," one of the men said. "Houser's the one that owns this place, ain't he?"

"Well, yes, but as I say, I'm the foreman, and that means that I am the one you need to talk to, if you're plannin' on workin' here. That's 'cause I'm the one that does the hirin' 'n the firin'."

"You ain't hirin' or firin' us. We'll be workin' for Houser."

"We all work for Mr. Houser," Turley said, his voice showing his irritation. "But like I said, I am the foreman."

"It's all right, Mr. Turley," Houser said, stepping out of his office. He looked up at the three mounted men. "This is Mr. Knox, Mr. Malcolm, and Mr. Dobbins. I did get those name right, didn't I, gentlemen?"

"Yeah," one of the men answered. He was a big, brutish-looking man, clean-shaven and bald so that his head looked like a cannonball sitting on top of a short neck. "I'm Knox. 'Hard Knox,' they call me." He grunted a few times in what might have been a chuckle. "This here is Malcolm, 'n this one is Dobbins."

"Mr. Knox is quite correct, Mr. Turley, I did hire these men," Houser said. "Please find billets for them."

"All right," Turley said, a bit chagrined at being left out of the hiring. "Come with me, I'll show you where you'll bunk, then we can ride out 'n take a look at the herd."

"There is no need for you to take them out to the herd. They won't be subject to your orders. And they will not be working as cowboys. Mr. Knox, Mr. Malcolm, and Mr. Dobbins will be supernumeraries to the outfit."

"They'll be what?" Turley asked, not understanding the word.

"It means that they will not be involved in the day-to-day operation of the ranch. They will be working directly for me. As I get more settled here, I intend to get quite involved in all the activities going on in the valley," Houser said. "You, yourself, Mr. Turley, have pointed out the lamentable fact that I am losing cattle to these smaller ranchers."

"No, sir, now, that ain't what I said. I didn't say nothin' 'bout it bein' the small ranchers that has been takin' the cows. I just said we've lost some of 'em."

"And who do you suppose took them?" Houser asked.

"Well, I . . ." He didn't want to accuse Slim and Dooley, who had been employees for some time now, in front of these three men who had just arrived. "I don't rightly know who it is that's took them. It's just that I know most all the small ranchers, 'n I just don't think it was them that took the cows that's missin'."

"Perhaps it is the result of rustlers and not the small ranchers themselves, but ask yourself, Mr. Turley, if we are the victims of, let us say, self-motivated and independent rustlers, just who would be their market? What use would the independent rustlers have for the cattle they are stealing from us, if not to sell them to the smaller ranchers? I intend to investigate this problem, and whether it turns out to be rustlers, or small ranchers, my inquest may well put me at risk. I have hired these three gentlemen specifically to provide security should there be any attack against my person. I am sure that, under the circumstances, you can understand why my personal bodyguards should be answerable to me, and to me, only."

Turley nodded. "Yes, sir, I understand," he said.

"Good, then that means we'll have no problems. Discourse among employees is a very bad thing.

"Now, you were concerned about Dooley Carson and Slim Hastings, I believe. Please send them in to see me. I wish to talk to them."

"Yes, sir," Turley agreed.

"You got another job for us?" Dooley asked anxiously when, a short while later, he and Slim showed up in response to the summons.

"No," Houser said. "I shall have no further need for you to perform those special jobs. I have hired three men who will take care of such things for me in the future. However, I do appreciate what you two have done, and while I shall no longer be needing you for such services, I would like to show my appreciation for what you have done."

Houser gave each of the men a one-hundred-dollar bill.

"I give you this money with the understanding that it is not only a token of my appreciation, it will also be a guarantee of your silence."

"Yes, sir, Mr. Houser," Hastings said with a broad smile. "We ain't never goin' to say nothin' to nobody about it."

Shortly after Slim and Dooley left, Houser sent for Knox.

"Mr. Knox, you came rather highly recommended to me," Houser said.

"Yeah?"

"I am told that if I needed a particular job done, one that might seem"—he paused—"rather extreme, that you would be able to handle it."

"You're wantin' me to kill someone?"

"Most perceptive of you, Mr. Knox."

"Most what?"

"Yes, I want you to kill someone. There are two men who have knowledge of an activity that, were it to get out, could be quite damaging. They are quite aware of just how damaging such information would be to my future plans, and I fear they may be tempted to blackmail me."

"It'll cost you two hundred 'n fifty dollars apiece," Knox said with an evil smile.

"Here are two hundred and fifty dollars now. I'll give you the other two hundred and fifty after the job is done."

"Who is it you're wantin' me to kill?"

Chapter Ten

The girls who worked at Fiddler's Green offered nothing but drinks, smiles, and friendly conversation. Dooley Carson and Slim Hastings wanted more than that, and they had the money in their pockets to be able to make that happen, if they went to the right place.

The Wild Hog Saloon was just such a place. There, one could arrange for just about any pleasure, as long as they could afford it. Dooley and Slim had both the means, and the willingness, to buy some of the pleasures thus offered. At the moment they were sitting at a table with two of the girls, enjoying the drink and the company, preparatory to taking the two young ladies upstairs for the ultimate pleasure.

Another customer came into the saloon, and he stood at the end of the bar, staring at Dooley and Slim.

"Hey, ain't that one of them new men that come to work at the ranch?" Slim asked.

"Yeah," Dooley said. "I think it is. It's that Knox feller."

"You two," Knox called out to them. "You're cattle

"We ain't goin' nowhere with you, Knox," Dooley said. "We're goin' back out to Twin Peaks 'n get this settled."

Knox shook his head. "No, you ain't. Mr. Houser has told me not to let you two boys come back to the ranch, 'n I aim to see that you don't. Now, come on over to the sheriff's office with me."

"The hell we will!" Dooley shouted, making a grab for his pistol.

Dooley's sudden grab caught Slim by surprise, but it committed him to draw as well.

Knox wasn't surprised at all. He had been expecting it, had in fact been pushing to bring it about. And whereas the expressions on the faces of the two young cowboys were of fear and desperation, Knox was wearing a triumphant smile. He drew and fired, twice.

Dooley got off only one shot, his bullet punching a hole in the floor. Slim didn't even manage to bring his gun to bear before Knox's second shot slammed into his stomach.

The sharp, acrid odor of the cloud of gun smoke drifted across the room. Nobody said a word, so that the saloon, which but a second earlier was filled with the roar of gunfire, was now ghostly quiet.

Knox put his pistol away then walked over to the two bodies and started going through their pockets. He took all their money and stuck it down into his own pocket.

"What are you doin', mister?" someone asked.

"They won't be needin' this money no more," Knox replied. He took another look around the saloon, then left.

* * *

Duff was at Fiddler's Green having a drink with Meagan when Knox came in. Shortly after Knox came into the saloon, another man came in and whispered something to one of the patrons. He whispered to another and yet another, so that word spread quickly. It was Biff, himself, who came over to tell Duff.

"That ugly, brutish-looking man just killed two of the Twin Peaks riders," Biff said, nodding toward the man.

"Has anyone told Sheriff Sharpie?" Meagan asked.

"Apparently not. He's still walking around," Biff said.

"Maybe I should walk over to the sheriff's office and . . ." Meagan started, but she interrupted her sentence when she saw Sheriff Sharpie coming into the saloon.

The sheriff had his pistol in his hand.

"Mister?" he called.

All conversation stopped.

"You talkin' to me?" the cannonball-headed man replied.

"Yes, I'm talking to you, whatever your name is."

"It's Knox. Hard Knox," he added with a grin.

"I want you to come with me, Mr. Knox," the sheriff said.

"Why should I do that?"

"Because you are under arrest for the murder of Dooley Carson and Slim Hastings."

"They drew on me first," Knox said.

"We'll let the judge decide that."

"Duff," Meagan said in quiet urgency.

"I see it," Duff replied.

Meagan was referring to the fact that Knox had drawn his pistol and was holding it down by his side, away from the sheriff.

Quietly and unobtrusively Duff drew his British Enfield Mark I revolver and aimed it at the gun Knox was holding. Only Meagan and Biff knew what he was about to do, so when Duff pulled the trigger, everyone in the saloon was surprised.

The most shocked was Knox, who felt the pistol being knocked from his hand, even though his hand wasn't struck.

"What the hell?" he shouted in a shaken voice.

For just a second, Sheriff Sharpie was as surprised as anyone, until he saw the pistol lying on the floor at Knox's feet. Glancing toward the sound of the shot he saw Duff holding a smoking pistol.

"Thanks, Duff," the sheriff said.

Duff nodded in acknowledgment.

The next morning Brad Houser showed up at the sheriff's office.

"Sheriff, I have a habeas corpus here, demanding the release of my employee. I also have the sworn statements of fifteen eyewitnesses who say Carson and Hastings drew on Mr. Knox. He shot them in self-defense."

Sheriff Sharpie examined the papers Houser presented, then shook his head.

"I would have thought you would show more concern for the two men who were killed. After all, they did ride for you."

"They did work for me, that is true. But yesterday I learned that they had been stealing cattle from me and selling to the small ranchers. Consequently I terminated their employment in absentia and I sent Mr. Knox into town with instructions to turn them over to you for proper adjudication."

Houser pointed to some of the papers he had presented to the sheriff. "As you can see by the witness accounts, my client . . . that is, my employee, Mr. Knox, made that abundantly clear when he confronted them. All he wanted to do was for them to accompany him, peacefully, here to your office to turn themselves in. But alas, that wasn't to be. Now they lie dead, the victims of their own misdoings, and Mr. Knox, who was doing naught but following my instructions to turn them over to you, has been incarcerated.

"And now I ask that you turn Mr. Knox over to me."

The sheriff looked at the assorted papers, then nodded.

"You can have him," he said.

"Thanks for gettin' me out," Knox said on the way back to the ranch.

"That's all right. You are no good to me in jail. And tonight, I shall have a special assignment for you, Malcolm, and Dobbins."

"Hey, Turley," Cooper, one of the cowboys from Twin Peaks Ranch said. "Did you hear what happened to Slim 'n Dooley?"

"No, but not much they can do would surprise me.

What happened, did they get drunk 'n get throwed in jail?"

"No, sir, they got themselves kilt is what happened," Cooper said.

"What? They've been kilt? How did that happen?"

"It was one o' them new fellers, Knox, that done it."

"Knox? If they know he done it, how come he ain't in jail? I seen 'im come ridin' in with Mr. Houser just a few minutes ago."

"Yeah, Mr. Houser, what he done was, he got Knox outta jail."

Later that afternoon, Houser asked Turley to call all the hands together so he could address them. It took only a few minutes to get everyone together, and they stood out in the yard between the bunkhouse and the Big House to listen to what their boss had to say.

"Men, by now you have heard that two of your own number, men who worked for me, were guilty of stealing cattle from this very ranch."

None of the hands had heard that, and they exchanged questioning looks.

"Dooley Carson and Slim Hastings had been spiriting cows away, at night, and selling them to some of the small ranchers around here. When Mr. Turley informed me of their despicable scheme, I sent Mr. Knox to see them." At his comment, Houser paused for a moment and pointed to one of the three men standing behind him.

"Mr. Knox approached the two men and told them that I was aware they had been stealing from me, and they drew against him. That was a terrible mistake, for Mr. Knox, who is quite skilled in the employment of the revolver, withdrew his own weapon much more rapidly and engaged the two men. The result of the engagement between the three men was the ultimate death of Mr. Hastings, and Mr. Carson.

"Sudden death is always a sad thing, but in this case it is even worse because these two men, who all of us considered as our friends, brought on their own demise by their precipitate and foolish action.

"Let that be a lesson to you."

Houser turned and walked back to the ranch office, with the three new men following behind.

"All them big words he was usin', what the hell is it he just said?" one of the cowboys asked.

"He said that Slim 'n Dooley got themselves shot," another replied.

A few days subsequent to Houser's address to his company, Turley saw Kenny Prosser riding up. Prosser was pushing ten cows, and Turley walked out to see him.

"Hello, Kenny, what's this?" Turley asked.

"This here is ten cows that don't belong to me," Prosser replied. "They're Twin Peaks cows."

Turley checked the brand, which was a horizontal line upon which two point-up carets were placed, making it look like a pair of mountains.

"Yeah, it's our brand, all right. How'd you come by them?"

"I don't have no idea," Prosser said. "They wasn't there last night, but this mornin' when I went out to check on m' herd, there they was. I heard what happened to Slim 'n Dooley, 'n knowin' how Houser is already suspicious of me, they wasn't no way I was goin' to let them cows stay so I figured I'd better get them back here, quick as I could."

"Thanks. By the way, did you have breakfast this mornin'?" Turley asked.

"I didn't get around to it, seein' as I needed to get these critters back."

"Come on, Cookie's got some breakfast left, you can eat 'n I'll have a cup of coffee with you."

The cowboys' dining room was empty, except for three men, Knox, Malcolm, and Dobbins. They were sitting at one of the tables and enjoying a late breakfast.

"Cookie, you got 'ny biscuits 'n bacon left? Turley asked.

"You still hungry, Mr. Turley?"

"No, but a feller just brought some of our cows back to us that had wandered off, 'n since he didn't have no breakfast this mornin', why, I figured it would be a nice thing to thank 'im for bringing the cows back by feedin' 'im."

"All right, I got some left. You'll want some coffee, I reckon."

"I would appreciate it."

"Who are those three men?" Prosser asked a few minutes later, nodding to the three new hires. "I figure as long as I've been here in the valley I've seen near 'bout ever' cowhand there is, only I ain't never seen none of them before."

"I hadn't ever seen 'em before they come here, neither, but they ain't cowhands. You can't tell now, 'cause they're all sittin' down when ever' one else is at work. But if you was to see the way they're wearin' their guns, you'd know, they ain't cowhands."

"If they ain't cowhands, what do they do?"

"You see the bald-headed one there? He's the one that kilt Dooley 'n Slim."

"Was they really stealin' from the brand?" Prosser asked.

"I don't know. We was missin' some cows, and they was actin' mighty peculiar. It could be that they was."

"I don't believe it," Prosser said. "I know most all of the smaller ranchers, 'n I don't believe none of 'em would buy cows they thought was stoled, let alone stoled from Houser. He's done got hisself a reputation of not bein' none too friendly with the small ranchers, which is why I brung these cows back."

"And you don't have no idea how they got there?"

"No, I don't. It's like I said, onliest thing I know is they warn't there last time I checked."

Shortly after Prosser left, Turley was watching a couple of men changing the wheel to a wagon, when Knox came walking up to him.

"Houser wants to see you," Knox said.

"What about?"

"That's 'twixt you 'n him," Knox said. He pointed to the wagon wheel. "That wheel's goin' to need grease. I 'spect all of 'em will."

"Yeah, you're probably right," Turley said. He walked over to the office and knocked on the door.

"Come in."

"You wanted to see me, Mr. Houser?"

"Is it true what Knox told me? Did you give Prosser breakfast?"

"Yes, sir."

"I provide food for the men who work for me," Houser said resolutely. "I can't afford to feed any saddle bum who happens by, especially one of the small ranchers who I know is stealing from me."

"Well, now, that's where you're wrong, Mr. Houser. Kenny ain't stealin' from us. Fact is, he brung some of your cows back to us that had, somehow, wandered over to his place. I thought that, since he done that, why, it would be all right to give 'im breakfast since he hadn't et yet. 'N Cookie was more 'n likely goin' to throw it away, anyhow, seein' as ever' one else had done et."

"He brought the ten cows back?" Houser said, the expression on his face registering his surprise.

"Yes, sir, that's what he done."

The surprised look was replaced by another expression, one that Turley couldn't quite read, though it almost looked like he was annoyed.

"All right. You can get back to work," Houser said with a dismissive wave of his hand.

Turley didn't ask, but he wondered how Houser knew it was exactly ten cows. He hadn't given him any number.

Chapter Eleven

Five hundred miles south of Chugwater, six men rode into the small town of Seven Oaks, Texas. All six were wearing long, brown dusters, and all had their hats pulled so low that it was difficult to get a good look at anyone's face. The town was relatively busy, with a couple of wagons rolling slowly down the street. In front of Bloomberg's General Store a woman was putting groceries into a buckboard as her six-year-old son stood beside her. At the hotel a man was standing on the roof that overhung the first-floor porch, washing windows on the second floor.

Two older men were playing checkers in front of the feed store, while a couple of gossips looked on.

"You've got a jump, Fred," one of them said.

"I see the jump. Leave me be, let me play my own game."

"I'm just tryin' to help."

"I don't need no help."

Abe Sobel was just coming out of the leather-goods store, wearing a new pair of boots, putting weight on them to see how they would feel, when the six men passed right in front of them.

"I'll be damn," he said quietly. He hurried two doors down to the sheriff's office, where he found Sheriff Munson reading a newspaper, leaning back in his chair with his feet propped up on his desk.

"Sheriff, we may be about to have some trouble comin' soon," Sobel said.

Munson put down the paper. "What sort of trouble?"

"Could be bad trouble. I just saw Sid Shamrock 'n a bunch of men ridin' into town."

"Sid Shamrock? Are you sure?"

"Yeah, I'm sure."

"How do you know, for sure?"

"I seen his scar."

"Lots of men have scars."

"Trust me, Sheriff. This here is Shamrock."

"All right, you said a bunch of men. How many men?"

"Five men with 'im. Six, counting Shamrock."

Sheriff Munson stood up, then walked over to a hook from which hung his belt and holster. He put it on, then took a rifle from the rack and tossed it to Sobel.

"What's this for?"

"You don't expect me to go up against six men all by myself, do you?"

"Wait a minute!" Sobel said. "I ain't gettin' paid for this. What about your deputy?"

"He ain't in town; he's takin' a prisoner down to Badwater. As far as gettin' paid is concerned, I'll make you my deputy. You can get a month's pay for one afternoon of work."

"Yeah, if I don't get killed."

"You comin' with me, or not?"

Sobel nodded. "I'm with you," he said.

As Sheriff Munson and Sobel were discussing the situation, Sid Shamrock and the five men with him stopped in front of the bank.

"Hawke, you 'n Wix hold the horses. Jaco, you, Pete, 'n Evans come in with me," Shamrock ordered.

Shamrock and Evans turned their reins over to Hawke, Pete and Jaco gave theirs to Wix, then the four men went into the bank. There was a man waiting at the teller's window, and a woman, with a little girl, standing at the table. A teller was behind the cage and another man was sitting behind a desk to the side of the room.

The four men drew their guns.

"Let's make this easy!" Shamrock shouted.

The woman screamed, and Evans brought his pistol down on her head, dropping her to the floor. Her screaming stopped.

"Mama!"

"Shut up, little girl, or I'll hit you, too," Evans growled.

The customer at the window stepped to one side with his hands up. "I'm not armed," he said.

"You," Shamrock said as he handed a cloth bag to the teller. "Fill this up."

The teller began to scoop the money up from his drawer. A quick glance made it obvious that there were only a couple hundred dollars in the drawer.

Shamrock pointed toward the closed vault. "That ain't enough money. Empty the safe," he said.

"I can't."

Shamrock raised the pistol and pulled the hammer back. "What do you mean, you can't?"

"It's on a time lock," the teller said. "It can only be opened at nine in the morning and four in the afternoon."

"If you don't want your brains scattered all over the floor, you'll open it now."

"Mr. Fitzhugh is correct," the man behind the desk said. "The safe can only be opened twice a day."

"Who the hell are you?"

"I'm the bank manager."

"Well, Mr. Bank Manager, you'd better find some way to override that time lock."

"There is no way."

Wix came into the bank. "We need to get out of here now," Wix said urgently. "There's a bunch of men beginnin' to gather down the street."

"Open the safe, now!" Shamrock ordered.

"If you're going to shoot me, shoot me," the bank manager said calmly. "Either way, that safe can't be opened until four o'clock this afternoon." Inexplicably, he smiled. "I would suggest that you might try coming back then."

It was the smile. Shamrock was ready to just leave, but the son of a bitch smiled at him, and that pissed him off. Shamrock pulled the trigger, and, gasping, the bank manager clasped his hand over the wound in his stomach and went down.

"Let's go!" Shamrock ordered as he and the others left the bank and leaped into the saddles.

* * *

"I heard a shot!" Sobel shouted.

"Shoot 'em, shoot 'em!" Sheriff Munson shouted, and he and Sobel began shooting at the bank robbers as they galloped away. There were two other armed men who had joined them, and though they were shooting as well, not one of the outlaws was hit.

When Sheriff Munson and several others rushed into the bank, they saw the still form of C. D. Matthews, the bank manager, lying on the floor. They also saw Fitzhugh, the teller, and the little girl, squatted down beside the little girl's mother.

"Was Mrs. Margrabe shot?" Sheriff Munson asked.

"No," Fitzhugh said. "She was struck with a pistol, but she's beginning to come around."

"Mr. Matthews?" the sheriff asked.

Fitzhugh shook his head sadly. "He's dead, I fear," Fitzhugh said.

Sheriff Munson looked at Sobel. "You say it was Sid Shamrock?"

"Yeah."

"How can you be so sure? The reason I ask is, I'm going to put out a telegram about it, and I don't want to say it was Sid Shamrock unless I can be absolutely certain."

"I uh." Sobel saw that everyone else was looking at him, waiting for his answer.

"I rode with him once," Sobel said quietly.

"Thanks," Sheriff Munson said. He put his hand on Sobel's shoulder. "As far as I know, there's no paper on you."

"I . . . I don't know whether there is or not."

"Sobel, you've not given me one lick of trouble from the time you come into town. And you could have kept quiet when you saw Shamrock riding into town, but you came in to tell me about it. So whether there is or not, as far as I'm concerned, there's no paper on you."

"Thanks, Sheriff."

"No, thank you for coming to the aid of the town when you were needed."

"Hear! Hear!" one of the townspeople said, and the others gave a friendly nod.

"Four hundred and thirty-seven dollars?" Hawke said. "That's all the hell we got, is four hundred and thirty-seven dollars? That's not even a hundred dollars apiece."

"Well, how much money did you have in your pocket this morning?" Shamrock asked, duplicating the same question he had asked Abe Sobel after the much more fruitful bank robbery in Sulphur Springs.

"Two dollars."

"Then you're money ahead, ain't you?"

"Hey, Shamrock, what do you say we find us some town where we can spend some of this money? It ain't much, but it's enough to get drunk on, 'n maybe get a whore," Wix said.

"Ha! You'll need to get the whore drunk, too, before she'll go with you," Jaco said, and the others laughed.

"It'll be best if we don't all ride in together," Shamrock said. "Just in case word has gone out to look for six men."

"How is word goin' to go out?" Jaco asked. "You know that there ain't nobody that's got up here this far before we did."

"Telegraph coulda done it," Evans said.

"Yeah, I forgot about the telegraph. We shoulda cut the wires. If we had cut the wires, we wouldn't have no telegraph to be a-worryin' about," Hawke said.

"Yeah, and if a frog had wings, it wouldn't bump its ass ever' time it jumps," Shamrock said. "It's too late to be worrying about it now."

Sid Shamrock woke up in a whore's bed in Whitcomb, Texas. During the night the sheet had pulled down to the woman's waist, exposing oversized, blue-lined breasts, one of which had burn scars from cigarettes. She was snoring, and a bit of saliva was dribbling from her lips.

"How damn drunk was I to choose this one?" he asked himself quietly.

He saw a fly land on one of the whore's breasts, and started to brush it away but decided against it. Instead he watched as it crawled up onto the nipple then sat there for a moment, rubbing its wings with its back legs. The whore twitched a couple of times, then brushed it away.

With a quiet chuckle, and without awakening her, Shamrock put on his clothes then went downstairs. The saloon was empty, so he walked across the street to have breakfast. Here, he picked up a paper from the counter and took it with him to read as he waited for the bacon and eggs to be brought to the table.

He was somewhat disturbed that a story about the

bank robbery was above the fold on the front page. He had hoped, and thought, that they would get a little more time than this.

Banker Killed in Seven Oaks

(BY TELEGRAPH) C. D. Matthews, manager of the Bank of Seven Oaks, was murdered during a bank robbery. Mrs. Pauline Margrabe received a skull fracture when one of the outlaws hit her on the head with the butt of his pistol.

The bank robbers were unaware that the vault is controlled by time lock, so the money in the vault was untouched. Only the money that was in the teller's cash drawer was taken, an amount that totaled $437.00.

That was small reward for the outlaws who are now wanted, not just for bank robbery, but for murder as well. One of the bank robbers has been identified, that person being Sid Shamrock. It is believed that Sid Shamrock is the leader of the gang.

Shamrock is about five feet ten inches tall, with blond, or very light brown hair. He is normally clean-shaven, and can be identified by a purple scar that cuts down through his left eye. The resulting scar has left a drooping eyelid.

Seeing his name and his description in the story startled him.

"What?" Shamrock said aloud. "How the hell do they know that?"

"I beg your pardon, sir, were you speaking to me?" the man at the next table asked.

"No, I wasn't, and mind your own damn business," Shamrock replied with a growl, and without further explanation.

How was it possible that he had been identified? Prior to the robbery, he had never been to Seven Oaks in his life. And unlike some outlaws who were widely known, who in fact took pride in their notoriety, Shamrock had purposely avoided being known, even changing his name when his previous name had been compromised.

Jaco and Wix came into the café while Shamrock was still eating his breakfast, and they joined him at his table.

"Do you know where the others are?" Shamrock asked.

"Yeah, I just seen Pete 'n Hawke over in the Brown Dirt Saloon. I don't know where Evans is, though," Wix said.

"Pete more 'n likely knows where Evans is, 'cause I seen them together last night," Jaco added.

"After breakfast, get 'em rounded up. We've got to get out of here," Shamrock told the others.

"Why?" Wix asked. "I've still got a little money to spend. 'N I've found me a good-lookin' whore to spend it on," he added with a grin.

"Because word has already gone out," Shamrock said. He tapped the story in the paper. "We have been identified. I don't know how they found out, but they know who we are."

Actually, only Shamrock had been identified, but by saying "we" had been identified, it gave more urgency to his suggestion that they leave the state.

"What are we going to do now?" Jaco asked.

"Like I said, we're gettin' out of here."

"Where at are we a-goin'?" Wix asked.

"We're going to Wyoming," Shamrock replied.

"Wyoming? What the hell is in Wyoming?" Wix asked. "Damn it, I don't like it that far north. It gets cold in Wyoming."

"Folks has most likely not never heard of us in Wyoming," Shamrock said. And his brother was there, Shamrock thought, though he didn't say that aloud.

Chapter Twelve

About forty miles south of where Shamrock and the others had spent the night, back in Seven Oaks, Sheriff Munson had invited Abe Sobel down to the sheriff's office.

"I have something I would like to show you," the sheriff said. "I've got a reward poster that you might be interested in."

"On me?" Sobel asked apprehensively.

"No, not on you. But I think you'll be interested in this one, nevertheless. It's one I just put out."

When they reached sheriff's office, Munson pulled out a just-printed flyer.

—WANTED—
SID SHAMROCK
$5,000 Reward
☞ **DEAD OR ALIVE**
$2,000 ea. for THOSE WITH HIM
(as yet unidentified)

CONTACT: Sheriff Munson, Seven Oaks, Texas

"That's an awful lot of money," Sobel said.

"Would you be interested in going after it?"

"Yeah," Sobel said, nodding. "Yeah, I would."

"Do you have any idea where to start?"

"He has a brother," Sobel said. "I told you I used to ride with him? Well, it was for only one job, 'n me 'n Shamrock 'n his brother did it together."

"Abe, you didn't . . . uh, what I'm asking is, was anyone . . . ?"

"There was nobody hurt in the job," Sobel replied.

Sheriff Munson nodded. "Good. If there was nobody killed, then I can disregard any paper that might come out about it."

Sobel went back to his room in Mrs. Rittenhouse's Boarding Home and began packing to start on the quest. He had $215 left from his share in the job he had done with Shamrock and his brother. That was all that remained from the $1,000 he had been given. He knew, without a doubt, that the brothers had netted a great deal more from the bank robbery in Sulphur Springs, but he was outnumbered and unable to do anything about it.

That had been his first and only foray beyond the limits of the law. Ever since his arrival in Seven Oaks, Sobel had earned his living as a mechanic and hostler for the Potashnick Stage Coach Line. The last thing he would have to do before leaving town would be to quit his job.

"I'm goin' to hate to lose you, Abe, you're a good mechanic and a dependable man," Morty Potashnick said. "But, if you're going after the sons of bitches who killed Mr. Matthews, then you have my blessings.

Wait a minute, you've got near a month's wages coming to you. I'll give 'em to you now."

Although only half of the month had passed, Potashnick counted out $55, which was actually the full month's payment.

"That's very generous of you, Mr. Potashnick."

"Glad to do it. Good luck to you, Abe."

Sky Meadow Ranch

"Damn, damn, damn!" Elmer said.

"Three damns, is it?" Duff said. "'N would ye be for tellin' me what calamity it is, that would elicit a three-damn fanfare?"

"The sucker rod on the windmill is busted."

"Do you suppose Mr. Guthrie would have a replacement?"

"Yeah, I know he does, on account of I've saw 'em there when I was in his place oncet," Elmer replied.

"Well, then, the broken rod doesn't seem to be that much of a disaster. Just send a couple of men into town and . . ."

"They mighten not get the right one," Elmer said. "I'd best go in my ownself. I know exactly what I'm lookin' for."

"All right."

"'N if you don't mind, I'll take Wang with me. I've got a hankerin' for Chinese food, 'n I think one of the waitresses at Lee Fong's Chinese Restaurant has set her cap for Wang, 'cause when he is with me, we get more food."

"Then, by all means, take Wang with you."

As the two men were talking, they saw a rider

thieves, 'n Mr. Houser wants me to take you down to the jail 'n turn you over to the sheriff."

"What? What do you mean, we're cattle thieves?" Dooley said.

"You've took twenty head of Twin Peaks cows," Knox said.

"We didn't do no such thing."

By now all other conversation in the saloon had stopped as they followed the exchange between the man whose head looked like a cannonball, and Dooley Carson and Slim Hastings. Nobody knew the man with the cannonball head, but everyone knew Carson and Hastings—they had worked at one ranch or another for the last couple of years.

"Mr. Houser said that you did take 'em. Are you callin' him a liar? I work for Mr. Houser, 'n I won't put up with nobody callin' him a liar. I'm loyal to the brand, unlike you two, who have stoled twenty cows. What did you do with 'em?"

"Wait a minute," Hastings said. "We took them cows, yes, but they wasn't stoled. We took 'em 'cause Mr. Houser told us to take 'em."

"Why would Mr. Houser tell me that you stoled 'em, if he told you to take 'em?" Knox asked.

"I don't know. All I know is we was told to take 'em."

Knox held out his hand, then crooked his finger. "Why don't you two come with me down to the sheriff's office? You can tell him that Mr. Houser told you to steal them cows, and Mr. Houser can tell him that you stoled them of your own account, 'n we'll see who the sheriff believes, you, or Mr. Houser."

Dooley stood up then and let his hand hang loosely toward the pistol at his side. Slim stood as well.

coming toward them, and as Percy Gaines had been doing a couple of weeks earlier, this rider, too, was pushing some cows before him.

"That's Poke Terrell," Elmer said. Poke was the twelve-year-old son of Ethan Terrell, a small rancher, whose ranch, the Diamond T, was somewhat larger than The Queen. Elmer chuckled. "For a boy, he's pretty good at pokin' cows, ain't he?"

"The Diamond T does quite well," Duff said.

"Yeah." By then Poke was upon them.

"What do you have there, Poke?" Elmer asked.

"These here is your cows, 'n Pa asked me to bring 'em back to you."

"I thank ye, boy," Duff said. "And I thank yer father as well."

"Pa said to tell you that he don't know how them cows got from your place over to our'n. I mean it bein' more 'n ten miles 'n all."

"I suppose they just wandered off," Duff replied. "But it was good of ye to bring 'em back."

"By the way, Poke, the heathen has made some doughnuts if you'd like to take a few with you when you start back home," Elmer invited.

"Yes, sir, I'd love that. Thanks!"

A few minutes later Poke started on the ten-mile ride back home, eating one doughnut and carrying almost a dozen with him.

"What would you like to bet that they don't a one o' them doughnuts make it all the way back to the Diamond T?" Elmer asked.

"I would nae be for takin' that bet," Duff said.

Duff was quiet for a moment before he spoke again. "Elmer, do ye think it be a strange thing that our cattle seem to be straying off now? First, it was Percy who brought them back, 'n now the young Terrell boy."

"I don't know," Elmer said. "I reckon I ain't give it that much thought. Most especial since we ain't actual lost none, I mean, what with Percy 'n the boy here, bringin' 'em back."

"Aye, should be nothing to worry about, but I cannae help but consider the wonder of it. Why have our cattle started to wander when they have nae done so before?"

"That is a puzzlement," Elmer agreed. "Well, I think I'll get me a team hitched up to a wagon so's me 'n Wang can go into town 'n buy us a sucker valve."

Twin Peaks Ranch

"Me 'n Pearson need to go into town 'n get some more grease," Cooper said. Cooper and Pearson had taken over the job of changing the wagon wheels since Slim and Dooley had been killed. "Some o' them wagon wheels is so dry that it'd cause a body to wonder how it is that they was a-turnin' at all. 'N what we done is, we run outta grease afore we could get 'em all packed."

"All right," Turley said. "I've been needin' a few things my ownself, so I'll just go into town with you."

"There ain't no need in them two boys goin' with you," Malcolm said. "Me 'n Dobbins will go with you."

"I thought you men weren't going to have anything to do with the regular work on the ranch," Turley said.

Malcolm chuckled. "Hell, we ain't goin' to change

the damn wheels or pack the grease. We're just goin' into town is all."

"Yeah 'n maybe get us a whiskey or two," Dobbins added.

Shortly after Turley, Malcolm, and Dobbins left, Knox stepped into the ranch office without being invited. Houser looked up, the expression on his face registering his irritation at the intrusion.

"Mr. Knox, this is my private office," Houser said. "I don't allow my employees to come in at their whim. You must either be invited or request permission to enter."

"Yeah, well I sort of thought that, bein' the way things is, that I wasn't like anyone else who works for you."

"Oh? And just what sets you apart from the others, may I ask?"

"Slim 'n Dooley."

"I beg your pardon?"

"You know, how you had me take care of Slim 'n Dooley for you? Well, it's more 'n likely that you'll be findin' more jobs for me like that. So what I was thinkin' is, maybe you'd like to pay me a little more 'n you're payin' me now."

"Mr. Knox, I gave you a special bonus for that job, and I am paying you one hundred dollars a month now. That is almost five times more than I am paying any of my hands."

"Yeah, but I know things that your hands don't know. Plus, I got Malcolm 'n Dobbins to look after. So I was thinkin', maybe, two hundred dollars a month."

"Suppose I meet your demand, Mr. Knox. What assurance will I have that you won't come back, asking for more?"

Knox held up his right hand. "Well, you got my word on it, Mr. Houser."

"Your 'word,' Mr. Knox, is a fragile guarantee at best. However, under the circumstances, I will have to depend on it. You shall have your raise."

Chapter Thirteen

It was just a coincidence that Elmer and Wang were going into town at the same time as Turley, Malcolm, and Dobbins. Elmer and Wang were on a mission to buy a new sucker rod for the windmill. Elmer was driving the wagon.

"You think Mai Lin will be the one to serve us?" Elmer asked.

"Yes."

"Good. She's got a hankerin' after you, Wang. 'N she always treats us real good."

"Yes," Wang said.

"She'd make you a good wife, you know. And she's a pretty thing, too."

"It is not good for a Shaolin priest to marry."

"But you ain't really a Shaolin priest no more, I mean, not since you come to America."

"Wherever I am, I will always be a Shaolin priest."

Elmer nodded. "Yeah, I reckon you're right. 'N I can understand about you not gettin' married. It's like Duff not marryin' Miss Meagan, though someday he might. 'N it's like me not marryin' up with Vi."

Vi Winslow and Elmer often kept company.

"Wonder what ole Le Fong has cooked up today."

"You will like it," Wang said.

"How do you know I'll like it?"

"Because you are always hungry, and all food tastes good to the hungry mouth."

"That's another one o' them Chinese sayin's, ain't it?"

"I am Chinese and I did say it," Wang replied with a smile. "So, yes, you might say it is a Chinese saying."

Elmer was saved from having to come up with some clever retort by the fact that they had arrived at Guthrie's Building Supply.

"All right, you wait here, I'll go in and buy the sucker rod," Elmer said as he climbed down from the wagon. "Then we'll go down 'n let you 'n Mai Lin make eyes at each other."

A short time thereafter, Turley, Malcolm, and Dobbins arrived in town and as they rode up Clay Avenue, they saw Wang leaning against the back of the wagon, with his arms folded across his chest.

"Look at that damn Chinaman, just a-standin' there like he owned the damned place," Malcolm said.

"Hey, Chinaman!" Dobbins called. "What are you doin' standin' out here in front of a white man's place of business? How come you ain't doin' laundry?"

Malcolm laughed at Dobbins's "joke" but Wang paid no attention to the taunt.

"What's the matter, Chinaman? Are you deaf?" Dobbins asked.

Wang didn't even glance toward him.

"Damn, Dobbins, looks to me like the Chinaman is ignorin' you," Malcolm said.

"What the hell? Don't you hear me talkin' to you, you yeller-skinned bastard?"

"Come on, Malcolm, Dobbins, we come into town to get some hub grease, 'n maybe have a drink," Turley said. "We didn't come into town to yell at Wang. I know him, he's a good man."

Malcolm dismounted. "I ain't goin' nowhere till I get this heathen bastard to talk to me."

"Maybe he don't talk English," Dobbins suggested. He dismounted as well.

"Oh, he speaks English, all right," Elmer said, coming out of the hardware store at that moment, carrying the long sucker rod. He put the purchase in the back of the wagon.

"Why is it, then, that he isn't talking?" Malcolm asked. "Why is it that we're doin' all the talkin'?"

"He who knows most speaks least. He who knows least speaks most," Wang said.

Elmer laughed.

"What?" Malcolm asked angrily. "What the hell did that Chinaman just say?"

"I think he just said you don't know nothin'," Dobbins said.

"Ahh, come on, you two," Turley said. "Leave Wang alone. The Chinaman ain't botherin' nobody." He glanced toward Elmer. "I'm sorry about this, Mr. Gleason."

"*Mister* Gleason? You're callin' that ole coot, mister?"

"I am."

"Well, maybe me 'n Dobbins will just have to take

care of *Mister* Gleason after we take care of the Chinaman." The two men dismounted.

"Now, boys, I don't think what you've got in mind is such a good idea. Trust me, it ain't goin' to turn out well for you," Elmer said.

"It ain't goin' to turn out well, huh? What do you say about it, Chinaman? Is it goin' to turn out bad for us?" Malcolm teased.

"A wise man thinks twice and acts once. A foolish man acts without thinking," Wang said.

"Now, what the hell does that mean?" Malcolm asked.

"I think he just said you was a fool," Dobbins said.

"We'll just see who is a fool after we whip your ass," Malcolm said.

"No, you won't," Elmer said with a little chuckle.

"What do you mean, 'No, we won't'? No, we won't what? 'N what are you laughin' at?" Dobbins asked.

"What I mean is, no, the two of you together cannot whip Wang's ass. Now, why don't you boys go on about your business?"

"Not until we take care of business with this here Chinaman," Malcolm said.

"Don't say you weren't warned."

"You're an old man, 'n this Chinaman ain't no bigger 'n a gnat's ass. Are you tellin' me that you're goin' to stop me from whippin' up on him?"

"There's no need for me to help. Wang can take care of his ownself."

"Really? Well, we'll just see about that," Dobbins said.

"Yeah," Malcolm added. "I think this Chinaman needs to be taught a lesson."

"You boys is kind of slow to learn, ain't you?" Elmer asked.

"Let's go," Turley said. "You have no business doin' this."

"We'll be along in a minute," Malcolm said. "Soon as we've taught the Celestial a lesson he ain't soon to forget."

Warily, Malcolm and Dobbins moved toward Wang, separating so that they were approaching him from either side. Wang had not moved, nor did he appear to take any notice of the two men who were now advancing toward him.

By now almost a dozen citizens and visitors to the town, who were in the vicinity of the showdown when it started, had gathered to watch the drama play out before them.

"Oh, somebody do something," a well-meaning lady said. "Those two men on that one little Chinaman? This isn't fair."

"I don't know, ma'am," one of the spectators said. "I kinda got me an idea that the Chinaman can take care of himself."

"There's no way that he can," another said. "Two of 'em against one? And the Chinaman ain't very big, as you can see."

"I'm tellin' you one last time, 'n for your own good. You two men had best leave him alone," Elmer said.

"Old man, you just wait your turn. After we take care of this Chinaman, I'm goin' to personally settle your hash," Malcolm said.

Elmer chuckled. "Oh, now, you see, that there just proves that you don't know what you're talkin' about. On account of there ain't a-goin' to be no 'after.'"

"Ha, the Chinaman don't hardly talk none at all, 'n you talk too much," Dobbins said.

"I reckon that's so," Elmer said. "Wang, I'm going to step into the drugstore here 'n get me some cough medicine. Soon as you get through with these two fools, we'll go have our dinner."

"You will get some lemon drops?" Wang asked.

Elmer chuckled. "Yeah, I'll get you some lemon drops. Damn, if you ain't like some kid, wantin' lemon drops all the time."

"I like lemon drops."

Elmer stepped into the drugstore.

"What are you wantin' lemon drops for? You ain't goin' to have no teeth when we're finished with you," Malcolm said.

"Hell, Malcolm, you don't really need no teeth for lemon drops. All you got to do is suck on 'em for a little while till they melt," Dobbins said with a little laugh.

Since asking Elmer for lemon drops, Wang hadn't moved, nor even looked at the two men. He continued to stare ahead, with his arms folded across his chest.

"The old man left," Malcolm said. "I reckon he didn't want to stay 'n watch his Chinaman friend get his ass beat."

"How come he ain't payin' no attention to us?" Dobbins asked.

"Maybe he thinks if he don't pay no attention to us, we'll leave 'im be," Malcolm suggested.

"For the last time, I'm tellin' you to leave him alone," Turley said. "You don't have no idea what it is that you two men is lettin' yourselves in for."

"Don't you worry none about it, Turley. We're goin' to end this quick, then we'll go get us that whiskey. You scoot over to the other side, Dobbins. Let's finish him off."

Malcolm and Dobbins both put up their hands and began to dance around like boxers in a ring. One of them moved to Wang's left, the other to his right.

"Both of them big men is goin' after that one little Chinaman?" one of the spectators said. "I agree with Miz Sidwell. This ain't fair. There ain't nothin' fair about it."

"You want to help the Chinaman out, do you, Boyce?"

"Me? No, sir, that's a couple of pretty big men," Andy said. "There ain't no way I'm goin' up agin either one of 'em. That's why I am sayin' that it ain't fair for both of 'em to go up agin that little Chinaman, him bein' all by hisself, 'n all."

"Now!" Malcolm shouted, and he and Dobbins both rushed Wang. As if his arms were spring-loaded, Wang snapped both of them straight out to either side, catching the two men in their Adam's apples with the knife edge of his extended hands. Both Malcolm and Dobbins went down, clutching their throats and gasping for breath.

With the two men writhing on the ground, Wang continued to stare blankly into space, his arms once more folded across his chest.

"Damn! I ain't never seen nothin' like that!" Andy said.

"How'd he do that?" another asked.

Elmer came out of the drugstore then, carrying two bags. He looked at Malcolm and Dobbins, both on their knees now, but with their hands still clutching their throats.

There were still several people gathered around the three Twin Peaks riders.

"You three boys shoulda listened to me. Especially you, Turley. You're a good man, you shoulda knowed better. I give you fair warnin', not to be messin' with Wang, 'n you can't say that I didn't. Now, I'm a little worried about you. Are you boys all right?" Elmer asked. "Wang didn't hurt you too much, did he?"

"Who . . . who the hell is he?" Dobbins asked, his voice raspy.

"His name is Wang Chow. He's a cook and all-around handyman for Duff 'n me, out at Sky Meadow. By the way, you can consider yourselves lucky."

"Lucky? How so?" Malcolm asked, his voice as raspy as Dobbins's voice had been.

"Because he could have kilt you if he had wanted to," Turley said.

"How'd a Chinaman learn to do stuff like that?" Andy asked.

"He is a Shaolin priest," Elmer said.

"A priest? He's a priest 'n he can fight like that?" Andy said. "He sure as hell ain't like no priest I ever seen."

"Yeah, well, how many priests have you seen, anyhow? I'll bet you ain't set foot inside of a church in four or five years, if ever at all. But he's not that kind of a priest. Here, you two boys have a lemon drop," Elmer said, taking a couple of pieces of candy from one of the two sacks, then holding them out toward Malcolm and Dobbins. "If you just suck on 'em real slow, it'll make your throat feel better."

Malcolm waved him away. "I don't need no damn candy. What I need is a whiskey," Malcolm said as he got up and started toward the nearest saloon. Dobbins and Turley followed him.

"I told you," Turley said. "You men wouldn't listen to me, but you can't say that I didn't warn you."

Elmer noticed that they were heading toward Fiddler's Green.

"Come on, Wang, let's me 'n you go down to Lee Fong's 'n have us a good dinner."

Wang and Elmer climbed into the wagon, then drove down to the other end of town toward the Chinese restaurant.

Chapter Fourteen

By the time Turley and the other two stepped into the saloon a moment later, word had preceded them about their encounter with Wang.

"I don't normally do this," Biff Johnson said. Biff owned Fiddler's Green Saloon. "But I'm goin' to give you three boys a drink on the house. I figure you could use one, seeing as you boys were outnumbered in the fight you were just in."

"Outnumbered? What are you talking about?" Dobbins asked with a rasp.

"I'm told that there were only the two of you. Is that right?"

"Yeah, two of us, one of him."

"I have seen Wang fight before, and figurin' that he was the one you were fighting, then, for all intents and purposes, you were outnumbered."

"Who . . . who is that Chinaman, anyway?" Andy asked. Andy, who had been one of the spectators, followed the three Twin Peaks men down to Fiddler's

Green. "That old feller said that he was a priest of some kind."

"Wang Chow is a priest, but not the kind of priest you know about." Biff chuckled. "Though to be honest, I doubt you know about any priests at all. Anyway, a Shaolin priest is something special. All they do all day long is practice martial arts."

"Art? You mean like paintin' 'n such?" Malcolm asked.

Biff chucked. "No, I mean practice fighting. If there had been ten of you, Wang would have prevailed."

"Lord Almighty," Andy said, shaking his head almost reverently. "I ain't never seen, nor even heard of, anyone like that."

"I must confess that though I had heard of them, Wang is the first such practitioner of the art that I ever actually saw," Biff said.

"I was in here once when somebody took it in mind to throw Wang out," Turley said. "I seen then, what he could do. You should have listened to Mr. Gleason and me."

"That old coot? What the hell does he know?"

"He knew that you were making a mistake," Biff said with a chuckle. "But there was no way anyone could have told you so that you would have believed it. It was something you had to see for yourself."

"Yeah, well, I seen it," Dobbins said. "What does that Chinaman do, anyway? He ain't a cowboy, is he?"

"He's a cowboy when he has to be, but the truth is, Wang Chow is the kind of man who can do anything," Biff said.

* * *

When Turley, Malcolm, and Dobbins returned to the Twin Peaks ranch, word of their adventure in town had preceded them, and they were met with laughter and a lot of derisive calls.

"Hey, Malcolm! Is it true that a little Chinaman whupped you 'n Dobbins?"

"Hell, I heard he done it 'n didn't even break a sweat!" another shouted.

There were many more taunts and jibes from the other hands, then Turley got word that Houser wanted to see him.

"Yes, sir?" Turley said a few minutes later as he stood across the desk from Houser in the ranch office.

"Is it true what they are saying, about you letting Malcolm and Dobbins be humiliated by a Chinese man?"

"Humiliated?" Turley paused for a moment then added, "Yeah, I guess that is the way I'd put it."

"You are my foreman, Mr. Turley. For you to allow two of your men to be humiliated by a mere Chinese man, is not conducive to discipline."

"Yes, sir, that may be so. But in the first place, Mr. Houser, I know Wang Chow, and I knew what he could do if Malcolm 'n Dobbins went after 'im. I tried to tell 'em, but they wouldn't listen to me. 'N in the second place, you told me yourself that neither Knox, or Malcolm, or Dobbins worked for me. 'N since I'm not their boss, there wasn't nothin' I could do about it except try 'n talk 'em out of it, 'n I did, only that didn't work out all that well. You see, the thing is, this here Wang feller ain't what you would call a mere Chinaman. He's a priest."

"A priest?"

Despite himself, Turley chuckled. "That's what ever' one says, soon as they hear he's a priest. But he ain't the kind of priest you think of, when you hear the word. I mean, he don't wear no collar or nothin'. But accordin' to Mr. Johnson at the Fiddler's Green, Wang Chow trained for most of his life to fight, only it ain't like ordinary people would fight. It's a special kind of fightin' 'n Johnson says he could probably whup up on ten men as easy as he did Malcolm and Dobbins."

Houser sighed, then ran his hand through his hair. "Yes, well, I can't let him do such a thing with impunity. I understand that he works for Duff MacCallister?"

"Yes, sir."

"I shall pay Mr. MacCallister a visit and register my complaint with him."

The next day, Elmer, Wang, and a couple other hands were busy mounting the sucker rod on the windmill when a surrey with a yellow leather seat came up into the yard. Duff, who was watching the men work, recognized the man driving the surrey, and he stepped forward to greet him.

"Mr. Houser," Duff said. "What would be bringing ye to Sky Meadow?"

"I want to know what kind of heathen monster you've got working for you, MacCallister."

"I'm afraid ye have me at a bit of a disadvantage,"

Duff said. "I've nae idea what heathen monster ye would be talking about."

"I'm talking about the Chinaman you have working for you. He made an unprovoked attack on two of my men. Mr. Malcolm and Mr. Dobbins are finding it difficult to breathe because of their crushed windpipes."

"They ain't crushed, Mr. Houser, or they would be dead. And you should know that had Wang Chow wanted them dead, they would be," Elmer said.

"Elmer, would you be for telling me now, what this is all about?" Duff asked.

"Yesterday, when me 'n Wang went into town, a couple o' Mr. Houser's men thought they would have a little fun with Wang, so they jumped on him."

He looked back at Houser. "That was a big mistake, Mr. Houser. Wang isn't like other men. He never starts a fight, but he never loses one."

"I understand he is trained in some sort of special technique of fighting, with which my men were unfamiliar," Houser said.

"Yes, sir, that's right. I tried to warn 'em not to start 'nything. Your own man, Ben Turley, tried to warn 'em, too, but they didn't listen. Maybe this here will teach them boys a little lesson so's they won't be a-startin' another fracas. They might run into someone who won't be as nice to 'em as Wang was."

"Nice? There was nothing nice about it," Houser complained.

"It's like I said, Mr. Houser. Did he want to, Wang coulda kilt them boys, just as easy as takin' a bite outta one o' Vi's pies."

"I don't know if you know it or not, MacCallister,

but I am an attorney," Houser said. "And I am quite prepared to sue you for damages due to injuries sustained by my employees from an unprovoked attack."

"There warn't nothin' unprovoked about it a-tall," Elmer said. "I seen the whole thing. Them two no-accounts of yours attacked Wang. All he done was defend hisself."

"There is no way one man could have prevailed against both of them in such a fashion unless he initiated the attack, and did so without so much as a word of warning."

"They was near 'bout a dozen people who seen it all happen," Elmer said. "I ain't no lawyer like you, but even I know that if you got a dozen people sayin' one thing, that there ain't no lawyer in the world can prove it another."

"I assure you, Mr. Houser, Wang is quite capable of handling not just two, but several attackers, at once," Duff said.

"You speak of him as if he can perform magic," Houser said.

Wang was at the top of the windmill, and because work had stopped, he was able to hear everything that was being said. And even though he was the subject of the conversation, he had not added anything to the discourse.

"Wang, would you come down, please?"

Wang started to climb down.

"Not that way," Duff said.

At Duff's suggestion, Wang turned around and leaped toward the ground, head first.

"What the . . . ?" Houser shouted, startled by Wang's action.

Wang caught hold of the windmill tower halfway down and used it, both to slow his fall and to turn a flip in midair to right himself. A second later he landed on his feet, alongside Houser and Duff.

"So, this is the Chinaman, is it?"

"Wang isn't an *it*, Wang is a *he*. I should think you would know that."

"Yes, well, I must say that while he exhibited a remarkable degree of dexterity by his rather . . . unorthodox . . . response to your call, that I find him rather unimposing."

Duff picked up a spanner wrench that was being used to repair the windmill and handed it to Houser.

"Hit him with this," Duff invited.

"So he can hit me back?"

"Wang, I don't want you to harm Mr. Houser in any way," Duff said.

"I will not harm him," Wang said, speaking for the first time.

"All right, there you go. Wang has said that he won't harm you. Now, go ahead and hit him."

"This is ridiculous. I have no intention of . . ." Suddenly in the middle of his sentence, and without warning, Houser swung the wrench at Wang. Had he connected, he would have injured Wang severely, but Wang, with only the slightest adjustment, avoided the blow.

Houser tried again and again, but each time Wang managed to elude his strikes, thrusts, and jabs with moves so subtle that to an observer it almost appeared as if Houser was missing on purpose. After half a dozen attempts, Houser stopped and just stood there for a moment, breathing heavily. He gave the wrench back to Duff.

"I . . . suppose it is possible that he handled them by himself," Houser said, gasping for air between words. "I'll be on my way, now."

"Come back for a visit, anytime," Duff called out to him as he climbed back into the surrey. Houser didn't respond verbally, but he gave a slight wave as he drove off.

"I tried to warn them fellers before they commenced tryin' to fight Wang that they was bitin' off more 'n they could take a chaw of, but they didn't listen. If they couldn't handle themselves, they shoulda found someone else to play with," Elmer said, and the others who were working on the windmill laughed.

Two days later, Houser drove the surrey into Chugwater then stopped in front of the law offices of Norton and Norton. It had been Dan Norton who handled the legal aspects of his buying Twin Peaks.

"Mr. Houser," Norton greeted when Houser stepped into his office. "What can I do for you?"

"Tell me what you can about MacCallister," Houser said.

Norton got a questioning look on his face. "Surely you aren't contemplating any legal action against Duff MacCallister, are you?"

"What? No, no, of course not. It is just that he is my neighbor and seems to be an important man in the Valley of the Chug, so I think I would like to know more about him. He speaks with a heavy Scottish brogue, so I'm certain he isn't a native American."

"No, he isn't, but he has adapted very quickly to our culture. He is, as you have observed, a very important man here, not only because he has extensive land holdings, but because he is in every way a gentleman, and someone we can count on when there is trouble.

"Of course, that comes rather naturally to him. You may not know this, but he was a reserve captain in the 42nd Foot, Third Battalion of the Royal Highland Regiment of Scots. He was a participant in the battle of Tel-el-Kebir in Egypt, and there, he received the Victoria Cross."

"The Victoria Cross? That's quite an honorable award," Houser said. "What do you know about the two men who seem to be closest to him . . . the one called Elmer, and the Chinaman, Wang?"

Norton chuckled. "Elmer Gleason is quite an interesting character. He was in the war, fighting for the South, though I believe he was with one of the irregular units. After the war, he went to sea, visited China, Australia, England, France. You would never know by looking at him, but he is quite a well-traveled man. Then he left the sea, wound up living with the Indians for a while before he relocated here, where he found some gold, I don't know how much, in what had been an abandoned mine. For a while people would see him so infrequently, that some began to think that he was a ghost. Shortly after Duff MacCallister arrived, Gleason went to work for him, but I think their relationship is more than just employer, employee. Gleason is a junior partner in the ranch, and there is a very strong bond of friendship between them."

"And the Chinaman?"

"He is a more recent addition to Sky Meadow. The word is that Duff saved Wang's life and, being a Chinaman, Wang sets a high value on honor and loyalty. It might also be good for you to know that Wang is quite skilled in some type of Chinese fighting technique, and it makes him quite formidable. But he is bound by his honor never to use his skills except in defense. I'm sure your questioning has to do with the little episode between Wang and some of your men."

"You are aware of that?" Houser asked.

Norton chuckled. "Oh, my dear Mr. Houser, the entire town is aware of that. Fully a dozen witnessed the event, and all have testified that it was your men who started it. I do hope you don't think you have a legal case against Wang."

"No, I'm satisfied that, under the circumstances, legal action would come to naught." Houser, who had been sitting in Norton's office, stood and extended his hand. "Mr. Norton, I want to thank you for providing me with information about my neighbor. You have been most helpful."

Chapter Fifteen

After leaving the offices of Norton and Norton, and taking care of some business at the bank, Brad Houser decided to have a drink at Fiddler's Green.

"Hello, Mr. Houser," Biff greeted. "What can I get for you?"

"I'll have a whiskey."

"Biff, give the gentleman a Scotch 'n put it on m' tab," Duff said, calling from his table.

"I thank you, sir," Houser said as he took the drink from the bartender.

"Would you be for joining me, Mr. Houser?" Duff invited.

Houser took his drink over to the table and sat down.

"Well, meeting you today is quite serendipitous, I must say," Houser said. He lifted the whiskey glass. "To your health, sir."

Duff lifted his glass as well. "And to yours, sir."

The two men drank, then Duff asked, "In what way is our meeting serendipitous, may I ask?"

"Well, for one thing, I would like to apologize to

you for my boorish behavior the other day, when I called upon you to protest the injuries your Mr. Wang inflicted upon my men. I have since heard from many witnesses that the incident was precipitated by my two employees. It was untoward of me, and I ask your forbearance."

"Dinnae be troubled over it, Mr. Houser. 'Tis more than one man who has underestimated Wang's rather remarkable skills."

"That's most gracious of you. But I've another thing I wish to discuss with you . . . you being the owner of the largest ranch in the valley. What do you think of all these . . . upstart . . . small ranchers?"

"I'm nae sure what ye mean by the question," Duff replied.

"A few weeks ago, I asked my foreman to move part of the herd into the Pine Flats. I am told that Mr. Prescott used the Pine Flats for grazing for as long as he owned Twin Peaks ranch, but Turley came back with the information that Prosser, one of these nuisance small ranchers, had moved his cows there, eating my grass and drinking my water."

"Ah, but 'tis nae your grass nor your water, Mr. Houser. The Pine Flats is open range."

"So I have been told," Houser replied.

"Then dinnae ye think that Mr. Prosser has every right to be there?"

"There is an unwritten law of inverse established domain, which grants to the prior user proprietary exclusion to public land, barring any government action to the contrary."

"Here now, Mr. Houser, 'n you'll be forgiving me for nae understanding the meaning of all your words."

"Basically it means that Twin Peaks has established a prior presence on the property, so that now I, as the present owner of Twin Peaks, have exclusive rights to the land."

"Aye, but dinnae ye say that 'twas an unwritten law?"

"Unwritten law, sir, is based upon custom, usage, and judicial decisions. And though it has not been enacted in the form of statute or ordinance, it does have legal sanction," Houser pontificated.

"And you bring up this unwritten law because Mr. Prosser grazed a few of his cows on open range?" Duff asked.

"Captain MacCallister," Houser started, then he interrupted his comment to ask a question. "I have recently learned that you were a captain in the Black Watch, is that correct?"

"Aye, but I'm nae addressed as such anymore."

"If you will allow me, I will extend you the courtesy of addressing you so. Captain MacCallister, it may well be that the usurpation of open range means little to you, as Sky Meadow is so large that you can manage your herd completely within the boundaries of your own holdings. But for those of us who depend upon open range, the proliferation of these pesky, small ranchers can be a problem."

Houser finished his drink then stood. "Thank you for the fine Scotch," he said. "And do consider my words, Captain MacCallister, for I have no doubt but that other larger ranchers are suffering loss of grazing area and water just as I am."

After Houser left, Biff came over to join Duff at the table. Knowing that Duff rationed his alcoholic beverages, he brought, instead of another whiskey, a cup of hot coffee to offer.

"What was Houser palaverin' about?" Biff asked.

"He seems to have a personal animus for the smaller ranchers in the area."

"Yeah, he would," Biff said. "He is so full of himself that it's a wonder his head doesn't explode. I don't mind tellin' you, Duff, I don't like the son of a bitch."

"Aye, he can be a bit unpleasant."

"A bit unpleasant? That's like saying the fight at Little Bighorn was a 'bit of a scuffle.'"

Somewhere in Eastern Colorado

"We need us a little more travelin' money," Sid Shamrock said to the men who were riding with him.

"How do you propose we get it?" Jaco asked. "There ain't no banks here 'bout."

"Which, even if there was, it would more 'n likely not do us no good anyway," Hawke said. "I mean, seein' as we didn't do all that good with the last one we robbed."

"Hawke, you can go off on your own, if you want to," Jaco said. "I know how well you were doing by yourself until you joined us."

"I didn't say nothin' 'bout goin' off nowhere," Hawke replied. "I was just sayin' as how we didn't get as much money as we thought we would, is all. They was all of us some upset about that, 'n you know it."

"It'll get better," Shamrock promised.

The six men came over the top of a hill and saw a stagecoach parked out in front of a building. The building appeared to be in the middle of nowhere.

"Damn, it's a way stop for stagecoaches," Shamrock

said. He smiled. "Boys, that's where we'll get our money."

"You mean we're goin' to rob a stagecoach?" Wix asked.

"Yeah, that's exactly what I mean. 'N seein' as this coach ain't even movin', it don't seem to me like it's goin' to be very hard to do."

"What if the coach ain't carryin' no money?" Evans asked.

"The passengers will have some money. 'N more 'n likely, the stagecoach station will have some, too. Right now we ain't got hardly two coins to rub together amongst us all, so anything we get will be better than what we've got."

"You got that right," Pete said.

As the six men approached the way station, the attached team stood quietly, as if the horses were mentally preparing themselves for the ten miles they would have to pull the coach before reaching the next way stop where they could rest.

"Hey, Shamrock, look at that," Evans said. "The shotgun guard didn't even take his rifle in with 'im."

"I don't know how much we're goin' to get from these folks, but whatever it is, it's goin' to be like takin' candy from a baby," Shamrock said.

The six men tied off their horses, then went inside. They saw seven people sitting around a table, being the five coach passengers, the driver, and the shotgun guard. The passengers consisted of one overweight man who appeared to be a drummer, a second man who had the worn look of someone who had worked hard for his entire life but had little to show for it, a woman and two children, a boy of about ten or eleven and a girl who couldn't have been over six. Neither of the male passengers was wearing a gun, but the shotgun guard and the driver were.

There was a man and a woman bringing plates of food to the table.

"Oh my," the station manager said when he saw the six of them. "If you fellers are here for a meal, I hope you like beans, seein' as that's all I'll have left after feedin' the stagecoach passengers. 'N they come first, you know."

"Take the driver and the shotgun guard first," Shamrock said quietly. "Now," he added.

Shamrock and the five men with him drew their guns.

"What the hell?" the shotgun guard shouted as he started to stand up. He was trying to draw his pistol at the same time, but was shot down before he could even get to his feet. The driver put his hands up, but that didn't stop him from being shot, either.

The station manager had started toward the counter as soon as he saw the men draw their guns, and he managed to bring up a shotgun but was cut down before he could shoot.

The two women screamed, and they were the next to be shot. The man who looked overworked made a desperate grab for the driver's pistol, but was shot before he could pull the pistol from the holster. The fat man who had raised his hands and made no move was the next to be shot. That left only the two children.

"We goin' to shoot them, too?" Wix asked.

Shamrock made no verbal response. Instead, he

shot the two children, who were on their knees alongside their dying mother.

The carnage the six men had wrought was over in less than a minute, and now all stood there, wreathed in gun smoke, the room very quiet.

Back in the kitchen Lorenzo Wilks, the black cook, had heard the shooting. When the shooting first started he ran to the kitchen door to see what was going on. He saw the women and children being shot, horrified by what he was seeing, but knowing there was nothing he could do about it without getting himself shot.

He knew he should run out the back door and put as much distance between the murderers and himself as possible, but he found himself completely unable to move. Instead he stood in the kitchen, looking through the barely open door.

He saw the man who appeared to be the leader, a man with the mark of Satan, in the form of a scar on his face.

"We'll eat first," Shamrock said, shoving the pistol back into his holster. "Then we'll see what we can come up with in the way of money."

Fifteen minutes later, after having gobbled down all the food that had been put on the table, the six men rode away from the way station. The six horses stood, immobile, unaware that their trip had been interrupted. Finding an unexpected feast, flies began buzzing around the nine bodies that lay spread out on the floor behind them.

The murder and robbery had netted them a grand total of $83.63.

"We ain't been makin' a whole hell of a lot of money, have we?" Wix asked.

"I've got somethin' in mind—don't worry about it," Shamrock said.

Lorenzo Wilks waited until he was sure the outlaws were gone, then he went out to the barn, saddled a horse, and rode into Wild Horse, which was the nearest town. Stopping in front of the sheriff's office, he went inside.

"Hello, Lorenzo," the sheriff said. "I thought you come into town for supplies just the other day. Mr. Booker think of somethin' you forgot?"

"He's dead, Sheriff," Lorenzo said.

"What? Who's dead?"

"All of 'em. Mr. Booker, Miz Booker, Mr. Woods, Mr. Parks, 'n all the stagecoach passengers. Them bad men kilt 'em all, 'n they was two kids they kilt, too."

Valley of the Chug

Ed Chambers could tell, just by looking, that his small herd had grown larger. Curious, he rode down to have a closer look, and that was when he saw at least ten calves.

"Whoa, I didn't have ten new calves born this year. Where'd you come from?"

Every calf had the Twin Peaks brand.

"How the hell did you get this far? Twin Peaks is at least fifteen miles from here."

Chambers sighed. He was going to have to take the calves back.

Or was he? Suppose he just kept them? He wouldn't make any attempt to change the brand, and if Prescott showed up, Houser could just say that he had been holding them for him, and the unchanged brand would validate his claim. But how likely was Mr. Prescott to come over here and examine his calves? And if he didn't show up, they would belong to Chambers.

Chambers was unaware that Prescott had died and that the Twin Peaks Ranch now belonged to someone else.

"All right, I know it's wrong," he said. "But if you wanted to live with me so bad that you walked fifteen miles, who am I to make you go back?"

Ten new calves? That was like seeing $350 lying on the ground, ready to be picked up.

Wild Horse, Colorado

It was the newspaper article that brought Abe Sobel to Wild Horse. The article told of a brutal murder and robbery at a stagecoach station just ten miles west of Wild Horse. The same article also stated that the station had been closed and not reopened.

The article said that there had been a witness who said there were six men, and one was a scar-faced man. Abe knew that it was a long shot, but the number of men and the scarred face were too much for him to ignore.

He dismounted in front of the sheriff's office.

There were two men playing checkers inside. A barred wall separated them, as one of the men was in jail.

"Now, LeRoy, you touched that man, 'n it means you have to move it," the player outside the cell said. He had a star pinned to his shirt.

"No, I didn't, I just kinda got close but I never touched that man, 'n you know it," LeRoy said. "You just think 'cause you're the sheriff 'n say that, why, I'll have to go along with it."

"All right, you can look for another move, but don't be puttin' your hand down there till you're ready to move."

"Sheriff?" Abe said.

"If there ain't somebody 'bout to get murdered, you just hold on for a minute," the sheriff said with a raised hand. He didn't look around.

LeRoy made a move, the sheriff countered, then, with a cackling laugh, LeRoy made a series of jumps.

"That just about cleans you out, Sheriff," LeRoy said.

"Damn!" the sheriff said. He turned back to see who had come into the office. "What can I do for you?"

"I'm looking for the men who killed all those people at the stage station," Abe replied.

"Who isn't?"

"Yes, but I think I know who they are. At least, I think I know who their leader is. But I won't know for sure until I can talk with the witness."

The sheriff nodded. "That would be Lorenzo Wilks. Come on, I'll take you to him."

* * *

Lorenzo Wilks was wearing a white apron and he had his arms elbow deep in soapy water. He was washing dishes in the kitchen of the Rustic Rock Café.

"Yes, sir, I seen it," Wilks said, answering Abe's question. "I seen it all. Like I tole the sheriff, the one that was leadin' 'em had . . ."

"No!" Abe said, interrupting the cook. "I'm going to describe the man to you, and I want to know if it is anything like what you saw."

"All right," Wilks said.

"He was about my height, he had dirty blond hair that hung down to his ears. And he had an ugly, purple scar that started here," Abe put his finger just below the brow of his left eye, "and it came down through his eyelid making it sort of purple and puffed up, then it ended right here."

Abe stopped his finger just at the top of his cheek.

"Lawd have mercy," Wilks said. "You done described the mark o' Satan he had on 'im so's I can see 'im, just like he was standin' right here."

Abe nodded. "It's Sid Shamrock," he said. "Thank you, Mr. Wilks."

"I hope you find 'im," Wilks said. "A man like that, 'n all those men that was with 'im . . . they don't deserve to live. What they done to all them people, 'n even the women 'n those poor little chilrun . . . they need to hang for it."

Chapter Sixteen

Turley saw the pinto approaching, and as it got closer he saw that the rider didn't appear to be any older than thirteen or fourteen years old.

"What do you need, boy?" Turley asked.

"I have a telegram for Mr. Houser," the boy replied.

"All right, give it to me, I'll give it to him."

"No, sir, I can't do that. Mr. Proffer, he said I can't give it to nobody but Mr. Houser his ownself."

"I work for Mr. Houser," Turley said, aggravated by the boy's response.

"I'm sorry, but I can't do it. I can only give it to Mr. Houser."

"Wait here," Turley said.

The boy dismounted and stood by his horse as Turley went into the ranch office.

"There's a boy out front with a telegram that he says he can only give to you," Turley said.

"A telegram? I can't imagine who would be sending me a telegram." Curious, Houser stepped out to see the boy.

"Are you Mr. Houser?" the boy asked.

"I am."

The boy handed Houser a yellow envelope, and Houser gave the boy a quarter.

"Thank you, sir!" the boy said enthusiastically.

"What does it say?" Turley asked.

"Mr. Turley, there is a reason that the boy insisted upon putting the telegram in my hands, and my hands only," Houser replied. "The reason is privacy."

"What?"

"It means that it is none of your business what the telegram says. It was sent to me, personally."

"Yes, sir, sorry. I didn't mean to pry. I was just curious, is all."

"I'm sure you have heard the expression *curiosity killed a cat*," Houser said.

"What? Now how the hell can bein' curious kill a cat?"

"Never mind," Houser said with a shake of his head.

Returning to his office, Houser opened the envelope and read the telegram.

I AM IN CHEYENNE WITH FIVE FRIENDS
STOP WE ARE LOOKING FOR A JOB STOP
CAN YOU MEET ME HERE STOP
SHAMROCK

At first, Houser slammed the telegram down on his desk in disgust. How dare Sid Shamrock contact him? Shamrock had taken a solemn oath never to contact him again. How did he even know where he was? Then he remembered the letter he had gotten from Rosemary Woods.

Well, he can just stay up there and rot.

No, wait, Shamrock obviously knew where he was, and if he had five men with him, then he could cause trouble.

Even as the agitation was building about the contents of the telegram, another thought began to take hold. And the more he thought about it, the stronger the thought became.

"Yes," he said aloud as a big smile spread across his face. Six men looking for a job? Houser knew exactly what job they could do. In fact, he could almost say that the arrival of Sid Shamrock could work out very well for him.

Stepping back outside, he saw Turley talking to a couple of his riders.

"Turley," he called.

Turley sent the two riders off on whatever task he had assigned them, then responded to Houser's call.

"Yes, sir?"

"I'm going to be gone for a few days. Keep things going here."

"Yes, sir. Uh, what about Knox 'n them other two?"

"Never mind about them. I'll tell them I'm gone, and I'm quite sure they will be able to take care of themselves."

"Yes, sir," Turley replied.

"You want to rent an entire stagecoach?" the manager of the Chugwater branch of the Southern Wyoming Stagecoach Company said, in reply to Houser's request.

"I do indeed. I have six men that I need to pick up in Cheyenne."

"Couldn't they just take the train?"

"I suppose they could, but I would like to set my own time schedule. Tell me, Mr. Walker, why are you so reticent to do business with me?"

"Why am I what?"

"Why are you trying to talk me out of renting a stagecoach? Do you not want my business?"

"Oh no, sir, no, sir, nothin' like that," Walker said. "I very much want your business."

"Then you will make a coach available to me?"

"Yes, sir, I would be glad to. If you will come back at one o'clock this afternoon, I will have a coach and driver ready for you."

As Brad Houser waited for the coach to be made ready for him, he stepped into the Valley Restaurant to have his lunch. There, he saw a pretty woman with blond hair and blue eyes, who was eating alone. He recognized her as the owner of the dress emporium. He had also heard that she was Duff MacCallister's lady friend.

"Miss Parker," he said, stepping up to her table. "Would you mind, terribly, if I joined you for lunch?" Houser smiled. "I would be happy to pay for the privilege of dining with you, by buying your lunch."

Meagan smiled up at him. "Of course you may join me, but it isn't necessary that you pay for my lunch."

A waiter came to see him as soon as he sat down.

"I'm taking a coach at one o'clock," he said. "So I'll take whatever is the fastest and easiest for you to serve."

"That would be our stew," the waiter replied.

"Very good."

"I didn't know we had a scheduled stagecoach that departed at one," Meagan said.

"This isn't a public coach; it is one that I have chartered for my private use."

"My, I don't think I've ever known anyone who chartered a stagecoach for their own use."

"It is one of the perquisites of being a wealthy man, my dear," Houser said. "As is dining with a beautiful young woman," he added with a smile that didn't reach his eyes.

"I assure you, Mr. Houser, your money had nothing to do with my accepting your offer to join me."

"Of course not. Please forgive me for turning what I meant to be a compliment into a crass statement."

"You are forgiven."

The waiter delivered the stew.

"I am particularly pleased that you did agree to let me join you, though. As I am sure you know, I am still relatively new in town, and affairs with running the ranch have not provided me with the opportunity to visit town very often, or even visit my neighbors. That has not allowed me to make many friends. To be honest with you, I wasn't sure you would even know my name."

"I am a businesswoman, Mr. Houser. And part of being successful in business is in being able to keep up with what is happening. I know that you bought Twin Peaks Ranch from Cliff Prescott's widow. And I know that you aren't married."

Houser smiled. "No, I am not married, and I'm flattered that you went to the trouble to find out."

Meagan laughed. "Oh, heavens, Mr. Houser, there is no need for you to be flattered. As I told you, I am a businesswoman, and my business is a dress shop. My inquiries into your marital status had to do with whether or not you might have a wife who could become a customer."

"Yes, of course, I can understand that. And who knows, it may be that somewhere in this beautiful valley I may find someone."

"That is a possibility, of course, and when you do, please don't hesitate to introduce us so that I can make her one of my customers."

"Oh, to be sure, I will definitely introduce you. In the meantime, perhaps you and I could see each other again, maybe for dinner and such other entertainment as may be available in this town?"

"Mr. Houser, I appreciate the invitation, but I am keeping company with Duff MacCallister."

"That would be the Scotsman?"

"Aye," Meagan replied automatically. Then, with a smile she said, "Yes. Do you know him?"

"We have had occasion to meet, yes," Houser said. "He has in his employ a common Chinaman with a rather remarkable ability to injure others in a street brawl."

"You would be talking about Wang, and believe me, there is nothing at all common about Wang," Meagan replied.

"Yes, I believe Wang is his name," Houser replied. "And I agree with you, there is nothing common about him. He was more than the measure of two of my men. I had to apologize to Mr. MacCallister on behalf of my men for causing the disturbance in the first place."

"Your men couldn't apologize for themselves?"

"I'm sure they could, but I am responsible for them, and therefore I have a certain obligation for their actions."

"That's quite honorable of you," Meagan said.

"Thank you."

For the rest of the meal the conversation across the table was incidental, with no further reference to Duff MacCallister. Finally Houser took out a gold pocket watch and examined it then closed it and turned his attention back to Meagan.

"Well, my coach should be ready now," he said. "Thank you for allowing me to share your table. It made lunchtime much more pleasant than it would have been had I dined alone."

"I have enjoyed the conversation," Meagan said.

After Houser left, Meagan smiled at the affectation of his examining his gold watch when there was a big clock on the wall, which was within the view of all in the café.

"Oh, there is no charge for your meal, Meagan," Katie said when Meagan went to pay her check a short while later. "Mr. Houser paid for it."

"Thank you," Meagan said.

"Hello, Mary Ellen," Meagan said when she returned to the dress shop. There was a young man with her.

"This is Ben," Mary Ellen said, smiling at the young man.

"Turley, ma'am. Ben Turley," the man said.

"Yes, I know you. You're the foreman out at Twin Peaks, I believe."

"Yes, ma'am, I foremanned for Mr. Prescott 'n now I'm workin' for Mr. Houser. Fact is, I brung 'im into town this morning."

"Yes, I had lunch with Mr. Houser. And speaking of lunch, Mary Ellen, you can go to lunch now."

"Thank you, I'll be back soon. Ben is taking me to the Chugwater Café," the pretty, young, dark-haired girl said with a happy smile.

Meagan thought about her brief visit with Houser. She had told him there was no need to pay for her lunch, and she wished he hadn't done so. He was clearly trying to ingratiate himself, and she wasn't interested. He was, she admitted to herself, a rather handsome man, and there was a sophistication about him that could be intriguing.

But there was something else about him, something she could feel, but couldn't see. If she had to describe it, she would say that he was like a piece of fine crystal that would be beautiful, if not for a slight flaw in its manufacture. In the case of crystal, the flaw can be seen. It was difficult to see the flaw in Brad Houser, but Meagan knew, instinctively, that it was there.

When Houser returned to the stagecoach depot he saw a coach standing out front with a six-horse team already attached. The driver was sitting on the high seat, dozing, as he waited for word to go.

"Is that my coach parked out front?" he asked as he stepped inside.

"Oh, it is indeed, sir, and you are in luck, as we had one of our finest drivers available."

"What do I owe you?" Houser asked.

"Suppose you settle when you return? That way I will know how long you have kept the coach, and it will give me a better idea as how to assess the amount."

"Very good," Houser said, turning around and walking back to the coach. Walker followed him outside.

"Sylvanus, here is your passenger," Walker called.

"Will you be ridin' up here with me, or down in the box, sir?" the driver called down to Houser.

"I will be in the coach," Houser replied.

"Well, sir, to be honest, the ride is a little softer up here, but you can do whatever you want."

"Driver," Houser replied, "we can save time and wasted conversation just by assuming that I can always do anything I want. At least with respect to this trip."

"Yes, sir," Sylvanus replied. "Just climb in and make yourself comfortable."

As the coach left Chugwater and started up toward Cheyenne, Houser thought back to his lunch with Meagan Parker. She was a beautiful woman, owned a successful business, and he already knew that she was quite well liked and respected by the people of Chugwater, and all over the valley.

She would make a great wife for him, but not in any kind of amorous way. He had no illusions of love or romance. He just believed that a marriage with someone like Meagan Parker, someone who was very smart and successful in her own right, would be like a good and effective business merger.

He smiled. And it didn't hurt that Duff MacCallister considered his relationship with her solid. Taking his woman away from him would be a great personal victory.

Chapter Seventeen

It was quite dark by the time the private stagecoach stopped in front of the Crooked Creek Saloon in Cheyenne, Wyoming. The Crooked Creek Saloon was on Fifteenth Street, separated from the Eagle Bar by the Western Hotel. Houser was the sole passenger, and on the stops the coach made to change teams, Houser avoided any conversation with the driver because he didn't want to give the driver any idea that he was anything more than a hired man.

"You want me to wait here, Mr. Houser?" the driver asked.

"Yes, keep the coach here until I return."

"Yes, sir."

Leaving the coach, Houser went into the Crooked Creek Saloon and stood just inside the batwing doors for a moment, perusing the two dozen or more customers. Because a man in a three-piece suit was seldom seen in a saloon, Houser was as much the viewed, as the viewer.

About a third of the drinkers were standing at the bar, the rest were sitting at the tables. He saw his brother sitting with several others at a table in the farthest corner of the room. He had no idea who the other men were, though he recalled that the telegram had said there would be five men with him.

Shamrock stepped over to the next table and, picking up the only remaining empty chair, without asking, moved it to his table. There were three men at the table that lost the chair, but they saw that there were five with the man who took the chair and decided that it would be better not to offer any protest.

The others at Shamrock's table made room for the chair that was brought over for Houser.

"I must say, Thomas, that I am rather surprised to see you in Wyoming. I thought you were in Texas," Houser said as he took his seat.

"See, what did I tell you fellers? Did you hear how he called me Thomas? He's just real polite, bein' as he's a lawyer 'n all."

"I no longer follow the legal profession," Houser replied. "I am not even a member of the bar in Wyoming."

"What do you mean you ain't in a bar?" one of the men with Shamrock asked. "Hell, you're in a bar now, ain't you?"

"Indeed I am," Houser said without further explanation.

"What I want to know is, why did you call Shamrock, Thomas? Don't you know his real name?" Wix asked.

"It's a name I used to use sometimes," Shamrock said. No further explanation was needed, as not one of the men who had come with Shamrock was using the name he was born with.

"What are you doin' now, if you ain't lawyerin'?" Shamrock asked.

"I own a ranch, some north of here."

"You need 'ny more hands?"

"No."

"We need a place to . . ."

"Hide out?"

"Yeah."

"What have you done?"

"Same thing me 'n you done down in Sulphur Springs, only this here 'un didn't turn out as good as that one did."

"You got a great deal of money from that, uh, incident," Houser said. "Fourteen thousand dollars, as I recall. What did you do with it?"

"You done a job that you got fourteen thousand dollars for?" Hawke asked, surprised by the amount. "Son of a bitch! That's a hell of a lot of money! I ain't never seen that much money in my whole life. How come we ain't never done nothin' to make that much money?"

"Tell them why," Houser said.

"Uh, 'cause I ain't never found another bank like that first one."

"Who found it?" Houser asked.

"You did."

"Yes. I did. What did you do with the money?" Houser asked.

"I spent it," Shamrock said.

"You spent fourteen thousand dollars, with nothing to show for it?" Houser asked.

"Yeah."

"Are there wanted posters out on you, Thomas?"

"Prob'ly down in Texas there is," Shamrock replied. "But they don't nobody know nothin' 'bout us up here in Wyoming."

"So you came up here to ask for my help, did you?"

"Yeah. I mean, bein' as we're brothers 'n all, I figured, where else could I go? Besides which, like I said, I ain't wanted up here, 'n I was figurin' that, well, you bein' so smart, maybe you could come up with another job like that one we done in Sulphur Springs."

"*We* didn't do that job," Houser replied. "If you recall, I kept my hands clean."

"Yeah, 'n got most of the money," Shamrock complained.

"Who else would you come to for help, if not for me?" Houser asked.

"Yeah, there is that. So, what do you say? Will you help me out, or not?"

Houser drummed his fingers on the table for a moment, then he smiled.

"As a matter of fact, you may have arrived at a most fortuitous time."

"What? What does that mean?" Shamrock asked.

"It means that I have been contemplating something, and you and your associates may just be who I need to put the plan into effect."

"What do you have in mind?" Shamrock asked. "Another bank as easy as that first one, 'n with as much money?"

"No, there is no bank involved. But there can be a great deal of money, even more money than before."

"All right!" Shamrock said, rubbing his hands together. "Let's do it!"

"You haven't asked what it is."

"I don't care what it is. I figure if it's somethin' you got planned, it'll be a lot of money, 'cause there was the last time," Shamrock said.

"Yeah, well, speaking of money, we ain't got hardly none at all now," Wix said.

"Who are you?" Houser asked.

"My name is . . . uh . . . Wix."

"Tell me who the rest of them are," Houser said to his brother.

"This here is Jeb Jaco, Pete, don't know his last name, Evans, 'n Hawke," Shamrock said, pointing out each of the men as he named them. "'N you done met Wix."

"Have you no money left from your recent activity?"

"We got maybe twenty dollars betwixt us all," Shamrock said.

Houser took six twenty-dollar bills from his pocket and handed one to each of them. "You can consider this an advance until I put my plan into operation."

"When will that be?" Shamrock asked.

"When I'm ready," Houser replied.

"All right," Shamrock said. "But how 'bout you buy us a couple of bottles now?"

"I just gave you twenty dollars apiece—buy them yourselves," Houser said. "But stay where I can get hold of you."

"All right if we get us some whores tonight?" Shamrock asked.

Houser started to say no, but he hesitated for a moment. "You may as well do it now, because once I get you up to Chugwater, I'm going to keep you too busy to visit with whores, or anything else."

"Just what is it you have in mind for us to do?" Shamrock asked.

"I'll tell you when the time comes," Houser replied.

"Come on, Shamrock, let's get us some whores," Evans said. "We're wastin' time, talkin'."

The next morning Houser was sitting in the outer chambers of the office of the acting governor of Wyoming Territory. He had no prior appointment with the governor, but a short while earlier he had given a $100 bill to the governor's appointment secretary with a request to "find a couple of minutes for me."

The appointment secretary glanced around the office quickly to see if the transaction had been observed, and seeing that it had not, he stuffed the money in his pocket and nodded.

Less than five minutes later, the appointment secretary stepped out of the governor's personal office.

"Governor Morgan will see you now, Mr. Houser."

Elliot Morgan was the acting governor of Wyoming Territory, having attained the position after the very popular William Hale died in office.

Governor Morgan was a relatively small man, with a mustache and long, flowing chin whiskers. He was standing in front of his desk and extended his hand to Houser.

"It's very good of you to see me, Governor," Houser said.

"I'm told that you are a cattleman of some standing," Governor Morgan replied. "And, as the cattle industry is significant to our territory, I would be remiss in not receiving an esteemed member of that estate. Now, Mr. Houser, to what do I owe the honor of this visit?"

"Governor, I've come on behalf, not just of myself, but for all of the larger ranchers in the Valley of the Chug. The national homesteader act has become a serious threat to the survival of our industry."

"How so?"

"Dozens, scores, and, no doubt, soon to be hundreds of men who know nothing of the cattle business have been flooding into the valley, denuding the open range of grass, denying water access to the traditional ranchers, and polluting the streams that our cattle can reach. In short, sir, the cattle industry of Wyoming is facing a serious crisis."

"That may be true, Mr. Houser," the governor replied. "But as you pointed out yourself, the homesteading act is a federal act, and I, as territorial governor, have no way to alleviate the problem."

"But there is a problem you can help us with," Houser said.

"Oh? What is the problem, and how can I help?"

"Cattle rustling," Houser said. "As it turns out, these small ranchers are not only having a poor effect upon the very grass and water our industry is so dependent upon, they are also augmenting their herds with cattle they have stolen from us. In some cases, I have no doubt, they are doing more than merely augmenting their herds with stolen cattle. A few, no doubt, have an entire herd that consists of cattle stolen from the larger ranchers, under the auspices of taking mavericks."

"Ah, I am aware of the practice of taking unbranded cattle that are found on open range and with no way of establishing ownership. That is quite legal."

"Yes, it is legal if the cattle are unmarked and taken from open range where they have wandered away from their home ranch so that there is no way of determining from whence they came. But these perfidious homesteaders have perverted the concept of acquiring mavericks and are actually coming onto privately held land, stealing our unbranded calves even before our ranch hands can gather them up in roundup. There is nothing legal about that, Governor."

Governor Morgan pulled upon his beard. "No, there is nothing legal about that. But I don't know why you have come to me with that problem. Shouldn't you take that problem to the local sheriff? Or, perhaps, to a U.S. Marshal?"

"I fear that the rustling is so pervasive that it would overwhelm the resources of a sheriff or U.S. Marshal. However, I do have suggestion as to how it can be handled, but that will require your official approval."

"Of course, I'll do anything I can. What do you require of me?"

After leaving the capitol building with the governor's approval of the plan he had proposed, Houser returned to the Crooked Creek Saloon, where he saw Hawke sitting alone at one of the tables.

"Where are the others?" he asked.

"Jaco is out back takin' a piss. Wix 'n Evans is still upstairs with the whores they got last night. Sid 'n Pete's next door havin' their breakfast."

Even as they were talking, Jaco came back into the saloon.

"I will go next door and retrieve my brother and Pete. You two go up 'n get Wix and Evans down here."

"I told you, they was both with whores right now," Hawke said.

Houser smiled. "Then you should have no trouble finding them, should you?"

"Ha!" Jaco said. "Come on, Hawke, I'm goin' to get a kick out of this."

"Yeah," Hawke said, also grinning at the prospect. "Yeah, come to think of it, I will, too. I'll take Wix. I want to see the look on his face when I pull him offen the whore."

"The first thing I want all of you to do is sell your horses," Houser ordered when they had regathered.

"Wait a minute, now, why should we do that?" Shamrock asked. "I got me a real good horse. It's a palomino, 'n 'bout the purtiest thing you ever seen."

"Think about it, Thomas. A horse like that is sure to stand out. By divesting yourselves of your horses you can sever one of the links that could lead the authorities to you. Because of the exposure, I don't even want to risk going on a train, so to ensure our privacy, I have rented a stagecoach to take us back to my ranch."

"What'll we do for horses once we get there?" Jaco asked.

"When we reach my ranch, I will provide you with fresh mounts."

"Wait a minute," Shamrock said. "This work you got in mind for us, ain't workin' on your ranch is it? 'Cause I ain't no ranch hand 'n they ain't none of these boys that's ranch hands, neither. If that's what you got in mind, you can just go on back to Chugwater, 'n me 'n the others will keep our horses 'n go somewhere else."

"I have no intention of employing you as cowboys," Houser said. "As you have so ungrammatically stated, you would be useless in such an endeavor. I have something entirely different in mind, and something that shall prove to be more lucrative for you."

"More what?" Hawke asked.

"He means something that will make a lot of money," Shamrock said. "My brother always has had him a highfalutin way of talkin'."

"Well," Hawke said with a broad smile. "Iffen he has a way of us makin' a lot of money like he made for you, why, he can talk any way he wants to. It sure as hell don't make no nevermind to me."

"Go down to the livery and sell your horses," Houser said. "I've already spoken to Mr. Abney, and he said that he would be happy to do business with you."

"Yeah? For how much?" Wix asked.

"You will take whatever he offers," Houser said. "We don't have time for any lengthy negotiations. I want to get under way as soon as possible."

"Yeah, well, I ain't goin' to sell my horse without I get a good price," Wix insisted.

"Understand this, all of you," Houser said. "If you are going to work for me, I will expect unquestioned obedience to my every command. If you can't do that, I'll have no use for you."

He looked directly at Wix. "And that includes my order to sell your horses. Now, you either sell your horse for the sum Mr. Abney offers, or you keep your horse and ride away. Your absence alone will not seriously impair the task I will be setting for the others."

"I'll sell my horse," Wix said, the challenge gone from his voice.

"I rather thought you would," Houser said.

Chapter Eighteen

As Shamrock and the men with him went about their business of selling their horses, at this very moment 250 miles south of Cheyenne, Lucien Bodine was in Colorado on his way north. He had learned that his brother was buried in Chugwater, Wyoming.

He was facing two problems now. He didn't know exactly where Chugwater was, and he had no money. He wasn't worried too much about the first problem. He figured he would be able to find Chugwater once he reached Wyoming, and he had just seen the solution to the second problem, that of no money.

He was at the crest of a hill, looking down at an isolated store ahead of him. There were actually two structures, one a small stable and the other, the store itself. The store was made of wide planks that had never been painted, and were sun-bleached gray. A sign across the front of the store had the name: GARLAND'S ROAD RANCH and beneath it: GOODS, GROCERIES, EATS, DRINKS.

There was a buckboard with the tongue lying on the ground parked alongside the store. There were two horses, which Bodine assumed made up the team, in the stable.

Bodine tied his horse off at the hitching rail in front of the store, then stepped up onto the porch. A white dog with black spots was sleeping in front of a sign that read: GOODS FOR ALL MANKIND, and though he opened his eyes as Bodine started toward the door, the dog was so comfortable with his position, and so used to seeing customers come and go, that he didn't rise.

A little bell was attached to the door and it made a tinkling sound as Bodine pushed it open to step inside. The store was redolent with the various aromas of its commerce: smoked meat, various spices, freshly ground coffee beans, tobacco, and stale beer. Looking around, Bodine saw only one man, and he was standing just in front of the counter. He looked to be in his fifties and was bald except for a fringe of white that was just above his ears. His protruding belly caused the shirt to gap open so that it pulled at the buttons that struggled to hold the shirt closed. Because he wasn't behind the counter, Bodine would have thought him a customer, had he not been sweeping the floor.

"Yes, sir," the man said, greeting Bodine with a smile. "Something I can do for you?"

"Would you be Mr. Garland?" Bodine asked.

"I am, sir."

"Well, Mr. Garland, I would like a pouch of tobacco and some paper for rolling cigarettes."

"Yes, sir," Garland replied, the smile still present as he walked around behind the counter, where he produced the tobacco pouch and the little packet of rolling paper. "Just travelin' through, are you?"

"I'm on my way to Wyoming."

"Wyoming, is it? Well, you got a ways to go, yet. By the way, I just got in a couple of cases of canned peaches," Garland said. "They're awful good, if I say so myself."

"All right, I'll take a can," Bodine said.

"Yes, sir." Garland turned around and reached onto the shelf behind him to grab a can, then he put it on the counter alongside the tobacco. "That'll be six bits," he said, opening the cash drawer.

"And all your money," Bodine added, pulling his pistol.

"I beg your pardon?" Garland replied, a surprised expression on his face.

"I'll be takin' all your money," Bodine repeated.

"What? You are robbing me?"

"Yeah."

With shaking hands, Garland cleaned out the cash drawer and tried to hand the money to Bodine.

"Drop it into a bag with the tobacco and peaches," Bodine said.

Garland did as ordered.

"Mister, this here is a real small store," Garland said. "You steal this money from me, 'n I'm likely not to make it."

"That's not my problem," Bodine said. With the gun still held in his right hand, he reached out with his left to grab the bag.

"You won't get away with this, mister," Garland said.

"We'll see," Bodine replied, starting toward the door.

There was a mirror just beside the door and, glancing into the mirror as he was leaving, Bodine saw that the storekeeper had brought a shotgun up from under the counter. Turning quickly, Bodine shot the man before he could raise the gun to his shoulder.

"Moe? What is it?" a woman shouted from a back room.

Bodine waited until the woman appeared, and seeing her husband on the floor, she raised her hand to her mouth and screamed.

"Moe!"

"You shoulda stayed back there, woman," Bodine said.

"No, no, no!" the woman cried.

Bodine shot her as she shouted the third *no*.

With both husband and wife lying dead on the floor, Bodine went back to the counter and cut himself a large chunk of cheese from a huge wheel that sat next to the roll of wrapping paper. Tearing off some of the paper, he wrapped up the cheese, then cut off another chunk and stuffed it into his mouth. Before he left the store, he found a can of kerosene, poured it on the floor, lit a match, and dropped it. The flames leaped up.

As he stepped out onto the front porch, the dog, which had been lying so peacefully a few minutes earlier, was now on his feet, growling, with his teeth exposed.

Bodine shot him as well, then rode away as smoke rolled out through the door behind him.

Half an hour and five miles down the road from Garland's Road Ranch, Bodine ate the peaches and counted the money. The robbery had netted him $146. That was enough to keep him going until he found the man who killed his brother.

"The truth is, Zeke," Bodine said aloud, "it ain't like me 'n you was ever all that close. Hell, if we had stayed together, I more 'n likely woulda wound up killin' you my ownself. But bein' as you was my brother I can't let somebody else kill you 'n not do nothin' about it. It just wouldn't look right. I don't know who it was that done it yet, but when I find out, I'll kill the son of a bitch."

Bodine wondered if it was Wynton Miller. He had never met Miller, but he had certainly heard of him.

"Miller, wherever you are, I hope it was you. I'm tired of hearin' people sayin' that you're faster 'n me."

Bodine turned the can of peaches up and drank the rest of the juice, smacked his lips in appreciation, then tossed the can away.

"Damn, I shoulda got me a couple more cans o' them peaches afore I burnt the place down," he said.

Bodine remounted and continued his ride north, toward Wyoming, and a place called Chugwater.

Twin Peaks Ranch

Ben Turley was surprised to see six new men arrive at the ranch, and as the men moved into the bunkhouse, they began staking out bunks, tossing aside the packs and cloth sacks that indicated the bunks were already taken.

"Whoa, hold on there!" Turley called. "Those bunks are already taken, and we don't have enough for all of you. A few of you men are going to have to throw out a bedroll on the floor," Turley said. "I don't know what you are doin' here anyway. We ain't got enough work for you."

"We'll keep the bunks we got," one of the men said.

"What's your name?" Turley demanded.

"The name is Shamrock."

"Well, Mr. Shamrock, just so's that you know, my name is Turley, 'n I'm the ranch foreman. So if you are goin' to work here, you'll do whatever I tell you to do."

"You may be the foreman, but these here men work for me, 'n you ain't got no say over me or them. So, it's like I said, we'll keep these here bunks," Shamrock replied.

Turley strode purposely from the bunkhouse to the ranch office.

"Yes, Turley, what is it?" Houser asked, looking up from something he was writing.

"It's about these new hands you have hired," Turley said.

"What about them?"

"Well, they have moved into the bunkhouse and they are taking over the place, layin' claim to bunks that some of the others already have. And to be honest with you, Mr. Houser, I don' know why you hired 'em in the first place. I can't see as we need any more riders."

"Are you trying to tell me how to run my ranch, Turley?"

"What? No, sir, I ain't tryin' to do nothin' like that. It's just that, well, if them new hands is goin' to be here, they need to know that I'm in charge."

"You aren't in charge of them," Houser said.

"You mean they're like Knox, Malcolm, and Dobbins?"

"In a manner of speaking, yes, that would be a good comparison."

"So they'll be working for Knox."

"No, my brother will be in charge of Knox, Malcolm, and Dobbins, as well as the men who just arrived with him."

"Your brother?"

"Mr. Shamrock is my brother. Incidentally, Mr. Turley, while you will continue to be in charge of the ranch hands, my brother will have superiority over you."

"What? Mr. Houser, I can see maybe him bein' in charge of all these new men, especially if they ain't goin' to be cowboys. But why are you puttin' 'im in charge of me? You didn't even put Knox in charge of me."

"Are you troubled by that, Mr. Turley?"

Turley was quiet for a moment, before he answered. "No, sir, I reckon it don't trouble me none."

"Very good. Make some arrangement for the men who were displaced by the arrival of Mr. Shamrock and the others, would you?"

"Yes, sir, I will.

"Very good. Is there anything else?"

"No sir."

* * *

Later that day Houser went into town, and when he stepped into Fiddler's Green he saw Duff, Elmer, and Wang standing at the bar, talking with Biff Johnson.

Houser glared at Wang, but said nothing to him.

"Good afternoon, Captain MacCallister," Houser said.

"Mr. Houser," Duff replied.

"Has your Celestial performed any more tricks lately?"

"Wang is nae 'my' celestial," Duff replied. "He is my friend, and my employee."

"I will grant you this, he is a man of most unusual athleticism," Houser said. He looked at Wang and nodded. "Mr. Wang, my apologies, sir, not only for questioning you, but also I apologize for the loutish behavior of my men. They had no right to do such a thing, and I have chastised them for it."

Wang returned the nod, without comment.

"Elmer, Wang, and I are about to go down to Lee Fong's Restaurant for Chinese food," Duff said. "Why don't you join us?"

"Very well, I will. Thank you for the invitation."

Lee Fong's restaurant was a relatively small building set between the Chinese laundry and an apothecary. It was painted in red and gold, and it had two waitresses, who wore the traditional cheongsam.

The young woman greeted them, holding her

hands together, prayerlike, smiling broadly, and dipping her head toward Wang Chow.

Wang Chow mimicked her hand position and returning the abbreviated bow.

"What was all that?" Houser asked.

"This pretty thing is named Mai Lin, and she's sweet on Wang. She just greeted him and he returned the greeting," Elmer said.

Elmer smiled at the waitress and addressed her in her native tongue.

"My word! You speak Chinese?" Houser asked, shocked to hear the words coming from Elmer, a man for whom he had very little respect.

"I was a sailor man for a while," Elmer said. "I was in China a few times and picked up some of the lingo. And Wang has helped me. I asked if she had anything good to eat today, but it was just to show off. The food here is always good."

"I will defer, and let you two gentlemen order for me," Houser said.

When the meal was delivered, Duff, Elmer, and of course Wang, ate with chopsticks. Houser didn't even try.

"Captain MacCallister, I would like to get your opinion about the pervasive cattle rustling that is going on in the valley," Houser said.

"Pervasive cattle rustling?"

"Yes. Surely, you are aware of that, aren't you? I have lost, just within the last month, nearly two hundred head. That is no insignificant loss."

"That is news to me, Mr. Houser, for I've lost nae cattle to thieves."

"Hmm, it makes one question how it is that Sky

Meadow, of all the ranches in the valley, is the only one that has not been hit by cattle rustlers."

"My closest neighbor would be The Queen Ranch, 'n I'm quite positive that Percy Gaines has nae been visited by cattle thieves."

"Percy Gaines? He's one of the smaller ranchers, isn't he?"

"Aye. Sometimes he works for me, but he is building his own ranch."

"Yes, well, that is my point. I am convinced that most of our losses are directly attributable to the small ranchers' perfidious raids against the ranches of their larger neighbors. Are you sure that this man Gaines isn't enlarging his own spread with some of your cattle?"

"Aye, that he is, but 'tis some cattle I gave him to help with the start. And, 'twas not too long ago that he brought in three cows wearin' the Sky Meadow brand, that he had collected while rounding up his own."

"Actually, I suppose you are somewhat protected, seeing as you are raising Angus while the rest of us are raising Herefords. It would be very difficult for Gaines, or any of the other small ranchers, to run your cattle in with their own."

"You forget, I gave some of m' own cattle to Percy for him to start, so 'tis Angus that he is raising. Young Percy Gaines is a good man."

"To you, maybe," Houser said with a growl. "But I am now keeping a very close eye on my own livestock. As I said, I have lost a considerable number of cows, just since I arrived here. And of course, there is no telling how many were stolen between the time of Prescott's demise and my arrival."

"I'm sorry to hear that, Mr. Houser. But if you have been losing cattle, I think 'tis unlikely that other ranchers be the rustlers. I know nearly all of them, 'n consider all of them to be good and honest men."

"You certainly have more faith in your fellow man than I," Houser said. "But then, of course, before I entered the cattle industry, I was a lawyer and, in that position, witnessed the dregs of all mankind."

"Aye, I can see how that might color your perception."

Houser put a dab of brown mustard on his egg roll. "Not to worry, however. I have been giving this a thought, and soon will be making a proposal to the other ranchers of the valley."

Chapter Nineteen

Warm Springs, Wyoming

Bodine dismounted in front of the Clayton and Barr livery.

"Yes, sir?" he was greeted. "You want to board your horse?'"

"Where am I?"

"You are in the wonderful community of Warm Springs."

"What state?"

The man chuckled. "You really are lost, ain't you? Well, sir, you're in Wyoming, but we ain't a state yet. There's them that says we won't never be a state, but most folks thinks that we will. But like I said before, are you a-wantin' to board your horse? Or was you just wantin' to find out where at it is that you are?"

"I want you to board my horse."

"That'll be fifty cents a night with hay, six bits if you want your horse to have oats."

"Hay is good enough for 'im," Bodine said.

"In advance."

"Here's for two nights." Bodine gave him a dollar, then looked down the street. There were three saloons interspersed with the other business buildings.

"Which one o' them saloons is the best?" he asked.

"Well, sir, you can get food in all of 'em. But the one that serves the best food is Lamberts. The best whiskey is at the Red Star Saloon, 'n the most accommodatin' women is at Frog City."

Bodine chose Frog City, and was greeted as soon as he walked in the door by someone saying, "Hello, cowboy."

At first, he didn't know who said it, then he saw a parrot in a cage, and never having seen one before, he went over for a closer look.

"Hello, cowboy," the parrot said again.

Bodine was fascinated by the parrot, but he saw something in the bottom of the cage that caught his interest right away. The bottom of the cage was lined with an old newspaper, and a visible story said, *Lucien Bodine killed in Chugwater.*

Since he was obviously still alive, he realized that the story must be about his brother.

Bodine smiled. If people thought he was dead, it would give him an opportunity to move around without fear of some old reward poster getting in the way.

At Twin Peaks Ranch, Brad Houser was having lunch with his brother.

"I'm going to have to give you a new name," Houser said. "You are wanted as Thomas Jefferson, you are wanted as Ray Kellerman, and now you are wanted as Sid Shamrock. I can't take a chance of being connected with any of those names." Brad chuckled. "You are running out of names, little brother, it's getting hard to keep up with them."

"Yeah, well, you're the one who made me give up my real name."

"You're the one that killed Angus Duncan. And Thomas Jefferson was no more your real name than John Tyler was mine. It was the nature of our mother's . . . let us call it, profession . . . that she didn't always know who got her pregnant. And, as she had an interest in past presidents, we were each named for one. I got rid of the name she gave me as soon I could. I needed nothing to remind me of the whore who, by accident, was our mother."

"Yeah, but then you wound up changin' that name, too," Shamrock said.

"Names are like shoes. You can put them on, or take them off as is convenient for the circumstances."

"What new name are you givin' me?"

"Harris. Paul Harris."

"I don't like it."

"Why not?"

"It don't stick with you like the name Shamrock does."

"Think about it, brother. Do you really want a name that sticks with you? A name that people, and the law, can remember? Or would you rather have a name that people can forget as soon as they hear it?"

"Yeah, that's why you got rid of your old name, ain't it?"

"Tell me, Thomas, just how many men have you killed?" Houser said, without responding directly to Houser's question. "Excuse me, I mean Paul. I had better get used to saying it, and you need to get used to hearing it. How many men have you killed?"

"I don't know. Six, maybe, seven. I ain't exactly kept count. I ain't kilt as many as Knox has. He told me he's kilt twelve men."

"Do you think you could kill him?" Houser asked. "Knox, I mean."

"Are you asking me if I'm faster 'n he is? I mean, that would be damn funny, comin' from you."

Houser shook his head. "I didn't ask if you were faster. What I want to know is, could you kill Knox if there was no chance of him killing you?"

"You mean could I shoot the son of a bitch in the back? Yeah, I wouldn't have no problem with that."

"That's good to hear."

"Why do you ask? Do you want me to kill him?"

"Not yet," Houser replied. "But he has given me some indication that the time may come when I find it necessary to get rid of him."

"What about them other two? Malcolm and Dobbins?"

"They are followers," Houser said. "Without Knox, they will need someone to follow." Houser smiled. "That will be you."

"What about Turley? You want me to kill him, too?"

"No. This is a cattle ranch, and everything else I am doing is designed to make the ranch bigger and more productive. Neither you, nor Jaco, nor any of the men you brought with you know the first thing about ranching. Turley does know ranching, and not only that, he knows this ranch. I need him, and I need the men under him. I may have made a mistake in having Slim and Dooley killed, but they knew too much about the strategy I've put into effect, and I didn't trust either one of them to keep it secret. Besides, they were neither ruthless, nor innovative, enough to react to unforeseen events, whereas Knox, Malcolm, and Dobbins are."

"I thought you wanted me to kill Knox."

"I do, but not until the time comes."

Trail Back Ranch

Leo Hartzog, foreman of Trail Back, made another circle around the cattle that had been pushed into the east range. Without even counting, he could tell that there were considerably fewer cows here now than there had been yesterday.

"Parker," he called to one of the riders. "Did you move some beeves out of here without tellin' me?"

"No," Parker said. "Why do you ask?"

"Take a good close look, then tell me if you still have to ask that question."

Parker stood in his stirrups and looked out over the milling cattle.

"Damn, some of 'em is gone, ain't they?"

"How many did we put in here?"

"We put five hunnert head in here."

"Get a count."

An hour later, Hartzog went up to the Big House to report to David Lewis. Hazel Prouty answered the door.

"Yes, Mr. Hartzog?"

"Ma'am, I need to talk to Mr. Prouty."

"He's just finished breakfast. Come on in, have a cup of coffee with him."

"Thank you, ma'am."

"Good morning, Leo," Prouty greeted when Mrs. Prouty escorted Hartzog into the dining room.

"We got a problem, boss."

Prouty shook his head. "That's not something a rancher likes to hear, first thing in the morning. What sort of problem?"

"Well, sir, we moved five hundred head into the east pasture a few days ago."

"Yes, I remember. Has the creek dried?"

"No, sir, it ain't that. What it is, is that there ain't five hundred cows there now. There's only three hundred 'n eighty-seven of 'em. We counted them."

"Are you sure that you moved five hundred cows to begin with?"

"Yes, sir, we counted 'em out as we moved 'em. And anyway, even if we hadn't counted 'em, you can tell the cows is gone, just by lookin' at the herd. That's how come I had Parker 'n the boys count 'em this mornin' in the first place."

"Rustlers," Prouty said.

"Yes, sir, that's sure what it looks like."

Two days after the conversation between Prouty and his foreman, a letter that Brad Houser had written appeared in the "Letters to the Editor" section of the *Chugwater Defender.*

To the EDITOR,

I address this letter not to you, but to the cattle thieves who are currently plying their iniquitous trade.

To you rustlers, I say that you have been stealing cattle without fear of reprisal, for the law in Laramie County has been unable, or unwilling, to hunt you down. I am, by means of this letter, giving you fair warning. Cease and desist your evil activity, for honest men will rise, and you will pay for your crimes.

BRAD HOUSER, *honest cattleman*
Twin Peaks Ranch,
Laramie County

Not long after Houser's letter appeared in the newspaper, Duff received an invitation to a meeting to be held by the Laramie County Cattlemen's Association.

"Well, now, this is rather odd," Duff said as he looked at the invitation.

"What's odd?" Elmer asked.

"The meeting is to be held in the boardroom of the Bank of Chugwater."

"Well, don't you s'pose most of the cattlemen here 'bout does their business with the Bank of Chugwater?" Elmer asked.

"Aye, but that's the point. I've seen the boardroom, 'n 'tis much too wee of a space to hold a meeting of all the cattlemen who belong to the Laramie County Association."

"Well, more 'n likely some of the folks up north will decide it's too far to come," Elmer suggested.

"Aye, that could be," Duff agreed.

When Duff and Elmer rode into town on the afternoon of the meeting, Duff expected to see a score or more surreys, buckboards, wagons, and horses. Instead, there were less than a dozen.

"Duff, do you think we've got time for a . . . ?" Elmer started to ask, but Duff interrupted him.

"Wee drop o' the dew? Aye, 'n 'tis a good idea. You go on down, I'm going to see if Miss Meagan would care to join us."

When Duff pushed open the door, Meagan was giving directions to Mary Ellen.

"Move the new bolts of cloth onto the front table so our customers can see what they have to choose from."

"Yes, ma'am," Mary Ellen said.

"Duff!" Meagan said happily. "What brings you to town in the middle of the day? Oh, wait, I heard there was a cattlemen's meeting."

"Aye," Duff replied. "But I've time to wet my whistle at Fiddler's and 'twas hoping, I was, that ye would be for joining me."

"I'd love to join you," Meagan said. "Mary Ellen, you can mind the store for a short time, can't you?"

"Oh yes, ma'am, no problem," the young lady replied.

"Now, let's step next door and have that drink," Meagan said.

"Oh, I don't mean join me just for a drink. As you are a partner in ownership of Sky Meadow, I want you to come to the cattlemen's meeting with me."

"Cattle*men's* meeting?" Meagan replied, smiling as she emphasized the word *men*.

"Aye, ye have a point. 'Twould rightly be cattlemen's and cattle women's meeting."

"No, cattlemen and cattle woman's meeting, as, no doubt, I shall be the only woman there," Meagan corrected.

"As ye wish, but you'll come?"

"I'll be there bright eyed, and by your side," Meagan said.

As Meagan's dress shop was right next door to Fiddler's Green, it took but a few steps for them to get there.

"Duff!" Biff greeted when the two stepped into the saloon. Biff was at his private table with Elmer. "Thank goodness you brought someone pretty to join us to offset all the ugly from this miscreant." He nodded toward Elmer, who was already sitting at Biff's personal table.

"You know, sonny, durin' the war, I used to shoot at blue bellies like you, sergeant major or not," Elmer replied.

Biff chuckled. "Well, my friend, the operative words there are *shoot at*. And in my case, I'm glad you missed. What'll it be, Duff, Meagan?"

Duff ordered a Scotch and Meagan ordered a white wine.

Biff stepped up to the bar, ordered the drinks, then brought them back to the table.

"Going to the cattlemen's meeting, are you?" he asked.

"Aye, and cattle woman," Duff replied.

"What?"

Meagan chuckled. "There's no need in going

through all this again. What he means is that I'm going as well."

"As you should, since you own part of the herd," Biff said. "What is the meeting about?"

Duff shook his head. "I've nae idea what it's aboot. 'Tis not a regularly scheduled meeting, 'n from the looks o' things across the street, 'tis not even a meeting to which ever' one was invited. 'Tis wondering, I am, why they would want to meet in a room as wee as the bank boardroom."

"Yes, Manuel Vazquez was in here earlier," Biff said. "He had found out about the meeting quite by accident, because he hadn't been invited. And when he asked about it, he was told that the meeting had nothing to do with him. I think he believed it was because he was a Mex."

"I dinnae know. That could be the reason, I suppose, but I'm for thinking that it might be something else. 'Tis for a fact that I know Percy Gaines wasn't invited, 'n Percy is a foine rancher. His ranch is still a wee one, aye, but I've nae doubt that it will grow. Percy is a good worker 'n as foine a lad as anyone would ever encounter."

"I'll say this about him. He watches his money," Biff said. "He comes in here from time to time and buys but one beer, and that's all."

"Aye, he is savin' money to marry his sweetheart. He plans to bring her here to help him run his ranch."

"Merlin Goodman just got here. I can see him goin' into the bank now," Elmer said, looking through the window.

"Perhaps 'tis time for us to go as well." Duff held his glass up. "Here's to older whiskey, younger horses, prettier women, 'n more gold in our pockets."

"What? Prettier women?" Meagan said.

"Forgive me, lass, for 'tis a Scottish toast I quoted without thinking."

"Ha! I'll say you weren't thinking," Biff said with a little laugh."

"Then we'll drink to younger horses 'n more gold," Duff suggested.

"Well, now, I didn't have anythin' against drinkin' to the whiskey, neither," Elmer added.

Chapter Twenty

Finishing their drinks, Duff, Meagan, and Elmer crossed the street and stepped into the bank. As they started into the board meeting room, however, they were stopped by someone that Duff had never seen before. Elmer recognized him, though; it was Dobbins, one of the men who had accosted Wang.

"You can't go in there. The cattlemen is havin' a private meetin' this afternoon," he said.

"Get out of the way, Dobbins, we're Sky Meadow, and we've been invited," Elmer said.

"There ain't no women allowed," Dobbins said. He pointed to Elmer. "And I know you ain't no cattleman, 'cause you was with that Celestial."

"The one I warned you about, but you wouldn't listen," Elmer said with a glint of humor in his eyes.

Subconsciously, Dobbins put his hand to his throat.

"Yeah, well, anyway, this here meetin' is for cattlemen only."

"It's all right, Mr. Dobbins," Houser called from just inside the room. "They may come in."

"All three of 'em?" Dobbins called back.

"Yes, all three of them, although Captain MacCallister, I do wonder at the sagacity of your bringing Miss Parker." He smiled at Meagan. "You are quite welcome, my dear, but as most of the conversation will be 'men's talk' I fear you may find the meeting somewhat off-putting."

"Oh, but I am very much looking forward to it, Mr. Houser," Meagan said, returning the smile. "And I am quite comfortable with 'men's talk.'"

"Then by all means, my dear, please do come on in," Houser invited. "The meeting will start in just a minute or two."

Duff looked around at the other attendees: In addition to Brad Houser, who seemed to be in charge of the meeting, also present were Clyde Barnes, Dale Allen, David Lewis, Merlin Goodman, Webb Dakota, and Burt Rowe.

Duff knew all the ranchers, some better than others, and what he knew about them was that they were the biggest ranchers in this part of Wyoming. Not only was Percy Gaines absent, but not one of the smaller ranchers was present, not even Ethan Terrell, whose ranch, the Diamond T, the largest of the smaller ranches, was nearly of the size to be considered one of the larger ranches.

Duff responded to the greetings of some of the others as he, Meagan, and Elmer took their seats.

"So, tell me, MacCallister, have you been eatin' any more lamb lately?" Goodman asked.

"Aye, but lamb is getting so hard to find that I'm thinking about bringing in a nice flock of say . . . oh, about a thousand of the woolly creatures. They aren't like cattle, you know. You can sell them for meat, or you can keep them and just sell their wool. 'Twould be quite a profitable enterprise, and I hope to convince others to join me in the raising of the creatures."

"What!" Goodman replied, gasping in displeasure. "You wouldn't dare!"

Webb Dakota chuckled. "My dear Mr. Goodman, I do believe that Captain MacCallister was joking with you. As an Englishman, it has been my observation that Scots are like that."

"Gentlemen, gentlemen," Houser called, holding his arms out. "If you would, please, I would like for you to direct your attention to the front of the room, so that we can get started."

"Mr. Houser, I thought this was a meeting of the cattlemen of Laramie County," Barnes said.

"That, it is, Mr. Barnes."

"Well, I don't know what you have in mind, sir, but there certainly are not many of us here. Laramie is a damn big county, and I know we've got more ranchers than just those who are here."

"That's true, Mr. Barnes, Laramie is a very big county, but this particular meeting refers only to those of us who have ranches here in the Valley of the Chug," Houser replied.

"Yeah, well, there are a lot more ranches in the Valley of the Chug than are here, too. Where are the other ranchers?"

"You would be talking about the small ranchers, of course."

"Yeah, men like Prosser, Terrell, Gaines, Patterson, and ten or twelve others at least," Barnes said. "They're cattlemen, and they have ranches in the valley. Why is it, then, that none of them are here?"

"Yes, and I heard that Vazquez tried to get in, and he was turned away," Burt Rowe said. "It wasn't because he's Mexican, is it? Vazquez used to work for me, 'n I can tell you now, that he is a damn good man."

"No, it has nothing to do with the fact that Señor Vazquez is Mexican. He was turned away for the same reason that the other men you have mentioned were not invited."

"And what reason is that?" Lewis asked.

"Before I answer that question, I have a question of my own," Houser replied. "How many of you have noticed, of late, a gradual diminution of your herds?"

"A what?" Dale Allen asked.

"Have any of you have been losing cattle?"

"Yeah," Goodman said. "I've lost some cattle, a hundred or more head, for sure. 'N they didn't die on me, neither, 'cause we ain't found no carcasses, nor even bones."

"I must say that Kensington Place has lost quite a few as well," Dakota added.

"I have lost several, just recently," Lewis said resolutely. "I'm glad that's the subject of this meeting, because I was going to bring it up myself."

"I share that problem with you, only more so. I have now lost over three hundred head, and I suspect it's because the rustlers realize I am new to the valley, and perhaps it has given them the mistaken idea that I am an easy victim."

"Rustlers?" Allen asked.

"Yes, rustlers. Gentlemen, that's precisely the

problem we're going to be talking about, a problem that, primarily, only we large ranchers have to deal with. And therein lies the answer to the question as to why the smaller ranchers were not invited to this gathering."

"Mr. Houser, are you suggesting something about the small ranchers?" Rowe asked.

"Indeed I am, Mr. Rowe. I'm suggesting that these upstart little ranchers have been augmenting their herds with our cattle."

"Here, now, Houser," Lewis said. "I know that the small ranchers may be rounding up mavericks. Hell, we all do that. But I wouldn't be callin' that rustling. Besides which, I didn't start losing cattle until just the last month. If it was the small ranchers, don't you expect it would have been going on all along?"

"Eddie Webb, the small rancher adjacent to Kensington Place, has been a very good neighbor, and quite often helpful," Dakota said. "I would have a most difficult time believing that he might be a rustler."

"Then who is doing it?" Houser asked. "I've already heard from some of you that you have lost cattle."

"But what makes you think it's the small ranchers who are doing the rustling?" Dale Allen asked.

"Tell me this. If it was anyone else, what are they doing with the cattle? I would estimate that, by now, nearly a thousand head have been stolen. That is a significant number of cows that would have to be sold in order to make the effort worthwhile. And in this valley nobody, who isn't a known cattleman, could do that without raising suspicion. No, sir, it has to be the smaller ranchers who could incorporate the purloined beeves within their own herds. All logic points to that inescapable fact."

"I don't know, you may be right," Allen said. "Like the rest of you, I've been losing cattle, and they have to be going somewhere."

"Yeah, I've lost a bunch, too," Burt Rowe said. "I didn't want to think it might be some of the smaller ranchers, but it's like Dale says, they have to be going somewhere. And this is the first year I've ever actually had this problem."

"What about you, MacCallister?" Barnes asked. "You got the biggest ranch of any of us. Have you lost 'ny cows to rustlers?"

"None to my recollection."

"It could be, Mr. MacCallister, that Sky Meadow is so large that you are incapable of taking an accurate inventory," Goodman suggested.

"No, gentlemen, as I have pointed out to Captain MacCallister in previous discussions with him, he is protected by the fact that he is running Angus, and as most of the rest of the cattlemen in the valley are running Herefords, it would be very difficult for any thief to hide any Angus they may have stolen from Sky Meadows, among their own cattle."

"Yeah, that's right, ain't it?" Barnes said. "Thieves ain't very likely to steal cows that can't be hid."

"Be that as it may, however, we can all agree that cattle *are* being stolen, and the purpose of this meeting is to address that problem."

"All right, we all agree there is a problem," Lewis said. "You called this meeting, Mr. Houser. I assume you have something in mind. So what do you propose to do about it?"

"Oh, I have already done something about it. That is, I have taken the first step. Where we go from here, is up to you."

"What is this first step you have taken?" Rowe asked.

"Gentlemen, I have contacted the governor, and he has granted me authorization to take specific action to locate, and bring to justice, those men who are stealing cattle from us."

"What sort of authorization?" Dale Allen asked.

"He has commissioned territorial deputies to look into the matter," Houser replied.

"Territorial deputies? I've never heard of such a thing. Who are these deputies?" Allen asked.

"I am one. I will introduce the other one in a minute. By the commission he and I both hold, we are duly appointed and certified by the governor to uphold the law here, in Valley of the Chug.

"As some of you know, I have recently moved here from Texas. In Texas we have a group of lawmen who can operate all over the state, without regard to county jurisdictional lines. The Texas Rangers have been a most effective means of controlling lawlessness in the state, and if I may be permitted to make a correlation, I would say that you can compare the territorial deputies to the Texas Rangers."

"Texas Rangers? Here? In Wyoming?" Goodman asked.

"No, Merlin, he was just sayin' they was somethin' like the Texas Rangers," Clyde Barnes explained.

"Oh."

"As special deputies, commissioned directly by the governor himself, we will have the authority to appoint more deputies," Houser continued. "And I have no doubt but that this cadre of law officers will bring this scourge of rustling to a halt."

"Look here, Houser, are you tellin' us that you'll be puttin' on a gun 'n goin' after the rustlers yourself?" Barnes asked.

"No, my position will be supervisory only. The gentleman I shall shortly introduce will be the field operative in charge of the aforementioned cadre."

"Mr. Houser," Duff called out.

"Yes, Captain MacCallister?"

"I would nae like to see any of m' neighbors being set upon by an angry group of men accusing them of stealing when they may be innocent," Duff said, "even though they be authorized by the governor."

"I assure you, Captain, it is not the innocent who should fear whatever we have in mind, but the guilty," Houser said resolutely.

"What, exactly, is it you have in mind, Mr. Houser?" Burt Rowe asked. "How are you going to determine who is guilty and who isn't? And how is it you're going to make the guilty suffer? What is it you are planning to do with these men you are calling territorial deputies?"

"It is simply as I have stated, Mr. Rowe. What I have in mind is putting the territorial deputies into operation so that they may determine who, among the small ranchers, are actually guilty . . . because I don't believe, for one moment, that all of them are. I'm quite sure that some of them, perhaps most of them, are innocent men just trying, without the slightest chance of success, to make a living as a small rancher. And in the case of the innocent small rancher, I think they couldn't but welcome our effort to take such action as is necessary to put things right, for, no doubt, their meager herds are also at risk."

"Yes, sir, but when you say 'such action as is necessary' to put things right, that's the part that I'm wondering about. What action would that be?" Rowe asked, still not satisfied with the answer.

"I'm afraid that is not a question that can be answered with any great degree of certainty. Whatever action is necessary would, of course, have to be dictated by the situation."

"How come you didn't ask no local law to be here?" Barnes asked. "I mean, if we're havin' a meetin' to discuss special agents to do some police work for us, don't you think Sheriff Sharpie should have been here?"

"Mr. Barnes, for your information, sir, I have paid a visit to the sheriff's office more times than I can count," Houser said. "Unfortunately Laramie County is so large, and Sheriff Sharpie has but one deputy, Mr. Logan, the problem we are facing now is much greater than his ability to cope. I realized, soon, that if we were going to be able to take care of this, we would have to have help from the territorial governor. So, last week I took a trip to Cheyenne, where I discussed the problem with the governor. It was his suggestion that he grant a special commission to me, and to another, whom I will shortly introduce. This commission allows me to organize these deputies, but disabuse yourself of any idea that they will play a role in the normal policing of the county. Violations of city, county, and territorial laws will continue to be the exclusive purview of Sheriff Sharpie. The territorial deputies will be unique, in that they will be specifically dedicated to the particular problem of cattle rustling, thus avoiding any conflict with the sheriff."

"Do you have these deputies yet?"

"No, not yet."

"Where do you plan to get them?"

"We will populate the territorial deputies with men who are known to have experience in dealing with outlaws."

"I'm still not sure of how, exactly, you are plannin' on usin' these deputies," Barnes said. "Do you plan to use them like a posse? I suppose if they know who it is that they are goin' after, why, it might work out. But right now, we don't have any idea who that may be."

"The whole purpose of this meeting, gentlemen, is so that I can alleviate any concerns you may have as to how the territorial deputies will function. I assure you, we will not be putting our trust into the hands of vigilantes. The very idea of vigilantes running un-restrained in our valley is abhorrent to me, as I'm sure it would be to anyone. But I promise you that the men I appoint will be legitimate deputies. The deputies will be composed of brave and dedicated men who will stay on the job until the violators are located and taken care of."

"Yeah, it's the *took care of* part that I'm wonderin' about. You still ain't said how it is that you're a-plannin' on takin' care of 'em," Goodman said.

"They will be dealt with in a way that is appropriate to their transgressions," Houser said, still avoiding specifics.

"By 'takin' care' of 'em, you don't mean by havin' these here deputies lynch 'em, do you?" Barnes asked. He shook his head. "'Cause if that's what it is you are plannin', then no, I'm sorry, but I can't go along with nothin' like that."

"Surely, Mr. Barnes, you know that I am a lawyer, and as such, I am an officer of the court. I would never approve of such a thing.

"State and territorial law enforcement agencies are nothing new, gentlemen. Why, they are more established than private detective agencies, and we all know the legitimacy of private detective agencies. Railroads routinely hire private detective agencies. In fact, during the war, the United States government hired the Pinkerton Agency, and by so doing, put the imprimatur of the federal government on such agencies so that the precedent was set. And that is exactly what we have done, here."

"So what you are saying is, these men are Pinkertons?" Allen asked.

"No, as much as I would like to, I'm afraid that the Pinkerton Agency would charge us way too much. They have established a name for themselves, you see, and they are quite willing to trade upon that name. However, fortunately for us, we don't have to. With the governor's authority, and the funding you grant me, these men that I shall assemble will be perfect for us."

"What do you mean by the funding we are to give you?" Lewis asked. "You've been telling us for this entire meeting that these men will be territorial deputies. Now, if the governor has authorized this, won't he also be funding it?"

Houser shook his head. "I'm afraid not, gentlemen," he replied. "Whereas the governor was able to provide me with the legal authority to form a group to serve our needs, he is not able, as a governor, to make funding available. That, I fear, would require legislative action. And we simply do not have time for that. We are going to have to come up with the money from our own resources."

"How much is it going to cost us?" Lewis asked.

"I think twenty-five hundred dollars apiece would get the job done," Houser replied.

There were a couple of low whistles.

"Must the subscription be so high?" Dakota asked. "Two thousand and five hundred dollars is quite a significant amount."

"The loss of as few as one hundred cows would cost even more, so I ask you, how much have you lost to cattle rustlers since this outbreak began?" Houser asked. "A better question might be, how many more will you lose if we don't do whatever it takes to stop it now?"

"Yes, I suppose if you put it that way, there may be some justification in such a steep assessment," Dakota said. "All right, I'll go along with it."

"I will, too," Barnes added.

Within a moment, every rancher but Duff had made a commitment of $2,500 to what was being called the territorial deputies.

"Captain MacCallister, we haven't heard from you, sir," Houser said. "Am I to understand that you have no intention of contributing your fair share to the protection of our interests?"

"Aye, your understanding is correct. I'll nae be contributing to the fund," Duff replied.

"If you don't pay for it, how do you expect us to provide Sky Meadow with protection against rustlers?"

"Oh, I'll nae be looking for such protection," Duff said. "As ye have already pointed out, 'tis unlikely anyone will be stealing m' Angus cattle."

"Captain MacCallister, I wish you would change your mind. Things always seem to go better when neighbors work together," Houser said.

"Aye," Duff agreed. "But these same wee ranchers that you're about to make war against are also my neighbors and friends. They are nae rustlers 'n scoundrels. Most have families, 'n 'tis only their wish to make a living for themselves."

"As I stated earlier, I'm the first to admit that not every small rancher is rustling cattle," Houser said. "But don't you see? That's the purpose of putting our special agents into the field. They'll be able to tell us who is, and who isn't, rustling. And look at it this way. The small ranchers who are innocent will be getting the same protection as the rest of us, only they won't have to be paying for it."

"Why not?" Allen asked. "Why shouldn't they pay for it?"

"It is precisely for that reason that I did not invite them to this meeting," Houser replied. "It is called the noblesse oblige."

"The what?"

"The obligation of the nobility to act honorably and generously to those less fortunate. We are not, strictly speaking, nobility. But, as the larger and more successful ranchers in the valley, we do carry the burden of looking out for the smaller ranchers who could ill afford the two-thousand-and-five-hundred-dollar subscription it would take to enroll them in the program. As Captain MacCallister has pointed out, and correctly, I must add, many of the small ranchers are honest people. I wouldn't want to embarrass them by asking them for money they can ill afford, and I don't think any of you would, either."

"You're a good man, Mr. Houser," David Lewis said. "I hope the smaller ranchers realize what you are doing for them."

"What *we* are doing for them," Houser corrected.

"Mr. Houser, you have stated that the governor appointed someone special to head up this constabulary that you are forming, but you haven't told us who he might be," Dakota said. He pointed to Shamrock. "May I take it that the person of whom you speak is this gentleman that none of us seem to know?"

Houser smiled. "I'm glad you brought that up. Stand up, Paul," he said.

Shamrock remained seated.

"Paul?" Houser said again, staring directly at Shamrock.

"Me?"

"Yes, Paul, you," Houser said.

"Oh." Shamrock stood.

"Gentlemen, this is Paul Harris. And as I stated, he holds a direct commission from Governor Morgan, as captain of the territorial law enforcement deputies. And whereas my commission is administrative, Captain Harris's commission is operative. He will be responsible for carrying out any actual investigation and law enforcement. By the way, in as far as the cattle rustling problem is concerned, Captain Harris's authority supersedes that of Sheriff Sharpie's, or any other lawman in the territory. He and his deputies will end our rustling problem."

"You have said that the constabulary is yet to be formed. Will you assemble them from among out own county citizens?" Dakota asked.

"No, they will not be local. Captain Harris needs men who have experience in dealing with law enforcement, and such men cannot be found here."

"I have a question," Duff said.

"All right."

"You have recently added three new men who work for you, but who are not cowhands. Their names, I believe, are Knox, Malcolm, and Dobbins. Do they also hold a commission from the governor?"

"No, they do not."

"If they are nae deputies nor hands, would ye be for tellin' us their purpose?"

"I will tell you as I told my men. Misters Knox, Malcolm, and Dobbins are supernumeraries to the operation of the ranch, and they will remain as such to the territorial deputies as well."

"You still haven't answered Mr. MacCallister's question," Burt Rowe said. "What is the purpose of these three men?"

"Gentlemen, and lady," Houser said, with a pointed reference to Meagan's presence, "if you look around you, you would see that every one of you are wearing pistols. I don't cite you for that—too often the continued existence of men who live here is dependent upon both their ability, and their willingness, to use a firearm. I do not wear a pistol, because I have neither the willingness, nor the ability, to do so. I also have an abhorrence to violence, especially as it may pertain to me."

Houser forced a smile.

"Therefore I have hired Mr. Knox, Mr. Morgan, and Mr. Dobbins to perform the service of personal bodyguards to me. And as such, they will have nothing to do with the deputies. The reason I have hired them should be obvious to all of you. Now that I have initiated this effort to rid our valley of the pervasive lawlessness, I do not fool myself with the false hope that I will not become a target of those whose rustling operations will be curtailed. As long as none of you take it upon yourselves to attack me, and I'm sure none of you are harboring such intentions"—again Houser forced a smile—"none of you need concern yourselves about the presence, or the activities of my *Pontificia Cohors Helvetica*."

"I am aware of some of the activities of these three men, Mr. Houser, and I would hardly call them the Swiss Papal Guard," Duff said.

Houser clapped his hands softly. "Oh, *very good*, Captain MacCallister, you recognize my Latin. You are right, of course, they are hardly up to the task of guarding the Pope. I do hope you will forgive me my little private joke."

"Yes, well, getting back to these deputies, how are we going to know who they are? I mean, will they be wearin' badges or anything?" Barnes said.

"I will provide them with badges, which will give them all the authority they need to carry out their mission. Mark this day on your calendar, gentlemen. This is the day the war against the cattle rustlers of the Valley of the Chug began."

Chapter Twenty-one

"I don't trust Houser any farther than I can throw him," Biff said. Meagan had returned to her dress shop, and Biff rejoined Duff and Elmer at his private table in Fiddler's Green.

"He sure talks fit 'n proper, I'll say that for him," Elmer said.

"That's because he was a barrister before he came here," Duff said.

"He was a barrister?" Elmer asked. "You mean he was a bartender? Hell, I thought the son of a bitch was a lawyer."

"I'm sorry. I should have said lawyer," Duff said without further explanation.

"Wait. Barrister, is that one of them Scottish words for lawyer?"

"Aye."

"Yeah, he was a lawyer, all right," Biff said. "Only what I heard was that he got in some kind of legal trouble down in Texas, 'n he was told he couldn't be a lawyer anymore."

"You mean he has been disbarred?" Duff asked.

"Yes, he was disbarred. That's what it is, I just couldn't think of the word."

"Why was he disbarred? Do you have any idea?"

"I've never heard why, I just heard that he was disbarred. He must have done pretty well as a lawyer while he was at it, though, because when he came up here and bought the ranch from Cliff Prescott's widow, he paid cash for it."

"Would ye be knowing how he came by the money he used to start his ranch?"

"I don't have the slightest idea. All I know is he put eighty thousand dollars in the Bank of Chugwater the very first day he got here," Biff said.

"I wonder if Mr. Blanton would be knowing anything about it," Duff asked. "If he has been disbarred from somewhere, 'twould likely have been a story about it. And all the newspapers share their stories."

"Could be," Biff replied. "Like you said, he gets all these stories sent to him from all over the country, so if it made the newspaper anywhere, Charley more 'n likely has it, even if he didn't print it in his own newspaper."

"What do you say, Elmer, that we pay a visit to Mr. Blanton? I would like to know a little more about the gentleman who has just hired his own private army."

"His own private army?" Elmer replied.

"Aye, for what else would you call these deputies who are responsible only to Mr. Houser?"

"I'll be damn," Biff said. "You know, I hadn't thought of it in that way before, but you are right. Houser does have his own army."

"Yeah," Elmer said. "Not only that, the slick-talkin'

son of a bitch managed to get all the other cattle ranchers to pay for it."

"Oh yes," Charley Blanton said as he searched through his morgue. "Here it is, reprinted from a Fort Worth newspaper. I didn't print it when the story came in, because Mr. Houser is obviously trying to make a new life for himself up here, and I saw no reason for my newspaper to place a burden upon any of our citizens."

"Aye, 'tis not asking you to print the story, only to let me read it," Duff said. "I think it would be a good thing to know a bit more about our newest rancher."

Duff examined the newspaper article.

Lawyer Disbarred

Brad Houser, a Sulphur Springs lawyer, has been removed from the Texas Bar for an act of dishonesty and corruption, committed in the course of his performance as an attorney-at-law.

It has been alleged that Mr. Houser lied to opposing counsel and to the court. Rather than face trial and possible incarceration, Mr. Houser pled guilty to the charge and accepted disbarment as the only assessed penalty. Houser has since left Texas and his current whereabouts is unknown.

"There is no doubt in my mind, but that this is the same man," Charley said. "How many lawyers could there be with that same name?"

"I don't trust nobody that talks like he does. All

them highfalutin words Houser spits out, he don't sound nothin' a-tall like no one I've never heard before," Elmer said.

Charley Blanton laughed. "Being as you're from Missouri, it seems highly unlikely that you have ever heard anyone use proper English."

"Are you sayin' I don't talk good?"

"No, Elmer. You talk just real good," Charley teased, mimicking Elmer's Missouri twang and idiom.

"Tell me, Duff," Charley continued. "Why are you so interested in Brad Houser?"

"We had a meeting of the Laramie Cattlemen's Association today," Duff replied. "Only, it was nae for all the ranchers, just for the larger ranchers. Houser let it be known that he is planning on going to war against all the wee ranchers of the valley."

"What? Why would he do such a thing? Some of the smaller ranchers are our best citizens. He'll never get the other ranchers to go along with him," Blanton said.

"He's already got 'em," Elmer said.

"He does?"

"Aye. He claims to hold a commission from the governor to raise a private army to go to war against the smaller ranchers. He's calling his army 'territorial deputies.'"

"Why in heavens name would he want to do that?"

"He's a-sayin' that all the little ranchers is stealin' cattle from the larger ranchers," Elmer said, answering Charley's question.

"You know what I'm thinkin', Duff? I think he just a-sayin' that the little ranchers is stealin' cattle so he can use that to sort of cover somethin' else he might have in mind," Elmer said. "Like maybe he don't like 'em usin' the open range."

"You may have a point there, Elmer," Charley said. "Tell me, Duff, would you mind if I did a little checking up, to see if the governor actually has given him such authority?"

"I don't mind at all. In fact, I think it would be a fine idea for you to do so."

"Then I shall get right on it," Blanton promised.

"I'm pretty sure that if Houser claims he has the governor behind him, he probably does," Biff said after Duff and Elmer returned to Fiddler's Green to give him a report on what they found out. "I mean, him bein' a lawyer 'n all, I would expect him to make certain everything is on the up-and-up."

"Aye, but it doesn't hurt to check up on him," Duff said.

"Well, would you look at what the cat drug in," Elmer said.

Elmer's comment caused both Duff and Biff to look toward the door, where they saw Percy Gaines.

At first Duff thought something might be wrong, but the broad smile on Percy's face told him otherwise.

"Percy, would ye be for joinin' us now?"

"All right, but I can only stay for a short while, because I've got a train to catch."

"Where are you goin' on the train?" Elmer asked.

"I'm goin' to Kansas City." Percy's smile got larger. "She's goin' to marry me, Mr. Gleason, Mr. MacCallister, Mr. Johnson. I wrote her a letter 'n asked if she would come out here 'n marry me, 'n she wrote back 'n said that she would. Sara Sue Cannedy is goin' to become Sara Sue Gaines."

"Well, now, this calls for a toast!" Biff said, and held his hand up, signaling to one of the girls who worked there. "Annie, drinks all around here, and from my special bottle of Scotch."

"Your 'special' bottle?" Duff asked. "Here, Biff, 'n are ye for tellin' me that I don't get your special bottle?"

"Of course you do," Biff replied easily. "And who do you think I keep the special bottle for? I was just givin' Annie her instructions, is all."

"I can't believe she's actually goin' to come out here to marry me," Percy said.

"What do you mean you can't believe it?" Elmer asked. "It's all you been talkin' about for the last year."

"I know, I know. But I wasn't ever just really sure, you know. But now, I've got me a nice little ranch, 'n it'll be growin', too."

"I'll send Keegan over to keep an eye on it while you're gone," Duff offered.

"Well, Mr. MacCallister, that's very nice of you, sendin' Keegan over to look after my herd, like that."

"That's what neighbors do for one another," Duff replied.

"Yes, sir, it is, ain't it? 'N we are neighbors, even if your ranch is near a hundred times bigger 'n mine."

Annie brought the drinks, and Duff raised his glass to propose the toast. "Percy, m' lad, may the best you've ever seen, be the worst you'll ever see."

The four men drank their toast.

"Let me ask you something, Percy," Duff said as he set his glass down. "Have ye lost any cattle to rustlers?"

"Lost any cattle? No, sir. Fact is, I've gained a few cows from some of the other ranches."

"What do you mean, you've gained a few cows?" Duff asked, curious about Percy's comment.

"Well, sir, it wasn't hard pickin' 'em out, seein' as they was Herefords. But, you know, it's the damnedest thing, just in the last few weeks I've had some cattle from Twin Peaks, Pitchfork, and Trail Back that's showed up on my ranch."

"How many?"

"Ten from Twin Peaks, four from Pitchfork, 'n two from Trail Back. 'N that's what is so funny about it. I mean, how come it is that all them cows has sort of wandered onto The Queen from all them different ranches at about the same time? I mean, I could see if they all come from one ranch, but from three different ranches?"

"Did ye take these creatures back?" Duff asked.

"No, sir, I wanted to, but I had some more brandin' 'n castratin' to do so's I could leave to go pick up Sara Sue. I left 'em back at the ranch, but I've got 'em separated out into their own corral, so's it'll be easy to take care of it when I get back."

"It's getting about that time. Come along, lad, we'll walk ye down to the depot," Duff offered.

It was a short walk from Fiddler's Green to the depot, but even before they got there, they heard the whistle of the approaching train.

"Do you think Sara Sue will like it out here?" Percy asked nervously as they waited for the approach of the train.

"It's a little late to be a-worryin' 'bout that now, ain't it?" Elmer asked.

"Oh! Do you think maybe she won't?" The tone of Percy's voice indicated a newfound concern.

"Come on, Percy, I was just a-funnin' with you," Elmer said. "What's there not to like about the Valley of the Chug? Besides which, I'll ask Vi to go out to your place 'n help Miss Sara Sue get settled in."

"Thanks, Elmer. I appreciate that. I appreciate that a lot."

By now the train arrived, and it rumbled through the station, the big drive wheels wreathed in ribbons of white steam, black smoke streaming from the stack, the wheels squealing, and couplers banging as the cars slowed against one another.

Nobody got down from the train, and Percy was the only departing passenger. Duff and Elmer stood on the depot platform until the train departed.

"There goes one happy man," Elmer said.

"Aye," Duff agreed.

Chapter Twenty-two

"Duff, what do you think about what Percy told us about them cows he found from some of the other ranches?" Elmer asked.

"I'm givin' the question some thought, Elmer," Duff said. "It's a good question, because having cows from three different ranches show up as they did was, indeed, quite puzzling.

"I suppose, what with roundup 'n all, that such a thing could happen," Duff said. "But I wish he had taken them back before he left. I don't know about this special detective 'n his crew of deputies 'n all, but I'd feel better if the creatures weren't in a corral on Percy's place."

"How 'bout me 'n Wang takin' 'em back to where they belong, tomorrow?"

"Aye," Duff said, nodding. "'Twould be a good thing for ye to do so."

"Wang will like goin' with me, 'cause he likes gettin' out 'n about," Elmer said. "'N you know what else he likes? He likes helpin' folks. It's kind of a honor thing with him. Actually, lots of Chinese are big on honor, I learned that when I was in China."

"I'm sure there are many honorable Chinese," Duff answered. "And I know for a fact that honor plays a significant role in Wang's makeup."

Houser and Shamrock were riding toward Twin Peaks alone. Wix, Jaco, and the others had been told that they were going to be used in a scheme that promised to bring everyone a rather sizable payroll, but as yet, they had no idea what that scheme might be.

"Paul," Houser started to say.

"Why don't you call me Sid when we are alone? I've had that name long enough that I've done got used to it."

"On your bank robbery in Seven Oaks, did you kill someone?"

"Yeah, I kilt the bank manager."

"Why?"

"The son of bitch grinned at me. The bank had what they called a time lock safe, 'n it couldn't be opened till four o'clock. He told me to come back at four o'clock, 'n he grinned at me while he was sayin' it."

"And for that, you killed him?"

"Yeah. You shoulda seen 'im, that big mocking smile like he had me just where he wanted me. It pissed me off so much that I couldn't help it, so I shot the son of a bitch."

"Yes, well, you should have controlled your temper. Did you not also say that you saw the name

Sid Shamrock in the paper for the bank robbery and murder you committed in Seven Oaks?"

"Yeah, I seen it. 'N seein' as I never was there before, I don't have no idea how it is that they knowed it was me. But, anyhow, that was down in Texas, that's a long way from here. So I don't see as how anyone up here can find out."

"Do you think we are on the back side of the moon up here?"

"What?"

"I was using an analogy."

"What's an analogy?" Shamrock asked again.

"Never mind. What I am saying is that, sooner or later, your name will be known up here as well. And the name Shamrock is just too easy to remember. In our business, it doesn't pay to have everyone know about you."

"Everyone knows about you," Shamrock said.

"Not as Brad Houser, and I'm quite comfortable with that name. You had better get used to being called Paul Harris. Anyway, when I secured your commission from the governor, I did it under the name of Paul Harris."

"What about the others? What names did you use for them when you was talking to the governor?"

"It wasn't necessary for me to even bring their names up. You and I were the only two who required a commission. We have the authority to appoint our own deputies. Thus, they will derive their authority from us. You are answerable only to me, and I am answerable only to the governor."

"What does that mean, that you are answerable only to the governor?"

Houser smiled. "That means that I can do anything I want. And, if you have my permission, you can do anything you want."

A broad smile spread across Shamrock's lips. "I can do anything I want?"

"Within reason, and as long as it has my approval."

"Ha! You know what I'm thinkin', big brother? I'm thinkin' this here is goin' to be a lot of fun."

"And profitable," Houser added. "For each miscreant standing in my way who's disposed of by you and your men, I'd be willing to pay a bonus of, say, one thousand dollars."

"Yeah," Shamrock replied with a grin. "Mighty profitable. Only how come I had to change my name, but you didn't have to change your name? You was involved in the robbery back in Sulphur Springs, same as I was."

"No, I wasn't involved. I set the job up for you, but I didn't actually take part in it, if you remember."

"Yeah, I remember. I wound up taking all the chances, but you got most of the money."

"What I've got set up for us now, why, you will be in position to make as much money as you did from the bank robbery in Sulphur Springs, and much more money than you earned from that job in Seven Oaks."

Shamrock smiled. "Yeah, I will, won't I?"

"The first thing you must do is instruct your men to refer to you as Paul Harris, not only in public, but even when you are alone. As I intend to do."

"Yeah, all right, if you say so."

"I do, indeed, say so."

* * *

As soon as Houser and Shamrock returned to the ranch, Shamrock rounded up Jaco, Evans, Wix, Pete, and Hawke, and told them that Houser wanted to talk to them.

"What about me 'n Malcolm 'n Dobbins?" Knox asked.

"He didn't say nothin' about none of you," Shamrock replied.

Turley didn't even ask about himself; he had already learned that there were two groups of men employed by Houser, those who worked, like he, Cooper, and the remaining cowhands, and those who, as far as he could tell, did nothing.

Turley shrugged. It didn't really bother him all that much that Houser had so much dead weight at the ranch. He wasn't paying their salary.

"What do you mean we're goin' to be deputies?" Jaco asked. "You signed us up to be deputies? I thought we was goin' to be makin' some money while we was here. What does a deputy make? Thirty dollars a month?"

"You won't be deputies for the sheriff, you'll be deputyin' for the governor of Wyoming," Shamrock said with a wide smile.

"The governor?"

"Yeah, I'm a special lawman for the governor of Wyoming. 'N from now on when you talk to me, you'll call me Captain Harris."

"Why the hell should we do that?" Wix asked.

"For two hundred dollars a month, 'n a chance to make a lot more money," Shamrock said.

"Two hundred dollars a month?" Jaco replied excitedly. "Damn, that's ten times more 'n a cowhand gets."

"Yes, it is. So, what do you say? Do you want to be my deputy?"

"I say you got yourself a deputy," Jaco replied.

"Two deputies," Wix added.

The others signed on as well.

"Here's a hundred dollars apiece to get you started," Houser said. He smiled. "And this, gentlemen, is just a bonus. It will not come out of your monthly salary."

Happily, and eagerly, the men took the proffered money.

"Hey, Shamrock, you ain't said what it is that we're goin' to be doin' as deputies," Hawke said.

"The first thing you're goin' to do is stop callin' me Shamrock 'n start callin' me Captain Harris. 'N then, after that, why, you're goin' to do whatever I tell you to do," Shamrock said.

"That's all right with me," Hawke said.

The others agreed.

"Hey, Sham . . . uh . . . Cap'n Harris, is it all right with you, if me 'n some of the others go into town tonight?" Jaco asked. He smiled. "I mean, what good is it to get a hundred dollars if you cain't go into town 'n spend it?"

Shamrock looked over at Houser, who, with a slight nod, gave his acquiescence to the request.

Chapter Twenty-three

The girls who served drinks at Fiddler's Green let it be known, very quickly, that a drink and smile was all they were willing to give. Jaco and the other men with him wanted more than that, so they took their business to the Wild Hog Saloon.

The newly constituted deputies were greeted by some working girls as soon as they stepped inside the saloon.

"Well," one of the girls said with a practiced smile. "What do you think, ladies? Here are some cowboys we've never seen before."

"We ain't cowboys," Pete said.

"Oh?" one of the other girls said. "Well, what are you, honey, if you ain't cowboys?"

"We're deputies," Jaco said.

"Deputies? My, my, you mean to tell me that Sheriff Sharpie has hired himself five new deputies?"

"Nah," Evans said. "We ain't deputies for the sheriff. We're deputies for the governor his ownself."

"Are we deputies for the governor, or just for Shamrock?" Wix asked.

"His name ain't Shamrock no more, remember?" Hawke asked. "His name is Harris now, Paul Harris."

"Oh yeah. Captain Harris," Wix said.

"My name is Cindy," one of the girls said, taking hold of Jaco's arm. "How would you like to buy me a drink?"

"Yeah," Jaco said. "I'll buy you a drink. 'N then maybe we can do somethin' else," he added with a salacious smile.

"Honey, as long as you got the money, we can do anything else you want," Cindy replied.

As the girls paired off with the men, it quickly became evident that there was one girl short of being enough to go around, Wix being the one who was left out.

"Hey, ain't there no other girls here?" Wix asked.

"Dianne is upstairs with a gentleman," Cindy said. "She'll be down soon."

"What room is she in?" Wix asked.

Cindy laughed. "It's the first door on the right as soon as you reach the top of the stairs. Don't worry, if she decides to go upstairs with you, she'll show you which room is hers."

"Yeah, well, I ain't plannin' on waitin'," Wix said, starting for the foot of the stairs.

"Fred! Fred, stop him!" one of the other girls shouted, pointing toward Wix. "He's going up to get Dianne."

"Hold on, mister, you can't go up there unless you're invited," the bartender called out toward Wix.

"I'm invitin' myself," Wix said, pulling his pistol and pointing it at the bartender.

The bartender put his hands up in the air. "You've got no right to do that!"

"Yeah, I do," Wix said.

Wix hurried up the stairs, then jerked the door open. A man and woman were in bed, and both of them called out in alarm when Wix stepped inside.

"What the hell?" the man shouted in surprise and anger. "Get out of here! Can't you see we're busy?"

"No, you get out," Wix said, pointing the gun at him. "The woman's comin' downstairs with me."

"I'm not goin' anywhere with you!" Dianne shouted angrily. She pulled the sheet up to cover herself.

"You're either comin' downstairs with me now, or I'm goin' to shoot this feller you're with."

"What? No, no! She'll go with you, she'll go with you!" the man responded, the anger in his voice replaced by fear.

Getting out of bed, the man hopped around on one leg as he began to pull on his pants.

"You better get dressed, too, missy, unless you want to go downstairs without no clothes on a-tall."

Dianne got out of bed then and, still clutching the sheet around her, reached for her clothes.

"Maybe you should just wrap a sheet around you to come downstairs," Wix said with a little laugh. "You'll just be takin' your clothes off again in a few minutes, after you've had a couple o' drinks with me 'n my friends."

"What makes you think I'll come back up here with you?" Dianne asked, still angry at the abrupt intrusion.

"How much did you pay her?" Wix asked the man who was dressed now, except for his boots, which he was pulling on.

"Three dollars," the man said.

"Here's ten. Go somewhere else 'n find yourself another woman."

The anger left the man's face as he reached for the ten-dollar bill. "Yes, sir!" he said, smiling.

"Your name's Dianne, ain't it?" Wix asked.

"Yes. How did you know?"

"Here's another ten dollars for you so that you'll treat me nice."

Now, like the man whose good humor had been bought with a ten-dollar bill, Dianne also smiled. She also noticed, for the first time, that there was a good deal of laughter coming from her friends downstairs.

"Sure, honey," she said, taking the bill. "I'll be glad to have a few drinks with you."

By the time they reached the bottom of the stairs, Sheriff Sharpie's deputy was standing there.

"Mister," the deputy said to Wix. "You've got yourself a peck of trouble, botherin' these people like this."

"What do you mean, Deputy Logan? I'm not bothered none," the man who had been with Dianne said.

"You sure this man didn't trouble you none, Buck?"

"I'm sure."

"What about you, miss?"

"I'm not bothered, either," Dianne added quickly.

Logan looked over toward the bar. "Fred, didn't you send someone after me, saying you was havin' trouble here?"

Fred looked at Dianne, obviously confused now by her reaction.

"Don't worry about it, Fred, it was just a misunderstanding is all," Dianne said. "But we've got it all worked out now, don't we, honey?" She put her hand on Wix's shoulder.

"That's right," Wix said. Wix extended his hand toward Logan. "I'm Deputy Wix," he said. "Looks like me 'n you's in the same business."

Now it was Logan's time to look confused. "You're a deputy? What do you mean, you're a deputy? I didn't know Sheriff Sharpie had taken on any new deputies."

"We ain't deputies for the sheriff," Jaco said, calling over from the table where he and the others were sitting with the remaining bar girls. "We're deputies for the governor. All five of us is."

"For the governor? I've never heard of deputies for the governor."

"You'll be hearin' about it pretty soon," Jaco said. "I reckon we'll be takin' over things here now."

"Does the sheriff know anything about this?" Logan asked.

"I reckon he'll find out soon enough. Mr. Houser, he's the one that got the governor to send us down here."

"Yeah," Sheriff Sharpie said a while later when Deputy Logan reported on what had happened. "I heard about it. They'll be working with the Cattlemen's Association, is what I'm told. It won't have anything to do with what happens here in town. Besides, there were no complaints filed, were there?"

Logan shook his head. "No, sir, I talked to Buck 'n

Dianne both, 'n both of 'em said there wasn't no trouble."

"Well, there you go, then," the sheriff said. "In a case like this, seein' as there was no damage done, 'n nobody was hurt, well, if there are no complaints, there's nothing we can do about it."

The next morning as Elmer and Wang rode up to The Queen Ranch, Keegan came out of the house to meet them.

"Hello, Mr. Gleason, Wang," Keegan said. "I've got a pot of coffee inside."

"Good man," Elmer said.

"What did you folks come over for? If you're here to check on me, well, everything's goin' fine. I hadn't had no trouble with anything," Keegan said as he served both Elmer and Wang coffee.

"Well, it's sort of to check up on you, 'n make certain you wasn't just lyin' aroun' on your ass for the whole time," Elmer teased. "But mostly what we're here for, is so's we can take some cattle back to where they belong," Elmer said. "Seems a few strays wound up in Percy's herd."

"Oh yeah, I wondered about that. They are out in the corral."

A cup of coffee and a short conversation later, Elmer and Wang rode away, driving the wayward cows before them.

"Trail Back is on the way to Twin Peaks, but we'll go to Pitchfork first," Elmer said. "Even though it's in the opposite direction, it's the closest."

* * *

"Captain Harris, I am about to give you and your men your first assignment. I want you to ride over to Percy Gaines's ranch," Houser told Shamrock. "I think you'll find some stolen cattle there. And whatever you find, bring back here. I'll have someone take the Pitchfork and Trail Back cows back to their owners."

"All right," Shamrock said.

"Oh, and you might administer a little justice for harboring the stolen cows."

"What kind of justice is it that you're talkin' about?" Shamrock asked.

"The kind of justice that will make certain that he doesn't wind up with any more stolen cows."

"Yeah," Shamrock said with an evil smile. "Yeah, I think I know what you mean."

"I'm sure you do."

Turley, who had not attended the meeting the day before, and who had heard none of the exchange between Houser and Shamrock, watched the six men ride off. Curious about it, he walked up to the ranch office to question Houser.

"I seen that your brother 'n them other five men rode off. Are they leavin'?"

"Mr. Turley, I told you not to concern yourself with those men. They are answerable only to me. But for your information, they are not leaving. You will learn, soon enough, that they are going to be dealing with the small ranchers who, I am convinced, are responsible for all the cattle rustling that has been going on of late."

"Mr. Houser, I know just about ever' one of the small ranchers here in the valley, I've rode with most of 'em. They're good men, all of 'em, and I just don't believe that they're the ones that's doin' the stealin'."

"You are looking at them through eyes that are distorted by previous amity. You feel a fraternity with them, and I can understand that, Turley, but you must look at it from my point of view. If we don't stop this now, in its earliest stages, then it will only encourage these small ranchers, these usurpers of grass and water, to continue to build their herds at the expense of those of us who, by the size of our operations, make perfect targets for them. Do you understand that?"

Turley didn't reply.

"Well, do you understand it? Because, Mr. Turley, if you are unable to understand this simple concept, then perhaps I need a new man."

"Oh no, sir!" Turley said quickly. "I understand just what you are talkin' about. A thing like this, stealin' cattle, I mean, is somethin' that you got to nip in the bud afore it gets way out of hand."

Houser smiled. "It is good that you understand."

"If I have to talk to 'em about something, should I talk to you, or to Cap'n Harris?"

"There will never be any need for you to initiate any conversation with them. As I said, they are working for me, they aren't working for you. And to the degree possible, I intend to keep the special police force separated from you and from the working cowhands. Do you understand?"

"Yes, sir."

"On the other hand, there may be occasions when it will be necessary for Captain Harris, or one of his men, to order you to do something. If he, or one of his men, should issue such an order to you, or to any of the hands, you may regard that as an order directly from me, and I will expect you to give them full cooperation."

"Yes, sir, I will do whatever needs to be done."

Chapter Twenty-four

Shamrock and the territorial deputies were coming close to The Queen Ranch, though as they were unaware of the name given his ranch by Percy Gaines, they didn't think of it in that way.

"Hey, Shamrock," Jaco started to say.

"It's Captain Harris," Shamrock corrected. "Remember, my name is Harris."

"I ain't forgot, but there ain't nobody here now but just us, 'n all of us knows you as Shamrock."

"If you call me Shamrock now, you're liable to forget 'n call me Shamrock in front of someone else. 'N don't forget, down in Texas they know all about us."

"Yeah, but that's in Texas. We're in Wyoming now 'n there don't nobody here know none of us."

"Do you think we are on the backside of the moon up here?" Shamrock asked, mimicking his brother's comment to him.

"What?"

"There are newspapers here just like ever' where

else, 'n who knows when they might have a story 'bout what we done down there?"

"All right, I'll call you Harris."

"Captain Harris," Shamrock corrected.

"Yeah, Cap'n Harris. But what I was goin' to ask you is, how come it is that Houser knows about them other cows 'n where they belong?"

"I don't know, 'n I don't care. He knows, is all I care about. That, 'n the money he's givin' us."

Half an hour later Shamrock and the deputies reached the ranch, which consisted of a small house, a barn, and a corral. As they rode up into the yard, they saw a man pumping water. He looked up, curious as to who they were.

"Howdy, gents, what can I do for you?"

"This here the Gaines's ranch?" Shamrock asked.

"Yeah."

"Gaines, I'm Captain Paul Harris. I am a Wyoming lawman, 'n I'm here to collect them cows that you stoled."

"My name ain't Gaines, it's Keegan." He smiled. "I'm just watchin' over the ranch for Gaines, seein' as he has gone to get hisself married. And anyhow, there ain't no stoled cows here, so you're just wastin' your time."

"We heard that there was," Shamrock said.

As the two men were talking, Jaco rode around so that he was behind Keegan, and, unnoticed by the young cowboy, he slipped a noose around Keegan's neck.

"What the . . . ?" Keegan started to yell, but Jaco urged his horse into a gallop, dragging Keegan with him and choking out any further protests.

Shamrock and Jaco had just earned themselves an extra thousand dollars.

When Elmer and Wang took the ten remaining cows up to the main area of Twin Peaks ranch, they were met by Ben Turley.

"What's this?" Turley asked.

"Accordin' to the brand, these here cows belong to the Twin Peaks ranch," Elmer said.

"Oh? Where did you find 'em?"

"It don't really matter none where we found 'em, does it?" Elmer asked. "Seems to me like 'bout the only thing that matters is that we brung 'em back."

Turley nodded. "I reckon that's right. Wait here, I'll just go get Mr. Houser."

Shortly after Turley stepped into the ranch office, Malcolm and Dobbins came out of the barn. They saw Elmer and Wang.

"Well, now," Malcolm said. "If it ain't the old man and the Chinaman. You're a little out of your territory, ain't you, Chinaman?"

Wang didn't reply.

"How come it is that you don't hardly never talk?" Dobbins asked. "Don't you know our lingo?"

"He talked some, Dobbins, don't you remember?" Malcolm said. "He called you a fool, as I recall."

"Yeah, I remember."

"Didn't you fellers get enough of my friend, here, when you was in town?" Elmer asked. He chuckled. "Actually, I'd say you got more 'n enough."

"Just how good are you with all them tricks 'n such?" Malcolm asked. "S'pose we was to get us three, maybe four more friends? You think you could do them tricks on all of us?"

Turley came back out then, and seeing Malcolm and Dobbins harassing Wang, hurried over to them.

"Malcolm, what makes you think you 'n Dobbins even have three or four friends?" Turley asked.

"What the hell, Turley? You takin' up for the China-man now?"

"Mr. Houser wants you two to take these ten cows 'n put 'em back out in the pasture where they belong."

"Where'd these cows come from?" Malcolm asked, looking at them very closely.

"It don't matter where they come from," Turley said. "Point is, they're back."

"Come on, cows," Malcolm said. "Why didn't you stay where you was took?"

The two men didn't bother to get mounted. Instead they pushed the ten cows before them, moving them toward the nearest pasture.

Turley watched them leave, then he turned his attention back to Elmer and Wang, who had remained mounted for the entire visit.

"Mr. Houser wanted me to tell you thank you, for bringin' 'em back," Turley said.

"You're welcome," Elmer said. Clicking to his horse, he and Wang turned and started riding away.

"Wang," Elmer asked after they were out of earshot from the others. "Did you hear what that Malcolm feller said, when he was talkin' to the cows?"

"Yes. He said 'Why didn't you stay where you was took?'"

"What do you think he meant by that?"

"It is a puzzle," Wang replied, without a specific answer.

"It's a puzzle, all right. What do you say we drop back by The Queen 'n tell Keegan that we got all the cows delivered? Most likely he'll still have a pot of coffee on, 'n I'd pure dee like to have another cup afore we get on back to Sky Meadow."

Wang saw them first, half a dozen buzzards making circles in the sky. He pointed them out to Elmer.

"Hmm, wonder what that is?" Elmer asked. "You reckon Percy's got 'em a cow down? More 'n likely a cat got one, or wolves maybe, or it could be one of his cows stepped in a prairie hole and broke his leg. That's goin' to be hard on Percy. A small rancher like him, who ain't got that many cows in the first place, why anytime one is took from him, that can be hard."

"Not a cow," Wang said quietly, and resolutely. "It is a man."

"A man? How do you know?"

Wang pointed to the circling buzzards. "See how the birds are slow to descend? They fear men, even if a man is dead, and are slow to approach."

"Come on, let's go!" Elmer called, and, slapping his legs against the side of his horse, his mount leaped forward with a sudden, cannonball-like burst of speed. Wang was right behind him.

When they got close enough to Percy's house, they saw a rope suspended from the large tree that provided shade for the house. And dangling from that rope was a man.

"What the hell?" Elmer said. "Wang, I think that might be Keegan!"

The two riders galloped into the yard and right up

to the tree. Keegan, with his arms hanging by his sides, was suspended about six feet from the ground by a noose. His head was bent to one side, his face was blue, his mouth was open, and his tongue extended.

"Who the hell would do something like this?" Elmer yelled in anguished rage. "And why?"

Wang rode all the way up to Keegan, cut the rope, then lowered his dead friend gently to the ground.

In Chugwater, Sheriff Sharpie came out of his office to examine Ollie Keegan's body. No longer draped across a horse, Duff had brought his young cowboy into town lying under a tarpaulin in the back of a buckboard.

"And you say they found him hangin' from a tree in Gaines's backyard?"

"Aye."

"Where's Gaines? What does he have to say about it?"

"Gaines is in Kansas City. I had sent Keegan out to Percy's ranch to look after it for him until he got back," Duff said.

"What kind of man was Keegan?" Sheriff Sharpie asked. "What I mean is, could it be possible that he got into a fight in town 'n made somebody mad enough that they might have gone out there to kill 'im? Maybe a fight over a woman or somethin'?"

Duff shook his head. "I would nae think such a thing. Keegan was a good lad and a friend to all. And he dinnae have a woman friend, or 'tis thinking I am that I would know."

"A whore, maybe?"

"Keegan was nae the sporting type."

"Well, this is quite the mystery then," Sheriff Sharpie said. "I'm sure you know, Duff, that a murder without a known motive is the hardest to solve."

"Aye, but I've nae intention of allowing the cateran who did this go unpunished."

"Cateran?"

"Aye, cateran, 'tis what we call a brigand, in Scotland."

"An outlaw," Sheriff Sharpie said. He pulled the tarp back over Keegan's head. "Will you be burying him here?"

"Aye. I'll be takin' the lad down to Mr. Welsh, now."

"You might want to have a closed casket," Gene Welsh said as he examined the body. "There's no way I can get rid of the discoloration in his face."

"Aye, a closed casket then, but make it one o' your finest. We can have the buryin' on Saturday."

Duff drove from the funeral home down to Fiddler's Green and parked the buckboard out front. He angled it in, then tied his team off at the end so that he didn't deny space for other customers who might want to use the hitching rail.

"I heard about Ollie Keegan," Biff said. "He was a good man, and it's a shame what happened to him. Do you have any idea who did it?"

"Nae, 'tis a complete mystery. As you said, Ollie was a good lad, 'n liked by all."

"He was at Percy Gaines's place? Maybe Percy was the target."

"It shoulda been Gaines," someone said from the other end of the bar. He didn't look up from his glass.

"I beg your pardon? 'N why is it that ye say it should have been Mr. Gaines?" Duff asked.

"Everyone knows that he built up his herd by stealin' cattle," the man replied.

"'N who might ye' be?"

The man turned to face Duff. "The name is Crenshaw. I ride for the Twin Peaks brand."

"What makes you say such a thing, Mr. Crenshaw?" Duff asked.

"It's like I said, ever' body knows it. It's why the cattlemen has all hired a bunch of deputies, so as to get the rustlin' stopped."

"And you know these deputies, do you?" Duff asked.

"Yeah, they're stayin' out at Twin Peaks."

"How many riders do you have out there?" Elmer asked.

"Well, countin' them that's guardin' Mr. Houser all the time, 'n the deputies, 'n all, there's eighteen."

"No, don't count them. I mean how many riders do you have for the brand, men that actually gets their hands dirty 'n the like?"

"That would be nine of us, countin' Turley," Crenshaw said.

"So there are nine of you who actually work, and nine of you who do nothin' at all," Duff said. It was a statement, not a question.

"Well, I wouldn't say they don't do nothin' at all, it's just that whatever it is that they do, do, don't have nothin' to do with ranchin'."

"Mr. Crenshaw, you said that you believed Mr.

Gaines has built up his herd at the expense of the other ranchers, I believe," Duff said.

"Yeah, I'm sure that's what he has done."

"Have you ever seen Percy Gaines's herd?"

"No, I ain't never seen it."

"It's too bad that you have nae seen it, because if you had, you would be for knowing that his herd is all Angus. And since every other herd in the valley is Hereford, it would be hard for the lad to be augmenting his Angus herd with Hereford cows, now, wouldn't it?"

"Yeah," Crenshaw admitted reluctantly. "Yeah, it would."

Like many young men of the West, Ollie Keegan had never shared any of his past. Nobody knew where he was from or if he had family anywhere. In truth, nobody knew for sure if Keegan was his real name. Because of that, Keegan was buried in the Chugwater cemetery, and the entire company of Sky Meadow became his family.

It wasn't just the hands from Sky Meadow who showed up, though. Keegan was well liked, and scores of ranch hands from the other ranches in the valley, large and small, turned out for the funeral, and for the burial.

When Duff arrived for the funeral, he was wearing the kilt of the Black Watch, complete with the *sgian dubh* and the Victoria Cross. He was also carrying with him a set of pipes.

The ranch owners, ranch hands, and townspeople who, in one way or another knew Keegan, gathered around the open grave as the Reverend E. D. Sweeny of the Chugwater Church of God's Glory, gave the final prayer.

"Our Lord and Savior who knows all, knows the history and the family of our brother, whom we bury today. Indeed, our Lord even knows Brother Keegan's real name, if it not be that by which we have known him. We humbly pray that you take this noble soul into your bosom. Amen."

Reverend Sweeny nodded at Duff, and he inflated the bag. The first sound was from the drones, then, fingering the chanter, Duff began playing "Amazing Grace," the steady hum of the drones providing a mournful sound to underscore the high skirling of the melody itself.

After the funeral Duff and several of those who had come to the burial gathered at Fiddler's Green.

"Me or Wang shoulda stayed there at Percy's ranch with 'im," Elmer said. "If I had been there, Keegan would still be alive."

"Maybe," Biff said. "But it could also be that you'd be dead along with him."

"Nobody has any idea why he was killed?" Charley Blanton asked.

Duff shook his head. "'Tis still a mystery."

Chapter Twenty-five

When the large ranchers returned home after the funeral, they were greeted with an unpleasant surprise. Every one of them, from Clyde Barnes of the Cross Fire Ranch to Webb Dakota of Kensington Place, had lost cattle, and not just a few. Dale Allen had lost the most, with 160 of his cattle gone. Burt Rowe had lost the least number of cows, and even he had lost 78.

Webb Dakota, whose losses were only slightly below that of Dale Allen, circulated a petition, then presented it to Brad Houser, calling for an emergency meeting of the Cattlemen's Association.

Like the previous meeting, this one was held in the meeting room of the Bank of Chugwater. Sid Shamrock, who the cattlemen knew as Captain Paul Harris, was there, and he was sporting one of the badges that had been fashioned for him and the other deputies.

"Mr. Dakota," Houser said as soon as the meeting was called to order. "I believe you are the one who circulated the petition. Therefore, you are responsible for this emergency meeting."

"I asked that the meeting be called. That is correct, sir."

"Then the floor is yours," Houser said with a welcoming sweep of his hand.

"I appreciate the invitation, Mr. Houser, but when you formed the constabulary, you also assumed, by your action, leadership of our organization. And because that is so, I shall defer to you, as I have no wish to conduct the meeting."

"Oh, you need not worry about conducting the meeting, Mr. Dakota. As the chairman I will be conducting this, as well as all the other meetings. I am merely inviting you to address the assembly so that you may apprise us of your perception of the magnitude of the problems we are facing."

"Very well, I shall."

Dakota stepped to the front of the assembly, cleared his throat, and then began to speak.

"When I returned to Kensington Place from the funeral that was held for the unfortunate young employee of Mr. MacCallister"—Dakota paused and nodded toward Duff—"I discovered that considerably over a hundred head of cattle had been stolen. This was in addition to the previous cattle I had lost. I have since checked with the others and learned that my situation is not unique. In fact, every one of us had been visited by cattle thieves."

"Except for Sky Meadow," Houser said, staring pointedly at Duff. "There were no cattle taken from Sky Meadow, isn't that correct, Captain MacCallister?"

"Aye, that is correct," Duff replied.

"Why didn't he lose any cattle?" Lewis asked. "Hell, it was his man that was killed. And he is the only one who wasn't hurt?"

"That is an awful thing for you to say, David," Burt Rowe put in. "We lost a few head of cattle. Duff had a man killed."

"Aye, and thank you for pointing that out, David," Duff said. "I would gladly trade places with any of you. That is to say, I would rather have lost a few head of cattle, than to have lost a friend."

Lewis looked chagrined. "I'm sorry, MacCallister. I had no right to say such a thing. I suppose I was just upset that I lost so many cows."

"We've discussed this before, gentlemen," Houser said. "Captain MacCallister enjoys a degree of protection by the very nature of his herd."

"Oh yeah," Goodman said. "There's no way a rustler can hide those black woolly bastards he raises."

The others laughed, including Duff. Then Houser raised his hand to reclaim attention.

"Gentleman, I do believe that Mr. Dakota was quite correct in calling for a meeting, and so I think perhaps we should decide what steps may be taken to deal with this problem."

"What do you mean, what steps?" Dale Allen asked. "We've already hired us some deputies. Seems to me that should be enough. If they will just get to work."

Houser smiled. "Yes, 'get to work.' That is exactly

what I wanted to hear you say." He turned to Shamrock. "Captain Harris, have you any specific plans in mind to deal with this outbreak of cattle rustling that is plaguing the valley right now?"

"Yeah," Shamrock said. "We're goin' to find the ones that's doin' this 'n put a stop to it."

Again, Houser addressed the cattlemen. "I am assuming, gentlemen, that by your expressed wish that something be done, that you are in full support of Captain Harris and his deputies."

"You are assuming too much, Mr. Houser," Duff said. "I've nae idea what your deputy has in mind, when he says he will 'put a stop to it' and I'll nae be giving my consent to action without knowing what that action may be."

"There's no rule in the association that says everyone has to agree, is there?" Dale Allen asked. "I mean, we already know that MacCallister didn't lose any cows on account of he's raisin' Angus 'n the rest of us are raisin' Herefords. Seems to me like, since he isn't dealing with the same things the rest of us are, then his vote should be discounted. Seems to me like if a majority of us are in favor of letting Captain Harris and his deputies do what needs to be done, that's all it should require."

"You are quite right, Mr. Allen," Houser replied. "I have examined the bylaws of the Cattlemen's Association and it clearly allows for action to be taken on a majority vote."

"Hear! Hear!" Goodman said.

"I have a question," Duff said.

"The chair recognizes Captain MacCallister," Houser responded.

"The Laramie County Cattlemen's Association has quite a number of members," Duff said. "If it requires a majority vote, we've nae near enough here to be a majority."

Houser smiled and held up a finger. "Ah, but my dear Captain MacCallister, this is the Chugwater Chapter of the Laramie County Cattlemen's Association. We are a subcommittee, an ad hoc group, gathered to deal specifically with such problems as may face us here, in the Valley of the Chug. And the rules of majority approval holds true for such committees as may be formed, as well as for the association as a whole. And by those rules, a majority at this meeting will dictate the actions we may take."

"Well, sonny, you can count my vote along with Duff's vote," Elmer said.

"Oh, I'm afraid we can't do that," Houser replied with a satisfied grin. "You see, we vote as corporate entities, not as individuals. That means that each ranch has only one vote, regardless of how many partners there may be. Why, you take Kensington Place, for example. As I understand it, there are at least ten partners in that ranch, but they are represented by Mr. Dakota, and he casts the vote that speaks for all of them."

"I move the question," Lewis said.

"Very well, all in favor of giving Captain Harris carte blanche to deal with these rustlers, hold up your hand," Houser said.

"What is carte blanche?" Goodman asked.

"It means give him absolute authority to do whatever he thinks is the right thing to do," Houser said.

"Well, if it's the right thing," Goodman said, holding up his hand.

Everyone voted yes but Duff and Webb Dakota.

"Mr. Dakota?" Houser said, surprised to see that the Englishman did not vote.

"I'm hesitant to give Mr. Harris . . ."

"Captain Harris," Houser corrected.

"Yes, well, I am hesitant to give Captain Harris carte blanche. I think we should have some input into his operation."

"If he, and the deputies, are limited by having to wait for specific authorization, I fear they will be so hamstrung that they will be ineffective," Houser said. "They must have the freedom to react to the situation at hand."

Dakota shook his head. "Then I'm sorry, I can't vote for that."

"Well, it doesn't matter," Houser said. "The vote is six to two, so the motion carries.

"Captain Harris, you are hereby authorized to take whatever action you deem necessary to rid the Valley of the Chug of the reprehensible activities of the rustlers. Can we count on you?"

"Yeah," Shamrock said.

Chapter Twenty-six

Buckhorn, Colorado

Abe Sobel was having his supper in the dining room of the Dunn Hotel, reading the *Buckhorn Herald* newspaper.

Chugwater, Wyoming, Deals With Rustlers

(special to the BUCKHORN HERALD*)* The Cattlemen's Association of the Valley of the Chug met on the fifth, instant, to discuss the problem of cattle rustling. The chairman of the organization put forth a proposal that the problem facing the ranchers may be met by a group of territorial deputies. The deputies mentioned have received a special commission of the governor of the territory as their authorization to work as lawmen.

By a majority vote, the deputies, headed by Captain Paul Harris, were given full authority to conduct their investigation, and bring the rustlers to justice. Brad Houser, who owns the Twin Peaks Ranch, is chairman of the organization, and has expressed the opinion that the herds of the larger cattlemen are being raided by the small ranchers, so that the purloined cattle may be added to their own herds. As such, he reports that the small ranchers will be the immediate targets of the investigation.

The name *Brad Houser* literally leaped from the page as Abe read the story. Brad Houser was the person who had set up the bank robbery in Sulphur Springs, and Sobel had learned during the robbery that Houser and Shamrock were brothers. If Sobel could find Houser, he figured there would be a good chance that he would be able to find Shamrock. Houser wouldn't be suspicious of him, as Abe had taken part, with him, in the Sulphur Springs robbery.

It was a fairly long ride to Chugwater, but there would be a nice reward at the end of the ride.

Twin Peaks Ranch

When Abe Sobel rode up to the ranch three days later, he was met by a tall, lean man with dark hair and piercing black eyes.

"The name's Turley," the man said. "I'm foreman of the place. What can I do for you?"

"Yes, I'm looking for an old friend, who may be here. His name is Sid Shamrock."

"Shamrock?" Turley shook his head. "No, sir, I don't know nobody named Shamrock. You sure you've come to the right place?"

"No, I'm not sure that Shamrock would be here. But I believe his brother owns the place. Brad Houser?"

"Houser? Yes, sir, he owns the place, all right, 'n he does have a brother here, but his brother's name isn't Shamrock."

"I see. Well, would you tell him that Abe Sobel is here to see him? He knows me."

"All right, wait here, I'll tell 'im."

Houser was writing figures in a ledger when Turley spoke to him.

"Sobel? Yes, I know him," Houser said when Turley told him of his visitor. "Tell him I'll see him in a few minutes. But before I see him, please ask Mr. Knox to come to the office."

"Yes, sir."

When Turley stepped back outside, Sobel was watering his horse at the trough.

"What did he say?" Sobel asked. "Will he see me?"

"Yeah, but he asked that you wait for a minute—he has some ranch business to take care of first. If you'd like some coffee, go on into the cookhouse there 'n tell the cook that I sent you."

"Thanks," Sobel replied. "A cup of coffee would go real good right now."

Turley stepped into the bunkhouse, where he found Knox playing poker with three of the deputies.

"Knox, Mr. Houser wants to see you."

"May as well go see 'im, I ain't doin' no good in this game," Knox said, getting up from the table. "What's he want to see me about?"

"Houser don't share nothin' with me that has

anything to do with you bodyguards or deputies," Turley said.

Knox chuckled. "No, I don't reckon he does, does he?"

When Knox stepped into the ranch office, Houser was standing at the window.

"You wanted to see me?"

"Yes, there is a man here named Sobel. He is here to look for my brother."

"You mean Cap'n Harris?"

"Yes, but Mr. Sobel knew him as Sid Shamrock. I'm going to send you with Sobel out into the Pine Flats."

"What for? Cap'n Harris ain't there. He's back in the bunkhouse. I just seen 'im."

"You don't understand. I don't want Mr. Sobel to find my brother; it could mean trouble for him, and for me. He is one of the reasons I hired you in the first place, to protect me from men like him. When you get Sobel out to the Pine Flats, I want you to take care of him in the same way you took care Slim and Dooley."

"You mean you want me to take him out there and kill 'im?"

"That is exactly what I mean." Houser opened a drawer on his desk, then took out some money. "Here is two hundred and fifty dollars. Once the job is done, wait there until my brother comes out there to meet you. He'll have another two hundred and fifty dollars for you, and he'll help you bury Sobel. I don't want any trace of him ever found."

"Yes, sir, don't you worry none, I'll take care of Sobel for you." Knox cracked an evil smile. "I told you there'd be times when you needed me to do things like this for you. You know, if we was partners, you wouldn't have to pay me nothin' extra to do things like this."

"Partners? In Twin Peaks?"

"Yeah, well, we wouldn't have to be full partners. I'm talkin' about somethin' like maybe thirty or forty percent."

"We'll discuss it when you get back," Houser said. "Now, wait here until Sobel comes."

When Sobel came into the office a few minutes later, Houser greeted him effusively.

"Mr. Sobel, it has been quite a while since the little adventure we shared."

"Yeah, it has," Sobel said. "I see that you done pretty good by it."

"I did indeed. Mr. Turley tells me that you are looking for my brother."

"Yes, I would like to see him again. Your foreman said that you had a brother here, but that it wasn't Sid."

Houser chuckled. "Oh, it's him, all right, but after a little adventure, or should I say, misadventure, he had in Seven Oaks, he found it necessary to change his name. Right now he is with the herd in an area we call the Pine Flats."

Houser raised his hand toward the other man who was in the room.

"This is Mr. Knox. I have asked him to take you to see my brother. Then afterward, if you are agreeable to it, I thought the three of us might have dinner in town tonight, at Tacky Mack's."

"Yes, yes, that sounds like a fine idea," Sobel said.

This might be easier than he had thought it would be, Sobel thought. If they were already in town, all he would have to do is find some way to excuse himself, then go to the sheriff with the wanted poster. The sheriff would arrest Shamrock, authorize payment of the reward, and Sobel could be on his way, $5,000 richer.

Houser stepped out of the office with them and stood there watching as the two men rode off. Not until they were gone, did he call out to one of the deputies.

"Mr. Wix, would you please ask my brother to come see me?"

Houser waited until Shamrock came to him a few minutes later.

"Whadda you want?"

"Mr. Knox has taken an old friend of ours out to the Pine Flats to look for you."

"What did he go out there for? I been right here, all along."

"That is why I sent him out there. The old friend I'm talking about is Abe Sobel. We don't want him to find you. As a matter of fact, we don't want him here, at all."

"Why not?"

"Think about it, Thomas. He knows what happened back in Sulphur Springs. He also knows that he could bring all this down on us. It makes us perfect candidates for blackmail."

"Blackmail? How could he blackmail us? He done that job with us, remember?"

"He could win amnesty by turning state's evidence. That's why I'm going to have Mr. Knox kill him."

"Oh yeah, right. That's probably a good thing."

"After Mr. Knox has done the job, he is going to wait for you to join him, out in the Pine Flats."

"What for?"

"He thinks it is because you will be bringing him two hundred and fifty dollars, and helping him bury Sobel, but that isn't the reason. Do you remember when I asked if you would be willing to take care of Mr. Knox?"

"Yeah."

"Now is the time. Mr. Knox has become a liability to us, and I want you to kill him."

"He's awful fast, Brad. I'm not sure I can."

"I'm not asking you to make a contest of it, Thomas. I just want you to kill him."

Shamrock smiled. "Yeah, I can do that. You want me to bury them both out there?"

"Take a couple of shovels with you so Knox will think you are going to help bury Sobel, but there's no need for you to bury either of them."

"If I don't bury them, they'll be found."

"We want them found."

"Why?"

"Don't worry about it, I know what I'm doing."

When Shamrock dismounted half an hour later, he saw Knox standing over Abe Sobel's body.

"You got the other two hundred 'n fifty dollars?" Knox asked.

"Yeah, and two shovels," Shamrock said, taking them down from where he had them tied to the saddle. He handed one of the shovels to Knox. "You start digging at that end, and I'll start at this end."

As soon as Knox turned his back, Shamrock swung his shovel around, catching Knox in the back of the head and knocking him down. Then, as Knox lay on the ground, Shamrock shot him twice.

Later that same day, Turley came into town driving a buckboard. Houser was in the seat beside him, and Shamrock, on horseback, was riding alongside. They stopped in front of the sheriff's office, and as Turley remained with the buckboard, Houser and Shamrock stepped inside.

Sheriff Sharpie was sitting at his desk, working on a kerosene lantern that was disassembled before him.

"Sheriff Sharpie, I don't know if you have met Captain Harris, a territorial deputy, specially commissioned by the governor," Houser said.

Sheriff Sharpie stood and extended his hand. "I haven't met you, Captain Harris, but I have certainly heard of you. Welcome to Chugwater."

"Thanks," Shamrock said.

"Unfortunately, Sheriff, this isn't a social call," Houser said. "Earlier today an old friend of ours, Abe Sobel, came to pay a visit. He wanted to take a look around the ranch, so I assigned one of my men, Knox, to show him around. My brother, hearing that an old friend had come to visit, rode out to catch up with them. That's when it happened."

"That's when what happened?"

"I'll let my brother describe the event," Houser said, looking toward Shamrock.

"Well, sir, just as I got there, I seen Knox robbin' poor old Abe of two hundred 'n fifty dollars, then as

Abe give 'im the money, he shot 'im. I yelled at Knox, 'n he shot at me, so I kilt 'im."

"Both bodies are in the back of the buckboard, parked out front," Houser said.

Once outside, Sheriff Sharpie pulled just enough of the canvas back to see their faces. He nodded. "This is Knox, all right, I remember him from shooting Hastings and Carson. And what did you say this man's name was?"

"Sobel, Abe Sobel," Houser said. "He is an old family friend." Houser shook his head. "How awful that he came all this way to visit friends and wound up like this. I blame myself, you know. After all, I'm the one that hired Knox. If I had had any idea that something like this would have happened, I would not have been so robust in defending him when you had him under arrest, earlier. If I had let him stay in jail, poor Mr. Sobel would still be alive." Houser pinched the bridge of his nose. "I guess you could say that, under the circumstances, I am doubly responsible for the demise of an old friend."

Houser put his hand on the canvas that covered Sobel's body. "I will make all the arrangements with Mr. Welsh. I want the best coffin for Mr. Sobel." He looked at Knox's body. "And the cheapest for this . . . this murderous despoiler of a young man's life."

There was no funeral for either one of the bodies, nor did anyone but Welsh and the two gravediggers show up at the cemetery when Sobel and Knox were buried. There were a few comments around town about Knox, none of them favorable, as the general consensus seemed to be that his death was no great loss.

There were some, however, who questioned why Houser, who had professed that Sobel was an old friend, and had even bought an expensive coffin for him, had not arranged for a funeral.

Two days after Knox and Sobel were buried, Asa Hanlon, who owned a ranch seven miles west of Chugwater, stepped into the kitchen, sniffed audibly, then smiled. "Honey, I don't know what you're cookin', but it sure smells good."

Jenny Hanlon, who was standing at the stove, laughed. "Asa, I do believe I could fry shoe leather in bacon grease, and you would tell me it smelled good."

"Jenny, my love, if you fried it, it would smell good 'n I'd most likely eat it, too." Asa walked over and kissed her on the cheek, then he bent over and kissed her swollen belly. "What do you think, little baby in there?" he asked. "Do you think it smells good?"

"You're crazy," Jenny said with another laugh.

"Yes, crazy for you," Asa said.

"How is it going?" Jenny asked as she whipped flour into the meat drippings to make gravy.

"I've got five of 'em cut 'n branded," Asa said as he grabbed a biscuit and took a bite from it. "We've got close to two hundred head now. You know what, Jenny? By the time little Johnny is old enough to help out on the ranch, we'll be big enough to start hiring some hands."

Jenny patted her protruding stomach. "What makes you think it'll be a Johnny? It could be an Alice, you know."

Asa shook his head. "No, the first one's got to be a boy. I'll need 'im to help me out, then we can . . ."

"Asa, there are some riders coming here," Jenny said anxiously, interrupting her husband in mid-sentence.

"Wonder who it is and what they want?" Asa said. With the biscuit still in hand, he stepped out onto the porch of the small, two-room house.

"What can I do for you gents?" he asked.

"This here your place?" the lead rider asked.

"Yes, sir, it is."

"How many head are you runnin'?"

The curious expression on Asa's face was replaced with a look of irritation. "Mister, I don't know that that is any of your business."

"Well, seein' as we're about to take 'em, I plan on makin' it my business."

"The hell you say!" Asa ran back into the house, then reached up over the door for his shotgun.

"Asa, what is it?" Jenny asked in alarm. "Why are you getting your gun?"

Before Asa could load his gun, two of the men came rushing in behind him, pistols in hand. Both men fired, and Asa went down.

"Asa!" Jenny screamed.

The two men shot her as well, and she fell on top of her husband. With her last, conscious act, she put her hand over his.

"Let's get them cows," one of them said.

"Let's eat first," another said as he grabbed one of the biscuits.

Chapter Twenty-seven

Meagan was standing in the front of her store, looking out onto the street, when she saw Ethan Terrell driving by. Seeing him come to town wasn't in itself unusual, but what he was carrying in the back of the buckboard was. Two pairs of legs were protruding from a canvas that covered a couple of bodies, and one pair of legs belonged to a woman.

By now several of the townspeople had also noticed the macabre cargo, and they followed the buckboard down to Welsh's undertaking parlor.

"Mary Ellen, watch the store for a few minutes, would you?" Meagan called.

"Yes, ma'am," the young lady replied.

Meagan knew that her curiosity was rather morbid, but the bodies were obviously that of a man and a woman, and that was too extraordinary to let pass. She had to know who it was, and what happened to them.

When the canvas was removed to reveal the bodies of Asa and Jenny Hanlon, Meagan felt tears burning her eyes. She wished she had not let her curiosity get the better of her. Jenny Hanlon had been in her dress shop just the day before.

"I'm so tired of being pregnant and having to wear large dresses. I want a beautiful dress that I can wear for the christening of the baby," she had said.

"How long before the baby will be born?" Meagan had asked.

"I think just within another couple of weeks. You should see Asa. He is so excited about it! And of course, I am, too."

"Well, that will be plenty of time to make a dress for you. And you'll look beautiful in it, too."

"Oh, I so want to. Asa·has been so sweet to me for this entire pregnancy, and I want to look good for him again."

But there would be no christening, and there would be no baby. Asa and Jenny Hanlon had both been shot.

Unable to hold back the tears, Meagan turned away and hurried back to her shop.

"Mary Ellen," she said when she got back. "I'm going to be gone for a while. You can stay, or close up the shop, whichever you choose."

"Miss Parker, what is it? Who were those two in the back of Mr. Terrell's buckboard?"

"It was the Hanlons, Mary Ellen."

"The Hanlons? But Mrs. Hanlon was just . . ."

"Yes, Jenny was in here just yesterday," Meagan said as she wiped a tear away.

"Meagan," Duff said when Meagan came riding up to Sky Meadow a short while later. "What a pleasant surprise! What brings you here, lass?"

It was not until Meagan dismounted that he saw the expression of extreme sadness on her face, and the red-rimmed eyes. She walked over to him and invited him to put his arms around her.

"What is it, lass? What has you in such a way?" Duff asked in a comforting tone, holding her close to him.

"Jenny Hanlon," Meagan finally said. "Ethan Terrell brought her and her husband into town today."

"He brought them in?"

"Dead. Both of them. Oh, Duff, they were shot. Someone murdered both of them. How awful it was!"

Duff continued to hold her in his arms for a long moment, letting her cry into his shoulders. He knew then why she had come to him. She had been holding the sobs in, and now, no longer restrained, she let them out.

Duff waited until she had cried herself out, pulled away, and put a handkerchief to her eyes.

"Do ye wish to go back into town, or would you be for staying the night out here?" Duff asked.

"I . . . I think I would like to stay here," she said.

That evening before dinner, Meagan and Duff waited in the living room for Elmer to return. Elmer and a couple other men had ridden over to the Hanlon ranch to see if there was anything that needed to be done. While they waited, Meagan told Duff how Jenny had come into her shop just the day before to make arrangements to buy a dress for the christening of the baby.

Once again, tears began to slide down Meagan's cheeks, though this time the crying was silent. Again, she dabbed at them with a handkerchief.

"I'm sorry," she said. "But I just can't get Jenny's face out of my mind—she was so happy. And now . . .

this. Oh, Duff, who could have done such a thing? And why?"

Just as she asked the question, Elmer came into the house.

"All his cattle is gone," Elmer said. "Ever' cow except for the milk cow. Funny thing, though, his horses is still there."

"Cattle thieves," Duff said.

"Yeah."

"Here, Houser is so dead certain that 'tis the small ranchers who are stealing the cattle, but it was Asa Hanlon who was killed, along with his wife. A small rancher he was, but 'twas his cattle that were stolen."

"I thought the territorial deputies were supposed to take care of that," Meagan said.

"Apparently the only thing the deputies have done is kill one of their own," Duff said, referring to the killing by Captain Harris of Knox, whose first name was unknown."

"Yeah, 'n there's somethin' that's just real peculiar about that, too," Elmer said.

"And what is that?"

"Well, sir, when I was talkin' to Mr. Welsh about the Hanlons, he told me about the bullet holes in Knox's body. It was bein' told that Knox shot at this Harris feller first, 'n then Harris shot back. But that don't seem very likely now."

"Why do you say that, Elmer?"

"'Cause Mr. Welsh said that Knox looked like he had been hit on back of the head by some kindly of a club, 'n then he was shot, two times." Elmer paused for a moment before he added, "In the back."

* * *

Although the burial of Knox and Sobel, three days earlier, had been an isolated event, attended only by the gravediggers, the joint funerals of Asa and Jenny Hanlon had been attended by almost everyone in town, as well as a large number of ranchers. Noticeably absent were Houser and his deputies. The cadre of deputies had now increased by two. After Knox was killed, Malcolm and Dobbins were "deputized."

Twin Peaks Ranch was, however, represented by one man, Ben Turley. Ben stood alongside Mary Ellen, his head bowed, and his hat in his hand. He spoke to no one, except when he was spoken to.

After the burial, as the mourners began to leave the cemetery, Sheriff Sharpie asked Duff if he would drop by his office for a few minutes.

"It's a sad day," Sheriff Sharpie said, filling two coffee cups and passing one to Duff. "Asa Hanlon was as fine a young man as you would ever want to meet."

"Aye, he was."

"Duff, I want to ask a favor of you. And if you feel you can't do it, I certainly understand, so don't feel bad about turning me down."

"Here now, Sheriff, ye have nae yet asked the favor, 'n it's turning you down ye would have me doing. Ask me the favor, mon, 'n let me be for deciding my ownself."

Sheriff Sharpie chuckled. "I guess you're right, that's not the best way to ask somebody for something if they're wanting a positive response. The favor I'm askin' of you is this. Would you be willing to let me make you one of my deputies? I don't mean a deputy that would have to come into town 'n make rounds 'n such. Fact is, there wouldn't even be anybody who would need to know you was deputyin' for me except me 'n you, 'n whoever else you might want to tell."

"The valley seems a bit overloaded with deputies now. Are you sure that you want another one?" Duff replied.

"It's those other deputies that I'm worried about," Sheriff Sharpie said. "I sent a telegram to the governor; he responded that both Brad Houser and Paul Harris hold commissions by him. The others have been deputized by those two.

"I'll be honest with you, Duff. As they hold their appointments by way of the governor, they have more authority than I do, 'n that means they will have more authority than any deputy that I might appoint. So if you agree to take the job, you will have two strikes against you before you even start."

"Two strikes against me?" Duff was clearly confused by the term.

"Oh, I forgot, you being a Scotsman that may be somethin' you don't understand. It's a baseball term, and it means that if you decide to take me up on my offer to deputize you, that the odds will be very much against you being able to actually do anything."

"Sheriff, 'tis quite a way you have o' recruiting someone. If you are for thinking that I can nae do anything, why is it that you want to appoint me?"

"Because there's something about all that's going

on around here now that doesn't ring true. It's going to take someone with a lot of courage, fortitude, intelligence, and good common sense to get to the bottom of it, 'n you have ever' one of those attributes. Fact is, I've never met anyone in my life who has more of those virtues than you do. Will you take the appointment?"

Duff took a swallow of his coffee before he responded. "Aye, Sheriff, I'll be your deputy, if you'll be for granting me a concession."

"What would that be?"

"I would be for wanting Elmer and Wang to be deputies as well."

A broad smile spread across the sheriff's face. "Consider it done," he said.

"Perhaps we could start with the killing of Knox," Duff said.

"You're talking about how he was killed?"

"Aye. Elmer told me he had spoken with Welsh about the condition of Knox's body."

"The back of his head was bashed in, and he had been shot twice in the back," Sheriff Sharpie said. "Yes, I know about it. I examined both bodies."

Sheriff Sharpie got up from his desk and walked over to a filing cabinet where he opened a drawer, then took out a paper and showed it to Duff.

WANTED
for **MURDER**
(DEAD *or* ALIVE)
ELWOOD ("HARD") KNOX
—*Reward: $1,000*—

CONTACT: Sheriff Tate *(Bent County, Colorado)*

"Because of the dead-or-alive provision of this dodger, it doesn't make any difference how Knox was killed." After Duff looked at the reward poster, Sheriff Sharpie returned it to the file cabinet.

"I've informed Sheriff Tate that Knox has been killed, but I also told him it was by an officer of the law." He slammed the file cabinet drawer shut. "At least the back-shooting son of a bitch won't be able to collect on it."

Chapter Twenty-eight

"You wanted to see me, Mr. Gleason?" Steve Emerson asked. Emerson was a grizzled old cowboy who had been working at Sky Meadow from the very year the ranch was started.

"Yeah," Elmer replied. He handed Emerson a cloth bag. "They's a side o' bacon in here, some beans, cornmeal, flour, coffee, 'n sugar. How 'bout ridin' over to Percy's place 'n give this to Kirk? He's watchin' out for it till Percy gets back."

"Woowee damn! With this much food, ole Sam's goin' to get fat 'n lazy. He won't be worth nothing when he comes back," Emerson teased.

"Yeah, well, we can't have him eatin' up all of Percy's provisions, now, can we? I figure he 'n his new bride will more 'n likely be comin' back home within another week."

"It's about time he married that girl. He was moonin' over her even when he was workin' over here, before he ever started his own spread," Emerson said.

"Well, you goin' to take that bag to 'im, or not?" Elmer asked, though his smile ameliorated the words.

"I'm goin', I'm goin', but I'll tell you this, I sure hope I don't never get as cranky as you are when I get your age."

"Now, seein' as you're already older 'n me, how the hell are you goin' to get my age, lessen you can turn aroun' 'n start goin' backward?" Elmer asked with a laugh.

Emerson took the cloth bag, saddled his horse, tied the bag to the saddle horn, then took the easy, four-mile ride over to Percy Gaines's ranch.

Emerson and Percy had been friends when Percy worked for Sky Meadow, and because of that Emerson had been to Percy's ranch several times. Emerson was a good chess player, and he taught Percy the game. They played chess when he visited, and Percy welcomed him because running a one-man operation could get very lonely.

"What do you think, Harry?" Emerson asked his horse. "After Percy 'n his new bride get back, do you reckon he'll still be willin' to play chess with an old man like me?"

The horse whickered, as if responding to Emerson's question.

"Yeah, that's pretty much what I was thinkin', too," Emerson said, with a little chuckle.

Percy looked out into the pasture to see how Percy's herd was doing. To his surprise, the herd wasn't there, not one cow.

"Well, now, just what do you reckon happened to all of Percy's cows?" he asked aloud. "Where'd Sam move them to? Percy don't have that much pasture to move 'em around. The grass ain't been over et here, 'n water is good so why would he move them?"

That would be the first thing he would ask Sam, though he knew Sam was an energetic sort, and he may have moved the cows around, just to have something to do.

"What the hell?" Emerson said when he crested a little rise that would afford him the first view of the house.

What he saw wasn't the house he knew so well, and had, in fact, helped Percy build. What he saw was a pile of blackened timbers where the house had once stood.

"Sam?" he called. "Sam, are you here, anywhere?"

The air was redolent with the odor of burnt wood, and Emerson dismounted, then walked up to look at it. It took but a cursory examination of what had been the house to see that there was nothing that could be salvaged.

"Damn," Emerson said aloud. "How the hell did this happen? And how come Sam didn't come tell us about it?"

Emerson's question was answered when he looked toward the barn and saw what he hadn't seen before. There was a body lying on the ground next to the watering trough, and even from here, Emerson could tell that it was Sam Kirk. He moved quickly to investigate. What was left of the top of Sam's head was lying in the dirt in a pool of blood and spilled brains. He had been shot in the head at very close range with a shotgun.

Emerson ran back to his horse and urged him into a gallop. It wasn't that he needed to report this right away—speed meant nothing to Sam Kirk now. But Emerson didn't want to be here, and he had to tell someone.

It took about an hour for Emerson to get to Sky Meadow and back, and when he returned, Duff and Elmer were with him. Elmer was driving a buckboard, so they would be able to take Sam Kirk's body back with them. When they arrived, the three men stood for just a moment, looking at the blackened pile of burnt lumber.

"Who would be mean enough to do somethin' like this? 'N poor Sam, look at 'im. A shotgun can sure make a mess," Elmer said. "What I don't understand is, how Sam let 'im get so close."

"His pistol is still in his holster," Duff said. Duff reached for the Colt, took it out, and gave it a closer examination. "It's fully loaded, except for the chamber under the firing pin. Apparently, he was nae expecting any trouble."

"Then that means whoever done this was pure dee cold-blooded about it," Elmer said.

"It also means he may have known them," Duff said.

"Steve, are you sure there's nae a steer on the place?" Duff asked. "Have you had a good look around?"

"No, sir, I didn't exactly look aroun', but I know this ranch just real good, seein' as me 'n Percy is real good friends. And it don't take a lot of lookin' to see that they ain't so much as a single cow on the entire place," Emerson replied.

"That's two of our men that have been killed now, Duff," Elmer pointed out. "Both of 'em right here, on Percy's ranch. Keegan 'n Kirk, 'n they was both good men, too."

"Aye, 'n Asa Hanlon 'n his wife, too," Duff said.

"This here ain't just rustlin'," Elmer said. "I been aroun' rustlin'." He paused for moment, then because he was with two close friends who already knew some of his background he added, "Fact is, I've done a little rustlin' of my own back in the day. But this here is murderin' 'n burnin' down a feller's house. It ain't just rustlin', Duff. For some reason, whoever done this thing wasn't satisfied with just stealin' cows. They're actual out to hurt people. And I tell you true, I just cain't hardly see no reason why somebody would be a-wantin' to do somethin' like that."

"I think it might be time that we had a meeting."

"A meetin' with who?"

"With the cattlemen of the valley," Duff replied. "Only this time, we'll invite all the cattlemen, the wee as well as the large."

"I don't figure Houser is goin' to be wantin' to invite the little ranchers, 'n besides which, the board-room in the bank ain't big enough to hold all of 'em, anyhow," Elmer said.

"Mr. Houser will nae be calling this meeting, I will. And I dinnae intend to hold the meeting at the bank."

After Duff put out word of the meeting, he waited at Fiddler's Green for the appointed time.

"Did you send word to Houser about the meeting?" Biff Johnson asked.

"Aye, I sent word."

"What did he say?"

"I have nae heard back from him."

"Do you think he'll show up?"

"We'll just have to see."

The meeting was held in the ballroom of the Antlers Hotel, a room that was large enough to hold many more people than the boardroom of the bank. And, as it was Duff who had issued all the invitations, this meeting, unlike the first one, welcomed any small rancher as might want to come.

Even with the extended facilities provided by the Antlers Hotel, the room was crowded as all the area ranchers, large and small, showed up for the meeting. And it wasn't just the ranchers; many of the smaller ranchers brought their wives, because after what had happened to the Hanlons, they were afraid to leave them alone.

Unlike the previous meeting, held by Houser, there was no guardian posted at the door to keep people out. That was because Duff believed that the subject of this meeting was germane to everyone who lived in the valley, whether they were ranchers or not, big or small.

The pre-meeting conversation of all those who had gathered was about the murders, not only of Sam Kirk, but of Asa and Jenny Hanlon and Ollie Keegan before.

"This ain't like shootin's we've had in the past where a couple of men get into a fight 'n shoot it out," someone said. "This is someone just goin' aroun' 'n murderin' people for no reason."

"No, they was reason. The cows was all took, so it was rustlin'."

"They wasn't no cows took when they kilt Keegan," somebody pointed out.

The conversation continued in that vein until, at the appointed time, Duff walked to the front of the room and stood there for a moment. That had the effect of getting everyone's attention, so the room grew quiet.

"Hello, friends. I would like to thank all of you for coming to the meeting today.

"As I'm sure you know, by now, one of my hands, Sam Kirk, was recently killed. I had sent him over to watch over Percy Gaines's ranch, while Percy was in Kansas City to get married."

"I heard that Percy's house got burned down, too," Ethan Terrell said. "Is that true?"

"Aye, 'tis true, all right."

"We've had cattle rustlin' before," Prosser said. "But I've never heard of any rustlers that kill ever' body then take the whole herd. That's two whole herds that's been took now."

"What is going on in here?" Brad Houser called angrily, charging into the room at that moment. "I called no meeting of the Chugwater Chapter. What right do you have to be gathering without due warrant and approbation?"

"I called the meeting, Mr. Houser. Did you nae get your invitation?" Duff answered, the agreeable tone of his response in direct contrast to the acrimonious timbre of Houser's challenge.

"I got the notification, yes, but it was not, nor could it have been, an official assembly. As I am the chairman, Mr. MacCallister, only I have the authority to convene meetings of the Chugwater Chapter of the Laramie County Cattlemen's Association."

It did not escape anyone's attention that Houser had dropped the title *Captain* when he addressed Duff.

"Aye, Mr. Houser, you are quite correct, 'twas not an official invitation, because as you have pointed out, only you can issue an official invitation to a meeting of the Chugwater Chapter. Also, as ye can see, many of the wee ranchers are present at this meeting, and as you have specifically prohibited them from participating in the Chugwater Chapter, then 'twould have been futile for me to ask you to convene a meeting. Therefore, this is merely a friendly gathering of neighbors, for to discuss events that affect every rancher in the valley, be they large or small. So my invitation was not official, you see."

"What good will it do? You can come up with no policy that will hold the weight of authorization by either the Chugwater Chapter, or the association as a whole," Houser complained.

"Aye, 'tis true, that we can only discuss the problem and perhaps make a few suggestions for anything that might require an official sanction by the Chugwater Chapter. The rest, we will come up with our own solutions."

"What do you mean, for the rest? You'll have no authority for the rest."

"Well, now, that's where ye may be wrong, Mr. Houser. You see, I plan to make any such suggestions as may be dealt with by the county constabulary to Sheriff Sharpie. He will have the authority to deal with it, personally, or to appoint deputies, to handle such problems as we may point out to him."

"You forget that we already have gubernatorial appointments for deputies whose authority supersedes any authority that any county official has," Houser said.

"Well, we'll just have to work along parallel paths, trying not to get in each other's way," Duff said. Again, he flashed a big smile. "Now, if you would please take your seat, Mr. Houser, we will continue with this meeting of"—he paused, then concluded the sentence with emphasis on the word—"*neighbors.*"

Ethan Terrell held up his hand.

"Aye, Mr. Terrell?"

"When Asa 'n his wife was killed 'n their herd was all took, that was all Herefords, so it was easy enough to hide them. But when Kirk was killed while watching Percy Gaines's ranch, Percy's herd was all took, too, which makes a man wonder what happened to 'em. I mean, he was runnin' Angus, just like you are. Where at would someone hide a bunch of Angus cows, unless it was with other Angus cows?"

"Well, now, that brings up a most cogent point, doesn't it?" Houser said.

"I beg your pardon?" Duff replied.

"It is common knowledge to everyone in the valley, in fact it was pointed out to me rather quickly, that your herd is composed entirely of Angus cattle. So, too, was Mr. Gaines's herd. Now his cattle are gone, and as Mr. Terrell has so correctly pointed out, where could you hide Angus cattle, except in another herd of Angus cattle?"

"Where indeed?" Duff replied, refusing to rise to the bait.

"Here's somethin' that's puzzlin' me," Prosser said. "I have been running my own ranch for three years now, and never until this year have full-grown, branded cows managed to drift into my herd. Almost every other day now, there will be one or two, or sometimes a bit more, cows mixed in with my herd, but wearing brands like Twin Peaks, Pitchfork, Trail Back, and such. How do the cows get there?"

"That's a good question, because that selfsame thing has been happening with me," Terrell said.

"Mr. Prosser, Mr. Terrell, would you be for answering this question for me? When these cows show up, mixed in with your herds, do you ever get cattle from any of the ranches, other than the large ranches?"

"No," Terrell said. "Now that you mention it, I've never gotten any of Kenny Prosser's cattle, or any of Ed Chambers's cows, and both their ranches are closer to mine than any of the big ranches."

"Have any of you who have seen branded cattle show up in your herd, ever had one of the cows that belonged to anyone but one of the larger ranches?" Duff asked.

The smaller ranchers all looked at one another and discussed the issue for a moment, then Ethan Terrell answered for all of them.

"None of us have ever gained any cattle, but what it didn't belong to one of the bigger ranches."

"'N we've always took them cows back," Spivey said.

"That is true," Webb Dakota said. "On at least three occasions, I have had errant cattle returned."

"There was never any of this going on when Prescott was alive," Terrell said. "Oh sure, there might have been a long rope thrown now and again, but nothing like that is happening now. We didn't have cows moving around from one ranch to another, we didn't have entire herds being rustled, and we didn't have folks being murdered."

"You are aware, are you not, Mr. Terrell, that when you say none of this happened when Prescott owned Twin Peaks, that you are inferring that these incidents may be the result of the present owner?" Houser asked. "I think, perhaps, you are coming dangerously close to making a charge here, and if you do, bear in mind that you can be held pecuniarily responsible for libel, and I will file suit."

"What the hell are you talking about, Houser?" Bert Rowe asked. "So far, there hasn't been anyone make any kind of a charge against anyone. We are discussing the facts in evidence: rustling has increased, people are being murdered, and the cattle of the larger ranches, and larger ranches only, seem to be wandering off, and that is rather peculiar, wouldn't you say so?"

"Yes, I suppose it is," Houser agreed. "I guess I may have jumped to conclusions here, and I apologize. Please, go on with the meeting."

After several more minutes of discussion, Duff once again addressed the meeting.

"I have a suggestion. For the wee ranchers, continue to look for cows that have wandered into your herd, 'n if you can't take them back, right away, let the owner know that you have them. That way he'll be for knowing that you dinnae steal them, 'n he'll know that he hasn't lost them."

"I've been doin' that," Prosser said.

A few of the other small ranchers made the same affirmation.

"And for you larger ranchers, if ye find yourselves missing cattle, give some time before you start worrying that your cows have been stolen. As we have all noticed here, of late, our cows have taken to wandering off on their own. If you'll but wait, they may be brought back to you."

"If a hundred cows are taken, they didn't just wander off," Houser said.

"Perhaps not, Mr. Houser," Duff said without further amplification. "Well, ladies and gentlemen, if there be no other subjects to discuss, this meeting is ended."

Chapter Twenty-nine

After the meeting Duff, Meagan, Elmer, and Vi had dinner at the Cattle Stampede Restaurant.

"Ha," Elmer said. "Did you see the look on Houser's face when he come into the meetin' 'n seen all of us there? He looked like he had just chewed up a whole hot pepper."

"Why was he so upset?" Vi asked. "Didn't you invite him?"

"Yeah, Duff invited 'im, but that was the thing. He said we didn't have no right to invite nobody, on account of he was chairman of the group 'n he was the onliest one who could do the invitin'."

"How did you handle it?" Meagan asked.

"Oh, I told him it was nae an official meeting, but was only a wee gathering of friends and neighbors," Duff replied.

"A wee gathering," Elmer said with a laugh. "We had nigh on to a hundred people there."

"Well, you would have had one more if I hadn't been working on Mrs. Trotter's new dress," Meagan said. "She wants it by Wednesday." She reached over to put her hand on Duff's arm. "But I know I was well represented."

"You got that right. We was all represented real good with Duff, 'cause he pretty much wound up givin' Houser pure ole dee hell."

"Be careful of that man, Duff. There's something about him, something in his eyes."

Meagan remembered sharing a table with him at Tacky Mack's, and she had a sudden thought.

"Duff, you don't think . . . ?" Meagan started, then she stopped as if not wanting to complete the question. "I mean, the Hanlons, Jenny and Asa, you don't think . . . no, it couldn't be."

"I know the question you fear to ask, Meagan, and I surely hope that Houser has nothing to do with it."

"Yeah, well, I wouldn't put it past 'im," Elmer said. "I ain't got a lot of book learnin' like some people, but there's somethin' I learned a long time ago, 'n that's how to see evil in a person. 'N I see it in Houser."

"Aye," Duff agreed. "He does have a touch o' the sulfur about him, that's for sure."

When Duff and Elmer returned home, they were met by Emerson. "Boss, we've got a puzzle here," Emerson said.

"And what would the puzzle be?"

"You know all them cows that was gone when I went over to Percy's ranch to take them provisions to Sam?"

"Aye."

"Well, they ain't gone no more."

"Are ye for telling me, Steven, that the cattle have been returned to Percy's ranch?"

"No, sir, I ain't a-tellin' you that at all, 'cause that ain't what's happened to 'em. They ain't back in Percy's ranch, on account of them cows is all right here at Sky Meadow."

"What?" Elmer asked. "Are you sayin' we have all of Percy's cattle?"

"Yes, sir, that's exactly what I'm sayin'," Emerson replied. "They're all mixed in with the Sky Meadow herd. It was Calhoun that seen 'em first, 'n he pointed 'em out to me. I started countin' em, 'n I done seen near a hundred of 'em. 'N here's the thing, Percy didn't have no more 'n a hundred 'n fifty head on his whole ranch."

"Now, how in Sam Hill do you think all them cows get here from Percy's place?" Elmer asked.

"We was talkin' 'bout just that same thing," Emerson said. "'N 'bout the onliest thing we can come up with is figurin' that maybe when the house caught on fire, that maybe the cows all got scared 'n run over here."

"That don't seem likely a-tall," Elmer said. "I mean, the whole herd just comin' over here?"

"We are the closest ranch to Percy's ranch," Emerson said. "'N what we got here is Angus cows, just like what Percy has. 'N remember, a lot of Percy's cows come from our herd to begin with. It could be that when them cows got scared they just wanted to come back to someplace they remember. And them that didn't come from here, just sort of natural followed the rest of 'em that did."

"Yeah," Elmer agreed. "I reckon maybe that could be."

"Have you separated Mr. Gaines's cattle from our herd?" Duff asked.

"Yes, sir, I got 'em all in the brandin' corral now. We're lookin' now to see if there's any more."

"Good. We'll keep them here until Mr. Gaines returns."

"What is it he's goin' to be comin' home to? He ain't got no house, no more," Elmer said.

"Yes, sir, 'n I got somethin' to say about that, too," Emerson said. "I been talkin' to some of the other fellers, 'n we got us an idea, that is, if you'll go along with it, Mr. MacCallister."

"What is your idea?"

"Well, sir, you might know that me 'n Percy was just real good friends all the time he was workin' here, 'n even after he started his own ranch, why, we was still good friends."

"Aye, I'm aware of that."

"What I was thinkin' is, after Percy gets back maybe me 'n the others could go help him build hisself another house. All the others is willin' to go along with that, but we'd need you to say we can do it, seein' as it might mean a few days off from our regular work. You wouldn't have to worry none, though, 'cause we'd keep some people back here."

Duff smiled. "I think that would be an excellent idea, 'n 'tis a good mon you are, Mr. Emerson, for to be thinking of such a thing."

* * *

Two days later, an item of interest to everyone in the Valley of the Chug appeared in the *Chugwater Defender* newspaper.

AN OPEN LETTER.

To Whom It May Concern:

I, BRAD HOUSER, owner of the TWIN PEAKS RANCH, by these presents make this public pronouncement.

I have filed a claim with the General Land Office and now hold deeded possession of the Pine Flats, as well as all water access on the previously open range land along Blue Elder Creek, Fox Creek, and Horse Creek. As a result of a change of status in the property herein described, and to which I hold exclusive title, no one shall be allowed to water their cattle at the aforementioned places without my specific consent.

Any livestock that may, whether under control, or by free migratory, violate this restricted area, shall be subject to seizure and acquisition by Twin Peaks Ranch.

Two days after the announcement appeared in the newspaper, Jim Spivey and his brother-in-law, Cecil, moved 118 head of Hereford down to Horse Creek.

"Look at 'em drink," Cecil said. "They're a bunch of thirsty little devils, ain't they?"

"Yes. I don't understand how the Wahite Ditch has dried up," Spivey said. "In all the time I've been here, it ain't never been dry."

"Damn, Jim, that's why," Cecil said. "Look over there."

The object of Cecil's attention was a dam, built across the Wahite Ditch, just as it branched off from Horse Creek.

"Who the hell would do somethin' like that?" Spivey asked.

"I'll get it tore down just real quick," Cecil said, taking his rope from the hook on his saddle.

"Cecil, wait," Spivey called. "There's a bunch of men comin'."

Cecil, with his rope in hand, rode back to be alongside Spivey.

"I wonder what they want," Spivey said.

"That feller in the lead is Harris. I've seen 'im in town. He's supposed to be some kindly of a sheriff or somethin'."

"What are you men doing here?" Shamrock asked gruffly.

"Hell, it ought not to be that hard for you to figure out," Spivey said. "I'm waterin' my cows."

Shamrock smiled, though there was no humor in it. "Uh-uh. You're waterin' Twin Peaks cows."

"What do you mean, Twin Peaks cows?" Spivey said angrily. "Check the brands, you'll see that they are my cows."

"You've brung 'em onto Twin Peaks land, 'n my brother has done put a notice in the paper saying that any cows that come onto his land can be confiscated," Shamrock said.

"This isn't Twin Peaks land, this is open range."

"Not 'ny more it ain't. This land has been filed on 'n now belongs to Twin Peaks."

"You can't just claim land 'n say it's yours. You have to improve upon it," Spivey said. "I know that, 'cause that's how I got my own land."

Shamrock pointed to the dam that had stopped water from flowing through the Wahite Ditch.

"There's the improvement, right there," he said with a cackling laugh.

"Improvement? What kind of improvement is that? You've stopped all the water from going to my land!" Spivey said angrily.

"Yeah, we have, haven't we? But, like I said, these ain't your cows no more, so you don't actual have no need for water now."

"All right, I'll take my cows 'n leave, but you ain't goin' to get away with this."

"I told you, they ain't your cows no more." Shamrock pointed to the badge on his shirt. "'N seein' as I'm a captain in the governor's territorial deputies, we'll be takin' 'em now."

"The hell you will!" Cecil shouted, reaching for his pistol.

Shamrock and two of the men with him were ready for just such a reaction, and all three off them shot Cecil, knocking him from the saddle.

"Cecil!" Spivey shouted.

Shamrock made a motion with his pistol. "Pick 'im up, 'n get 'im outta here."

Sheriff Sharpie shook his head. "I'm afraid there's nothing I can do about it, Jim," he said to Spivey. "There are four witnesses who swear that Cecil drew first. Is that true?"

"Well, yeah, he did draw first, but he was just trying to protect our property. Harris stole my entire herd, Sheriff."

Sheriff Sharpie sighed. "I'm lookin' into that. I've checked the land claims, and they are legitimate. And there was a notice put in the paper that any trespassing livestock was subject to seizure. Harris, bein' a governor's deputy 'n all, is authorized to confiscate any cows that come onto the land."

"That ain't in no way fair, Sheriff," Spivey said.

"I admit that it don't seem fair," Sheriff Sharpie said. "But, Jim, this is somethin' that you should fight out in court, not the way Cecil did. Look what happened. He got himself killed, and you lost a friend as well as your herd."

Jim Spivey wasn't the only one to lose his herd. Ed Chambers lost his herd as well. Of all the ranches in the valley, Sky Meadow was the most favorably situated, as it was watered by Bear Creek, Little Bear Creek, and the Chugwater River itself. Duff let it be known to any rancher who had a need for water, that they could bring their cattle onto Sky Meadow for water.

Ethan Terrell's ranch, the Diamond T, was also on the Chugwater River, and Terrell let it be known that he would allow others to use his ranch as well.

None of the larger ranches had been hurt by Houser's acquisition of the open range, for the same streams that flowed through his land, also flowed through theirs.

Chapter Thirty

When Percy Gaines returned to Chugwater with his new bride, he was blissfully unaware of the tension gripping the valley. Sara Sue was a pretty woman, tall and slender, though certainly rounded enough that no one could doubt her sex, even from a distance. She had high cheekbones and a dusting of freckles across her nose. Her hair was a bright red.

"Here it is," Percy said, taking in the town with a sweep of his arm. "What do you think?"

"It's very . . . small," Sara Sue said.

"Well, yeah, maybe so, but that just means you'll get to know everyone. Come on, I'll introduce you to some of my friends before we go out to the ranch."

"Oh, I don't know," Sara Sue said. "We've been on the train since five o'clock yesterday morning. I must look a mess."

Percy laughed. "Darlin', if you was covered in mud right now, you'd still be the most beautiful woman in Chugwater. You'd better come on, now, because once we reach the ranch we won't be coming back into town that often."

Sara Sue smiled and put her hand to her hair. "All right," she said. "At least I'm not covered with mud," she added with a laugh.

The first place Percy took her to was Fiddler's Green. Sara Sue hesitated just before they were about to go in.

"Percy, isn't this a saloon?"

"Yes, but that's all right, because it's almost like some sort of fancy club. Nice ladies come in here all the time. Miss Meagan comes in here, 'n there's not a lady with more quality in the whole town than Miss Meagan."

"Oh?" Sara Sue said, lifting an eyebrow. "Should I be worried about your Miss Meagan?"

Percy laughed. "Darlin', you don't need to be worried 'bout no other woman in the whole world. 'N anyway, she ain't 'my' Miss Meagan. She belongs to Mr. MacCallister."

"Are you talking about the MacCallister who is our neighbor?"

"I sure am. There ain't no finer man anywhere than Duff MacCallister."

"I can't wait to meet him."

"I expect you'll be seeing him real soon. But for now I want you to come on in and meet Biff Johnson. He's another real good man."

Percy led Sara Sue into the bar, and Biff, who was talking to one of his lady servers looked up, saw him, and smiled.

"Percy Gaines," he said, starting toward him. "Welcome home, my friend, welcome home!" He smiled at Sara Sue. "And so this is your new bride?"

"Biff Johnson, I would like you to meet Mrs. Sara Sue Gaines."

"Mrs. Gaines, it is a pleasure to meet you," Biff said with a broad and welcoming smile. "Percy, she is every bit as beautiful as you said she was. Please, come join me at my table."

"Oh my," Percy teased. "Sara Sue, you must have really made an impression, because Biff doesn't invite just everyone to his special table."

"That's only part of it," Biff said. "Mim?" he called back to the girl he had been talking to when Percy and Sara Sue came in. "A bottle of champagne for the newlyweds."

"Champagne? I don't know," Percy said. "I've never had any champagne before, I don't know what it tastes like."

"You'll like it," Biff promised.

A moment later Biff popped the cork to the squeal of delight from Mim, who was standing by. He poured the champagne, then held the goblet out in a toast toward Percy and Sara Sue.

"To a fine young man, and a beautiful young woman, may your days together be long and fruitful."

They drank their toast, then the smile left Biff's face and he grew more serious.

"Have you heard from anyone here while you were gone?"

"No, why?"

Biff shook his head. "Things aren't going well. Houser has laid claim to all the open range in the valley, and he has cut off water supply to half a dozen of the small ranches."

"There's nothing he can do to me. I've got enough

grazing area that I don't need any of the open range, and the Bear and the Little Bear creeks that I use for water come from Sky Meadow."

"Are you about to go out to your ranch now?" Biff asked.

"Yes, I parked my buckboard down at the livery. I figured I would need it to carry all of Sara Sue's things, and I was right. I think she brought half of Kansas City with her," Percy teased.

"Duff asked me to tell you if I saw you, to stop by Sky Meadow before you went out to your place."

"Oh, I'll do that for sure, because I want him to meet Sara Sue," Percy said. "But I'd rather do that later. Right now I'm anxious to get back home, and I'm anxious to show off the place." He smiled at Sara Sue. "I can't wait until you see it."

"No, you don't. Listen to me!" Biff said rather sharply. "I'm telling you, that you need to go see Duff first."

"What?" Percy asked, surprised by the sharpness of Biff's words. "Biff, what is it? What has happened?"

Biff was quiet for a moment.

"Percy, please, don't go home now," Biff said, now his words soft and pleading. "Because if you do, you'll see that there is nothing to go home to."

Percy felt a hollow sensation in the pit of his stomach, and a light-headed dizziness.

"Biff, please tell me what happened."

"Your house is gone. It burned down."

"What? You mean it caught on fire and there was nobody there to stop it? I thought Mr. MacCallister was going to have someone watch the place for me while I was gone."

"There was someone there, Percy. Sam Kirk was there."

Percy nodded. "Well, Sam's a good man. I know he would have prevented the fire if he could. But what happened to Ollie? I thought Ollie Keegan was the one who would be watching out for the ranch."

"Ollie Keegan was killed the very next day after you left."

"Keegan killed? Who killed him?"

"Nobody knows. And about your house, Percy, it was no accident. It was arson. And they found him—Sam—shot dead, lying on the ground outside what was left of your house."

"What? Ollie and Sam both killed? At my place?"

"Yes. And Percy, I think there is something else you should know," Biff said, the tone of his voice as somber as when he told of the burned-out house and the killing of Ollie Keegan and Sam Kirk.

Percy shook his head. "Whatever it is, it couldn't be any worse."

"It's bad enough," Biff said. "You have no herd left. All of your cows are gone. Whoever killed Sam and set fire to your house, also took your herd."

"Oh, Percy! What sort of place have you brought me to?" Sara Sue asked.

Percy didn't answer his wife's question. Instead he was quiet for a long moment, then he nodded.

"You're right, Biff. I think we do need to stop by and see Mr. MacCallister."

As Percy and Sara Sue approached the ranch, they passed under the name SKY MEADOW RANCH, which was worked in wrought iron letters between the open rails of the arch that spread its curve over the entryway.

"Oh, what a beautiful place," Sara Sue said.

"Yeah, it is. Mr. MacCallister's a pretty rich man, but he's real nice about it. I mean, he ain't like some rich men who think they're king of the roost."

Before they reached the house, they were met by Steve Emerson, who greeted them with a broad smile.

"Welcome home, Percy. It's good to have you back," Emerson said.

Percy introduced Sara Sue to the man he described as his best friend.

"I think you're goin' to like it out here, Mrs. Gaines," Emerson said.

"I hope she likes it," Percy said. "But I must say I brought her home to an absolute mess. I heard about my house being burned 'n my herd being rustled."

"Your herd wasn't stoled," Emerson replied.

"What do you mean? Biff said that my herd was gone."

"Yeah, they're all gone from your place. But they ain't really gone, seein' as they are all here, on Sky Meadow. We're holdin' 'em in the corral for you."

A happy smile spread across Percy's face. "That's really good news," he said. "Thanks."

"You don't need to thank me. As far as any of us can tell, your cows all come here by their ownself. Go on up 'n see Mr. MacCallister. He has some other news that I think you will like."

"Really? I don't see how it can beat what you just told me."

A few minutes later Duff and Elmer greeted the couple.

"Steve told me that my cows were here, on your place," Percy said. "I want to thank you for that." The smile left his face. "Oh, and I heard about Ollie and Sam. I'm sorry about that . . . I feel responsible for it."

"There is nae need for you to feel so," Duff said. "The only one responsible is the blackhearted cretins who killed them, whoever they may be. And I'm sure they are the same people."

"I'm sorry, Sara Sue, I seem to have brought you home to a mess," Percy said.

Duff smiled. "As they say, 'tis always darkest before the dawn. By the way, we were expecting you today, so Wang is preparing a feast for you, and Meagan and Vi will be here as well."

"That's very nice of you, Mr. MacCallister," Percy said.

"Percy told me he had nice neighbors, and I can see that he was telling the truth," Sara Sue said. "That nice older gentleman that Percy just introduced me to told how some of the men will help us rebuild the house."

"Older gentleman," Elmer said with a little laugh. "Yeah, we're goin' to help with the new house, but you ain't seen nothin' yet."

Wang had prepared Peking duck. Because there were so many for dinner, he had cooked two of them, and was now slicing the birds in front of the diners. The skin of the two birds was especially crisp, and served with sugar and garlic. The meat itself was served with scallions, cucumbers, sweet bean sauce, and Chinese pancakes.

"Oh, I've never seen such a thing," Sara Sue said.

"Just seein' it is only half of it," Elmer said. "Wait till you taste it."

The meal was every bit as good as the presentation had promised, and everyone ate with gusto.

"You must tell me how to prepare that!" Sally Sue said.

"He won't be able to tell you how he done it," Elmer insisted. "It's prob'ly one o' them things he has to keep secret."

"I cannot tell," Wang said.

"See there, what did I tell you?" Elmer crowed.

"It is not a thing that can be told, but it is a thing that can be shared. I will teach you," Wang said.

"Well, I'll be damn. Percy, your bride must have made quite an impression on Wang," Elmer said. "I never thought he'd tell her nothin' at all like that."

After dinner Duff invited everyone into the parlor.

"Let's talk about your house," Duff said.

"Yes, Steve said that my house would be rebuilt."

"Nae, lad, your house will nae be rebuilt."

"Oh well, I . . ."

Duff smiled. "This is the house that will be rebuilt," Duff said, walking over to a table upon which was spread a large piece of paper.

"What?"

"Come and have a look," Duff said.

Curious as to what he was talking about, Percy and Sara Sue walked over to the table to look. There, on the sheet of paper, was the drawing of a house, three times as large as the one that had burned. The house had a front porch, covered by a roof that was supported by four posts spread across the front. It had wings that spread to either side. And below the drawing was a floor plan that showed a kitchen, dining room, living room, and three bedrooms.

"I . . . I don't understand," Percy said.

"Well, 'tis sure I am that there will be wee ones coming along someday," Duff said. "And when they do, you'll be for needing a bigger house than the one you had. So, I had the architect in town, Swayne Byrd, draw these plans out for us to follow when we build your house."

"We're goin' to build it for you, Percy," Elmer said. "All the boys from the ranch here."

"But the building material . . ."

"All your friends and neighbors pitched in to buy the material, and Bob Guthrie at Guthrie Building Supply, gave us a very good price."

"And there's enough money left over to furnish the house," Meagan said. "Sara Sue, Vi and I will help you pick everything out, and then we'll help move you in, won't we, Vi?"

"Oh yes indeed!" Vi said.

"Oh," Sara Sue said as tears began to roll down her cheeks. "I can't believe all this. What a wonderful thing for you to do!"

"What did I tell you, Sara Sue? I told you that we had the best neighbors in the world, didn't I?"

"Yes, you have told me that, and I can see now that you weren't exaggerating at all. You actually do have the nicest neighbors in the world."

"No, I don't have the nicest neighbors in the world," Percy said resolutely.

"Oh, Percy, how can you say such a thing, knowing what they have done?"

Percy smiled broadly and reached over to put his hand on Sara Sue's cheek.

"*We* have the best neighbors in the world." Percy emphasized the word *we*.

"Oh! As soon as we are moved in, I want to invite all of you over to be our very first houseguests."

"In the meantime . . . you will need a place to stay, so I've made arrangements for you to stay here," Duff said.

"I can't stay here without doing something to repay you," Sara Sue said. "I shall keep your house spotless."

"Except for the kitchen," Elmer said.

"Why not the kitchen?"

"The kitchen belongs to Wang," Elmer explained. "Oh, I suppose you can go in there, if you aren't afraid of Wang coming after you with a cleaver."

Sara Sue and the others laughed.

"I shall leave Wang with his domain," she promised.

Chapter Thirty-one

When Lucien Bodine arrived in Chugwater his first thought was that it was no different from any of the other small towns he had been in over the last ten years. But as he rode north on Clay Street, he saw a town of industrious people. There were a couple of freight wagons moving in the street, half a dozen buckboards, and that many more on horseback. Wooden plank sidewalks lined each side of the street and they, too, were filled with people, all of whom seemed to have some place to go.

As he rode past the sheriff's office, he saw a man, wearing a badge, leaning against the post that supported the porch roof. He was smoking a cigar and greeting people who passed by. Bodine dipped his head slightly and looked away from the lawman as he passed. He had never been in Wyoming before, so he had no way of knowing whether or not the lawman would recognize him, but he thought it would be better not to take a chance.

He knew, from the newspaper article, that Chugwater

was where his brother was killed, but the article had not identified the man who killed him. Bodine intended to find out that bit of information, though he wasn't quite sure how he should go about it. If he started asking questions he might arouse a little more attention than he wanted.

Bodine was in no particular hurry. His brother was dead and would stay dead for as long as it took for Bodine to avenge him.

Bodine was tired, hungry, and thirsty from the long ride up. He still had most of the money he had taken when he robbed Garland's Road Ranch, for the simple reason that there had been little opportunity for him to spend it. The Wild Hog Saloon seemed to call out to him, so he stopped in front, looped the reins around the hitching rack, and went inside.

"What'll it be?" the bartender asked, making a swipe across the bar with a wet and smelly rag.

Bodine ordered, and was served, a beer.

"You got 'nything to eat here?" Bodine asked after taking his first swallow.

"Ham, beans, biscuits."

"Bring it to me over at the table."

"That'll be two bits."

Bodine slapped a quarter down, then took his beer to a table that he chose specifically so that his back would be in the corner, making it very difficult for anyone to approach him without being seen.

When Sid Shamrock stepped through the batwing doors of the Wild Hog Saloon, he saw an old familiar face. Lucien Bodine was sitting alone at a table in the back of the saloon. He was eating, and paying more attention to the food on his table than to anyone in the room.

For just a moment Shamrock considered going over to talk to him, but then he decided against it. Bodine was one of the most volatile men Shamrock had ever known, and if he happened to see the badge pinned to his shirt, Bodine could start shooting before Shamrock could explain its purpose.

Shamrock needed to avoid being seen by Bodine until he was able to figure out how best to handle the situation. Although he preferred spending his time in the Wild Hog Saloon, he decided that under the circumstances, and to avoid being seen by Bodine, it might be best for him to give Fiddler's Green his business. He eased back out before Bodine looked up from his beans.

"Captain Harris," Biff greeted when Shamrock stepped up to the Fiddler's Green bar a few minutes later. "I must say that I'm surprised to see you here. I had been given to understand that the Wild Hog is your preferred watering hole."

"It is, but there's a feller in there right now that I would just as lief not see."

"You and your . . . deputies . . . have been busy, I hear. Damming up the water sources for half a dozen ranches, and, how many herds have you taken?" Biff asked.

"It's all legal," Shamrock said. "It ain't like we was stealin' or nothin'."

Shamrock ordered a beer, then glanced down at

the other end of the bar where a couple of cowboys were in animated conversation.

"Well, it's causin' ever' body a lot more work but Terrell is lettin' his neighbors use his water so's the cows don't all die off," one of the men said.

"So is Mr. Dakota over on Kensington Place," another said.

"And don't forget Duff MacCallister."

"What kind of man is this feller Houser, anyhow? I mean, it takes one mean son of a bitch to come in here 'n start makin' life bad for ever' one. Why, I wouldn't be surprised if he warn't the one that kilt Keegan, Kirk, 'n then burnt down Percy Gaines's house."

"Not him. Have you noticed that he don't never even wear a gun? Hell, a real gun would more 'n likely scare 'im to death. 'N he don't never ride a horse, neither. He just drives aroun' in that surrey of his'n."

"Yeah, well, if he didn't do it his ownself, there ain't no doubt in my mind but what he had some o' them men that works for him do it."

"Not Turley or Cooper, 'cause I know them two boys, 'n they're pretty good men."

"No, I don't mean none o' his cowboys. I know all of them, 'n they're all pretty good men. I'm talkin' about some o' them deputies he's got workin' for 'im. You got to wonder, though, why it is that Turley 'n Cooper is still workin' for Houser?"

"The way I figure it, they ain't workin' for Houser a-tall. Both them boys rode for the brand when ole

Mr. Prescott owned the place, 'n I think they're just still ridin' for the brand."

"Yeah, you may be right. But hey, we was talkin' 'bout Gaines gettin' his house burnt down a while ago. As it turns out, that could wind up bein' 'bout the best thing that ever happened to Gaines."

"What? Now, why would you say somethin' like that? When is it ever a good thing if a man's house burns down 'n he loses ever'thing?"

"I can say somethin' like that, on account of he's havin' a new house bein' built that's a lot bigger 'n nicer 'n the old one ever was."

"He's got that kind of money? How is it that Gaines can afford a house like that?"

"Oh, he ain't havin' to pay for none of it. Most o' the other ranchers has took up a collection 'n that's what's payin' for it, though folks is sayin' that it's MacCallister hisself that's payin' for the most of it. 'N as for the work, well, all the hands that works for MacCallister is doin' the actual buildin' of it."

"Why's MacCallister takin' such a interest in it?"

"I don't know for sure, except that Gaines used to work for MacCallister, so prob'ly that's why."

Having heard enough, Shamrock drained the rest of his beer and set the empty mug down on the bar.

"Another one?" Biff asked Shamrock. There was no welcome in the tone of his voice.

"No, I gotta go."

Leaving the saloon, Shamrock rode out to Percy Gaines's ranch to see for himself what the two men in the saloon were talking about. He was surprised to see how far they had come, and equally surprised to see the kind of house that was being built. Unlike the earlier structure, which had been wood, the house going up now was of brick. There were at least nine people working on the house, some laying brick, some mixing mortar, others carrying bricks, while one was up on the new gables.

Steve Emerson, having seen Shamrock arrive, walked over toward him. Shamrock had not dismounted.

"Hello," Emerson said. "Did you come to help?"

"No," Shamrock replied bluntly. Jerking on the reins, he turned his horse around and left at a rapid trot.

"Who was that?" Percy asked.

"That was . . . Captain . . . Harris," Emerson said, slurring the word *Captain*. "He's the head of this bunch of no-account deputies I told you about."

"I wonder what he wanted," Percy mused.

"More 'n likely, the son of a bitch was out here spyin' on us."

"Spyin' on us for what?"

"Who knows for what? Who knows anything about him or, for that matter, any of the rest of those deputies? You've done been told how they stoled Spivey's 'n Chambers's cows. 'N they shot 'n kilt Cecil Gibson."

"And the sheriff didn't do anything about it?"

"No, he didn't do nothin' about it. First of all, Harris 'n the others that shot 'im is deputies for the governor, 'n they was just carryin' out orders in takin' the herd. 'N in the second place, all the witnesses says that Gibson drawed first."

* * *

Some distance away from the Gaines ranch, at Twin Peaks, Brad Houser sat behind his desk, drumming his fingers on the desktop as he contemplated the information Shamrock had just given him.

"His house is being rebuilt?" Houser asked.

"Yeah, they's nine or ten people out there workin' like beavers," Shamrock said.

"Who are the people who are helping him? Where do they come from?"

"Most of 'em is from MacCallister's ranch. But they's a couple of the smaller ranchers that's helpin' 'im, too. I've seen Ethan Terrell out there, 'n his boy."

"Terrell? Correct me if I'm wrong, but isn't he providing water access to the ranchers who have been cut off from water by our recent acquisitions?"

"Yeah, that's the one."

The drumming of Houser's fingers became even more pronounced. "This new house that is being built. You say MacCallister is behind it?"

"Oh yeah, he's for sure behind it." Shamrock smiled.

"I had no idea that our Scottish neighbor would wind up being as much of a fly in our ointment as he has been."

"You want me to kill 'im?"

"No. MacCallister is a man who commands a great deal of respect, not only for the size of his ranch, but also because of the dominance of his personality. I fear that his untimely demise, at this time, could wind up causing more problems than getting him out of the way would solve."

Back at the Gaines house, where everyone had put in a full day's work, Ethan Terrell put down a hammer and looked toward the western sky. The sun had lost its heat and glare, but none of its brilliance as it was a glowing, orange globe, hanging just above the horizon. "Boys, it's gettin' a little late," Ethan Terrell said. "I think the boy's ma was going to fry some chicken for our supper, 'n if it gets cold before we get home, she'll be some upset."

"Ha, I know Lottie," one of the others said. "And believe me, you don't want her upset."

"Come on, Poke, we gotta go."

"All right, Pa," Poke replied.

"What do you say, men, that we call it quits for the day?" Percy said. "I want to thank all of you for coming, and hope to see all of you tomorrow."

"We'll be here," Terrell promised. "I'm anxious to see what this house is goin' to look like when it's finished. Why, I might even hire Byrd to design a new house for me."

After all the tools were put away, and good-byes exchanged, the men left the worksite to return home, home for most of them being the bunkhouse at Sky Meadow.

Ethan Terrell and his son, Poke, had the farthest to go, and though it wasn't yet dark, the sun was completely below the horizon by the time they got home.

"You got here just in time," Lottie said. "The

chicken is done, the potatoes are mashed, the gravy is made, and I'm taking out the biscuits now."

"Ma, when I get married, do you think she will be as good a cooker as you?" Poke asked.

"Well, if not, we can always have your ma teach her," Ethan said. "My ma taught Lottie. Why, before we were married, she couldn't boil water."

"Ha! Do you want to eat tonight, Ethan Terrell?" Lottie teased.

Poke was tired and pleasantly full when he went to bed that night, and because of that, went to sleep very quickly. He wasn't sure what time it was when he awoke in the middle of the night, but he lay comfortably in bed, about to drift off again, when he saw a strange, wavering light playing against the wall of his bedroom.

Confused, he sat up and looked through the window.

The barn was on fire!

"Pa!" he shouted, running into his parents' bedroom. "Pa! The barn is on fire!"

"The horses!" Ethan said. Getting up, he pulled on his boots, but didn't put any clothes on over his long underwear.

"Get your shoes on, Poke, come help me!" Ethan shouted as he started toward the front door.

Poke returned to his bedroom, but unlike his father, he pulled on a pair of trousers, then reached for his boots. He was just pulling them on when he heard shots from out front.

Almost immediately after the shots, he heard his mother cry out.

"Ethan!"

There were more shots, and Poke hurried to the living room. His mother came back inside, and Poke saw that the front of her nightgown was covered with blood.

"Ma!"

"Run, Poke, run!" Lottie said. "They've killed your father . . . and me. Run, hide!"

Chapter Thirty-two

Poke had heard the scream of the horses when he crawled out through the back window. One of the horses, he knew, was his horse, Cody. He had had Cody since he was nine years old, and the thought of him dying in such a way just added to the hurt he was feeling over the sudden death of his parents. But he knew there was nothing he could do about it.

He ran through the night, not only to escape the men who had come to kill, but also to get away from the panic and pain-induced screams of the horses.

When he first started out he had no specific plan in mind other than to escape. But after a few minutes he realized that it was as important for him to be going toward something as it was for him to be running away from something. Without having to think hard about it, he started the long, fifteen-mile trek toward Sky Meadow.

About an hour after he started, he heard horses coming up the road. It was still dark, and he had no idea who would be out riding this time of night, but he didn't want to take any chances, so he left the road and hid in the trees.

The riders stopped right in front of him, though it was so dark that he could make out only the shapes and shadows. The good thing was, he knew they wouldn't be able to see him back in the trees.

"You sure they was a boy in the house?" one of the men asked.

"We was told there was, but I didn't see nobody."

"Well, if they was a boy, I don't think he coulda got this far. Come on back, we're just wastin' time here."

"Yeah, we need to help get the herd moved."

Poke stayed perfectly still for nearly an hour after they were gone, getting up to leave only because he was afraid he would fall asleep, and he didn't want to do that until he reached Mr. MacCallister's place.

Sara Sue Gaines had begun helping Wang in the kitchen, doing so with his permission, and under his guidance. Elmer's prediction that such an arrangement could only lead to trouble, proved to be false. Wang took well to his position as instructor, and Sara Sue was a very good student.

Sara Sue opened the oven door to look in at the biscuits she had rolled out and put in to bake a short while earlier.

"Oh, they are browning quite nicely," she said. "Your idea of baking them in an iron skillet is wonderful."

"I will get water for the coffee," Wang offered.

"I'll grind the beans."

Wang stepped out onto the back porch and began

pumping water for breakfast, when he saw the boy coming up the long front drive. It was Poke Terrell, and Wang wondered why he was walking, instead of riding. As he saw the boy approaching, he realized that something was wrong. He was walking in a staggering, hesitant motion as if hurt, or exhausted. What was he doing here like this? Where were his parents?

"Madam Sara Sue," he called through the kitchen door.

"Yes?"

"Tell Duff that he will be needed."

There was enough urgency in Wang's voice that Sara Sue didn't question him. Instead she started back into the house to summon Duff.

After giving Sara Sue the order, Wang put the bucket down, vaulted easily over the porch rail, than ran to meet Poke Terrell.

"Poke, why have you come here in such a way? Why do you not ride your horse? Is there trouble?"

"They're dead, Mr. Wang. Ma 'n Pa are both dead. Some men came in the middle of the night and shot 'em. They burned the barn and the house down, too."

As if it had taken all his strength to make that pronouncement, Poke collapsed into Wang's arms.

It was midmorning when Elmer and Wang returned from the Terrell ranch.

"They're both dead, like the boy said," Elmer said. "The barn 'n house has both been burnt down, 'n all the cattle has been took."

"Where are the bodies?" Duff asked.

"Steve 'n Percy went over to get 'em. They'll be takin' 'em to Mr. Welsh. How's the boy doing?"

"Mrs. Gaines is with him," Duff said. "The lad is having a hard time, but Mrs. Gaines is very good with him."

"Did Poke see any of the men who did this?" Elmer asked. "Will he be able to tell us who it was that done it?"

"I asked, and he says that it was dark and he dinnae see anyone close enough to identify them."

"Whoever the sons of bitches is, they've been damn busy," Elmer said. "They killed Ollie 'n Sam, 'n burnt down Percy's place, 'n they killed Asa Hanlon 'n his wife and took all their cows, they kilt Cecil Gibson, 'n now they've kilt Poke's ma and pa 'n stoled their cows, too."

"Cecil Gibson was killed by Houser's deputies," Duff said. "'Twas reported that he drew on them when the deputies confiscated Spivey's herd."

"Yeah, well, how do we know they ain't all the same?" Elmer asked.

"That is a very good question, Elmer," Duff replied. "And 'tis one that we should investigate. I'll be for taking a ride over to Twin Peaks."

"Good, I'll be comin' with you."

"You can both come," Duff said, referring also to Wang.

It was Shamrock who saw the three riders approaching Twin Peaks, and he stepped into Houser's office to report it.

"Three riders comin'," he said. "One of 'em is MacCallister."

Houser nodded. "I was wondering when he might show up. All right, as soon as they get here, show them in."

In one part of Houser's ranch office there was a comfortable sitting area consisting of a leather sofa and two overstuffed leather chairs. The sofa and chairs were separated by a low-lying table, onto which Houser spread a white tablecloth, then he got out a bottle of Scotch and four shot glasses. He had just put the bottle and glasses on the table when the front door opened, and Shamrock brought in the three men.

"You said you wanted me to bring 'em in, so here they are," Shamrock said.

"Thank you, Captain Harris. Would you excuse us please, so I can talk to these gentlemen alone?"

"Yeah, all right. I'll just be outside, if you need me."

"Drinks, gentlemen?" Houser offered after Shamrock left.

"Aye, thank you," Duff replied.

"I do not wish a drink of whiskey," Wang said.

"I'm sorry, I'm not better prepared to be a host," Houser said. "But I must confess that my knowledge of the drinking habits of Chinese is quite deficient."

"He drinks wine," Elmer said.

"Now, I am really embarrassed, for I have no wine to offer."

"Be not concerned," Wang said.

Houser poured the drinks, handed a glass to Duff and Elmer, then took one for himself.

"And now, gentlemen, to what do I owe the pleasure of your visit?"

"There is no pleasure in this visit, I'm afraid," Duff said. "Last night some brigands visited the Diamond T."

"Oh? And the Terrells?"

"They were both killed."

"Both? But, wasn't there a third? Their son, I believe?"

"Aye, he survived. 'Twas a costly mistake the murderers made, for young Terrell saw them."

"He . . . he saw them?" Houser asked.

"Aye. He can give no names, but if he sees any of them again, he will know."

"Where is the boy now?" Houser asked.

"He is in a safe place."

Houser shook his head. "It is just as I have been saying. Ruffians running wild, killing innocent people like the Hanlons so they can steal the herd. I may have been wrong in suggesting that the small ranchers are guilty, because the implication was that there were several involved. Now I'm thinking it may only be one, who is plying his evil trade upon not only the large ranchers, but the smaller ones as well."

"How did you know?" Duff asked.

"I beg your pardon?"

"How did you know that the Terrell herd was taken?"

"Why, you, yourself, just said that the herd was taken."

Duff shook his head. "I made nae such a remark."

"Oh. Well, I suppose that because the Hanlons were killed and their stock taken, I naturally assumed that Terrell's herd was taken as well." He forced a laugh. "As a lawyer, I should know better than to assume anything. I hope you will forgive my mistake."

"There is nae to forgive."

"Tell me, Captain MacCallister, was there any other purpose for your visit, other than to inform me of the unfortunate fate which fell upon the poor Terrell family?"

"Aye. I've come to tell you that I'll be investigating the murder, and to ask your cooperation if I need to question any of your men."

"*You'll* be investigating? I don't understand. Have you set yourself upon a personal mission for some reason? Why would you be investigating?"

"Oh, I dinnae tell you? I'm a deputy sheriff, 'n though your deputies have preeminent authority with regard to the cattle rustling, the county sheriff has the responsibility for investigating murder. And, in the last two months we have had eleven murders."

"Eleven murders? I am aware of but six murders. Your two men, Mr. Keegan and Mr. Kirk, Asa Hanlon and his wife, and the unfortunate incident last night when Mr. and Mrs. Terrell were murdered."

"Aye, but there is also the murder of your two ranch hands, Hastings and Carson, as well as Sobel, Knox, and Cecil Gibson."

"Oh, but you are mistaken in calling those murders. When Slim Hastings and Dooley Carson were killed by Knox, you might remember that those were deemed to be justifiable homicides, and no charges were filed. Later, Mr. Sobel was killed, also by Knox, and I will grant you that, that was a murder, which resulted in Knox himself being killed. But when my brother killed Knox it could be classified as a line-of-duty shooting, not only because Knox had just murdered Mr. Sobel, but also because Knox was a wanted man, with a dead-or-alive warrant placed upon him. And as for Mr. Gibson, well, that was most lamentable, but it, too, was a case of justifiable homicide. When the territorial deputies confiscated Spivey's cattle, which was quite legal because the cattle had infringed upon private property, Cecil Gibson drew his gun in an attempt to shoot the deputies. He was, himself, shot."

"'Tis perhaps only a coincidence, Mr. Houser, but have you considered that all those killings have happened just since you arrived in the valley?"

"Are you making a correlation between my presence and these killings?" Houser asked.

"A correlation, aye, for that they have all happened since you arrival can nae be denied. But whether ye be answerable . . . 'tis something that I will study."

"Surely, sir, you are not suggesting that I am a subject of your investigation?" Houser challenged.

"Aye, that is exactly what I am suggesting," Duff said.

"Why, I don't even carry a gun."

"Neither did Arabi Pasha in Egypt, but he managed to have a great number of my fellow soldiers killed. 'Tis a fact, Mr. Houser, that one can be responsible for killing, without being the one who pulls the trigger. And if I find, in my investigation, that you are accountable, I will see that you stand trial."

Chapter Thirty-three

"You want me to kill him?" Shamrock asked after Duff left.

"No," Houser replied. "That is, I want him killed, but I don't want you to do it. I need him killed in a way that cannot be traced back to me."

"Bodine," Shamrock said.

"Who?"

"Didn't you tell me that MacCallister kilt Zeke Bodine?"

"Yes, or so I have been told. The story I heard is that Bodine and two others attempted to hold up a stagecoach on which MacCallister and the Chinaman were passengers. The Chinaman killed one of the would-be robbers and MacCallister killed the other two. One of the two men that MacCallister killed was Zeke Bodine. But what does that have to do with the situation at hand?"

"Lucien Bodine is in town. I seen 'im yesterday. All I have to do is tell 'im that MacCallister is the one what kilt his brother, 'n he'll kill MacCallister for us."

"What makes you think he will believe you?"

"He'll believe me," Shamrock replied. "Me 'n him's old friends."

"Thomas! I know you have lived a most checkered life, but I can't believe that you actually have been friends with someone like Lucien Bodine."

"Yeah? Well, knowin' 'im comes in handy now, don't it?" Shamrock replied with a self-satisfied laugh.

For the last three days, Lucien Bodine had spent much of his time in the saloons of Chugwater. He talked little and listened much, trying to learn who killed his brother. He had never been here before, so he wasn't concerned that someone might recognize him.

At the moment he was in the Long Horn, playing a game of solitaire, just listening to the buzz of conversation. He was looking for a black queen, and he dealt the three cards with no luck. He was studying the card layout when someone approached his table. Cautiously, he looked up.

"Hello, Bodine."

"Shamrock," Bodine said, surprised to see him. "What are you doing here?"

"I live here. My brother and I own a ranch just outside of town." Houser had never offered a share of his ranch, but Shamrock was sure that was going to happen, especially if he was able to get rid of MacCallister.

Bodine's only response was a nod, then he dealt out three more cards.

"Do you know who killed your brother?" Shamrock asked.

Bodine looked up again. "No. Do you?"

Shamrock smiled. "Yeah, I know."

Meagan was making a new dress for Barbara Woodward, and as Mary Ellen Summers was about the same size as Barbara, Meagan had her put it on so she could take up the hem.

"Oh, Miss Parker, this may be the most beautiful dress I have ever seen," Mary Ellen said.

"Turn to your left just a bit," Meagan said, though her voice was somewhat muffled because she had a mouthful of pins.

The bell on the front door dinged as someone came in.

Meagan took the pins out of her mouth and laid them on the table. "I had better go see who that is."

Just as she stood up, two men came into the back of the shop. She recognized one of them as Captain Harris. She had never seen the other one before.

"Oh, Captain Harris, I don't allow any of my customers back here," Meagan said, being careful not to allow her agitation to show. She smiled. "Besides, all the displays are out front. What can I do for you?"

"I am told that you are a friend of Duff MacCallister."

"Yes."

"I want you to ride out to MacCallister's ranch and see to it that he comes to town."

"Why should I go get Mr. MacCallister? I'm sure he is too busy to come to town right now."

"This is Lucien Bodine," Shamrock said.

"Oh?" Meagan replied anxiously. She recognized the name.

"You may recall that it was MacCallister who killed Mr. Bodine's brother."

Meagan didn't answer.

Shamrock pulled his pistol and pointed it at Mary Ellen, who had been watching the conversation with an expression that was halfway between fear and curiosity.

"Oh!" Mary Ellen said, startled at seeing the gun pointed toward her.

"If he does not come to town within two hours, I will kill this girl," Shamrock said.

"What? Have you gone crazy?"

"And if I see the sheriff come through the front door, the girl dies."

"Oh, Miss Parker!" Mary Ellen said in a choked voice.

Meagan held out her hand. "Don't do anything," she said. "I'll get Duff."

Shamrock looked, pointedly, toward the grandfather clock that stood against the wall.

"Now you have only one hour and fifty-nine minutes. You'd better get started."

"I'll be back, Mary Ellen. I promise you, I'll be back," Meagan said as she headed for the door.

Elmer was the first one to see Meagan as she came riding up the road at a gallop. When he stepped out to meet her, he saw that the horse was covered in sweat.

"Here, girl, what's wrong? Why would you come galloping in like that?" Elmer asked.

"Oh, Elmer, get Duff. He has to come to town!" Meagan said, the tone of her voice reflecting her distress.

Elmer didn't have to go for Duff, he had just noticed her and was coming to greet her, but when he saw the condition of the horse, and the expression on her face, his smile faded.

"Meagan! What is it, lass?"

"Oh, Duff, Captain Harris is holding Mary Ellen! They say if you aren't in town by three o'clock, they'll kill her."

"They?"

"Lucien Bodine is with him."

Duff nodded. "I wondered when he might show up. What I don't understand is his connection to Harris."

"Duff, I . . ." Meagan started. "You know he wants to kill you. I would say don't go, but . . ."

"I understand. The lass is in danger. Of course I'll go."

"Wang and I will go with you," Elmer said.

"Not with, ahead of me," Duff said. "I dinnae want us to be seen riding in together. You and Wang go in alone and . . ."

"I know," Elmer said. "Take a look around."

"Aye."

"I'm going back with you," Meagan said.

"There is nae need for you to go back. 'Twould be much safer for you here."

"I promised Mary Ellen that I would be back. I'll not be going back on that promise."

Duff nodded. "Aye, Meagan, I understand."

Duff and Meagan gave Elmer and Wang a fifteen-minute head start, then they started out as well.

"Here he comes," Shamrock said, looking through the front window of the dress emporium. "That's him, the tall feller ridin' alongside the woman."

Duff stopped in front of the leather goods store, which was at the far end of the street Meagan's Dress Emporium was on. Dismounting, he tied off both his and Meagan's horses.

"I want you to stay here until this is finished," he said.

Duke Rudd came out of his leather goods store, and the druggist, Harry White, came out of the apothecary that was next door.

"What's goin' on?" Rudd asked.

Duff held his hand out. "Best you stay out of the street," he said as he loosened the pistol in his holster, stepped out into the middle of the street, and started walking toward the dress emporium.

"Bodine!" he called. "Bodine, I'm the man who killed your brother. If you have an argument, take it up with me and turn the young lass free."

Duff's shout alerted several of the citizens of the town who were going about their business on Clay Street, which was Duff's intention. They hurried off the street, which was his purpose.

"Bodine!" Duff called again.

From the front of Meagan's store, a rather short, narrow-faced, hollow-cheeked man with a large, hooked nose came outside. He stepped out into the middle of the street.

Shamrock was watching through the front window of the dress shop, smiling that he had put into motion the event that would kill his brother's principal enemy. After this, Brad would have to make him a partner in the ranch.

Because he was watching the street, he was no longer paying any attention to the young woman in his charge. Mary Ellen sneaked out through the back door, then locked it behind her to keep him from coming out after her. Once out of the building, she ran down the alley.

"My brother wasn't much of a man," Bodine said in a harsh, raspy voice. "If you hadn' kilt him, I prob'ly would have gotten aroun' to it m' ownself someday. But you done it first, so now I'm goin' to have to kill you."

"'N would ye be for tellin' me, then, Mr. Bodine, if ye had no love for your brother, why 'tis you would be wanting to kill me?"

"It just wouldn't look good, I mean, me lettin' you get away with killin' my own blood like that."

"Are you sure you're nae doing this for the bidding of Brad Houser?" Duff asked.

Bodine shook his head. "I ain't never heard of anyone named Brad Houser."

"What about Paul Harris?"

"Ain't never heard o' him, either. Did you come

to talk? Or did you come to settle this thing that's between us?"

"I came to . . ." That was as far as Duff got before he saw Bodine's hand start toward his pistol.

For just a split second, Duff wasn't watching a hand dip toward a pistol, he was seeing Wang's palm close around a pebble.

The Enfield Mark I revolver seemed to leap into Duff's hand of its own accord and was spitting flame as Bodine was still in the midst of his draw. Duff saw a little spray of blood from the hole his bullet had put in the middle of Bodine's chest.

Bodine dropped his gun, slapped his hand over the hole, then looked down with shock and disbelief as the blood streamed between his spread fingers. He sat down, and Duff moved up quickly, to kick the pistol away.

"You beat me," Bodine said, almost as if fascinated by the fact that it could be done. "I didn't think anyone could beat me but you . . . you . . ."

He took one final gasping breath, then fell on his back. By now, all the people who had left the street a moment earlier were coming back and crowding around Duff, who still held the pistol in his hand, and the prostrate form of Lucien Bodine.

"Damn!" Shamrock said aloud. "I woulda never thought anyone could beat Bodine!"

Suddenly Shamrock grew frightened. Duff MacCallister had killed Bodine, now he might be coming for him. Unless he could use the girl.

"Come here, girl, we're goin' . . ." Shamrock

stopped in midsentence. The girl wasn't there. "Where the hell did you go?"

Looking back out through the window, he saw the girl running toward the woman who owned the dress shop. They embraced in the middle of the street. How the hell did she get away?

The back door. Yes, she left through the back door, and Shamrock would do the same thing.

Hurrying to the back door, he tried to open it, but found it locked.

"Harris!"

The shout came from the street.

Hurrying back to the window he saw, not only Duff MacCallister, but Deputy Logan.

"Harris, come out with your hands up!" Deputy Logan called.

Shamrock opened the front door, then tossed his gun out into the street.

"I'm comin' out!" he called. "I'm comin' out with m' hands up!"

Jeb Jaco had watched the gunfight from the boardwalk just in front of the Wild Hog Saloon. He was shocked by what he had seen, not only because he didn't think Bodine could be beaten, but because he had never seen anything as fast as the Scotsman's draw.

And now he was watching Shamrock walking down the street with his hands up.

Houser would need to be told.

Chapter Thirty-four

"Bodine is dead, 'n they got your brother in jail," Jaco told Houser.

"How was Bodine killed?"

"MacCallister kilt 'im. I'm tellin' you the truth, Mr. Houser, I've seen some fast gunmen in my days, but I ain't never seen nothin' like MacCallister. I never even seen 'im draw. He was just standin' there one moment 'n the next moment the gun was in his hand."

"Is my brother injured?"

"No, he ain't hurt none. He's just in jail, is all."

"Thank you, Mr. Jaco."

"You want me 'n the others to go into town 'n break him out of jail?" Jaco asked.

"No, that wouldn't be prudent. We will need to take some other approach. Let me think about it."

"Harris is in jail," Cooper told Turley.

Turley smiled. "As far as I'm concerned, that's

where the son of a bitch belongs. What happened? How did he wind up in jail?"

"From what I heard in town, he 'n a feller named Bodine took that girl that works for the lady that runs the dress shop prisoner and . . ."

"Mary Ellen? Is she all right?" Turley asked anxiously.

"Yeah, that's right, I forgot you're kind of sweet on her. Don't worry, she's fine." Cooper laughed. "You know what she did? Harris was holdin' her in the dress shop where she works, but somehow she got out through the back door, then she locked it, 'n that trapped the son of a bitch inside. After that it was easy for Deputy Logan to arrest 'im for holdin' her like he done."

Turley smiled. "Yeah, I can see Mary Ellen doing something like that."

"Will this do for you Mr. Houser?"

=A PROCLAMATION=
of the GOVERNOR OF WYOMING

$10,000 REWARD

Dead or Alive

DUFF MacCALLISTER
for MURDER *and* CATTLE RUSTLING

Houser was in the office of the *Hawk Springs Herald*, a newspaper in the nearby town of Hawk Springs, and he examined the printer's proof the editor of the paper had handed him.

"Yes, Mr. Denman, that will do quite nicely, thank you," Houser replied.

"I've never met Mr. MacCallister," Denman said. "But I know he's a big cattleman over near Chugwater."

"Yes," Houser replied. "And now we know how he acquired his wealth."

"I must say that I've never heard anything bad about him."

"He managed to hide it quite well for some time," Houser said. "But Governor Morgan, and Governor Hale before him, had long been suspicious of Duff MacCallister. That's why I was appointed a special deputy by the governor. Now I have the evidence I need to make the arrest."

"What I don't understand is, if you know where he is, why do you need a reward poster?"

"Oh, MacCallister is quite the wily one. If he gets word that we are onto him, he might well make good his escape. If so, I'll have these ready."

In the bunkhouse at Twin Peaks that night, Turley was awakened by a conversation going on between the deputies.

"First thing we're goin' to do," Jaco said, "is go out to the Pine Flats 'n take about a hunnert o' them cows we stole 'n move 'em over to Sky Meadow."

Even though Jaco thought he was speaking in a harsh whisper, Turley was able to overhear every word that was spoken.

"Why are we goin' to do that? Hell, we was the one that stoled the cattle, 'n we're s'posed to be gettin' some money for them cows. Why are we goin' to give 'em away like that?" Pete asked.

"We ain't actual givin' 'em away, we're just movin' 'em over there so's it looks like MacCallister is the one that stoled them."

"So we're goin' to accuse MacCallister of stealin'? Who's goin' to do that? Didn't you say he was the fastest man you ever seen?"

"We won't have to arrest him. All we have to do is kill 'im. 'N we'll most likely have some help with that," Jaco said.

"Have help? Help from who?"

"From anyone who wants the ten-thousand-dollar reward."

"What reward?"

"This one," Jaco said.

"Damn!" Pete said. "You mean there's actual dodgers out on MacCallister?"

"Yeah. Now, come on, we got to get them cows moved before it gets daylight."

Moving the stolen cows onto Sky Meadow wasn't the only nefarious act that the deputies did during the night. When the residents of Chugwater awakened the next morning, they were surprised to see a sudden plethora of wanted posters.

"Duff MacCallister murderin' and stealin'?" Duke Rudd said as he examined the reward bill that was posted to the front of his leather goods store. "I don't believe it."

Rudd's rejection of the charge that Duff was a murderer and cattle thief was nearly universal, as nobody else in town believed it, either.

Rudd took the poster to the sheriff's office, where he found Deputy Logan sitting at the sheriff's desk, drinking coffee.

"Deputy Logan, where's Sheriff Sharpie?"

"The sheriff won't be back till tomorrow. He took the train up to Cheyenne last night."

"Have you seen this?" Rudd asked, holding the poster out to show it.

"No," Logan said after examining it for a moment. "I'll be damn, accordin' to what it says here, this dodger comes direct from the governor his ownself. 'N look at the reward! Ten thousand dollars! Who but the governor could authorize that much money? Where did you get it?"

"This here one was nailed onto the front wall of my office."

"There's somethin' fishy about this," Logan said. "I've known Duff MacCallister ever since he settled here in the valley, and for as long as I have known him, he has been an honest and upstanding citizen. And how is it that these posters didn't come to the sheriff in the mail like all the others?"

"I don't know," Rudd answered. "But this isn't the only one. They're plastered all over town."

"I'm going to ride out to Sky Meadow and see what this is all about," Logan said, but as he and Rudd stepped out onto the front porch, they saw eight riders coming into town.

"That's Jaco 'n the territory deputies," Logan said, "but I don't know who the one in front is."

"I'll be damn," Rudd said. "That's Houser."

"Yeah," Logan agreed. "Yeah, you're right, that is Houser. What happened to that little beard he always wears?"

"Yeah, well, it ain't just the beard. He ain't wearin' a suit like always, 'n I don't think I've ever seen him on a horse before, neither."

Instead of the three-piece suit that Houser normally wore, today he was wearing black trousers, a black shirt, and a black, low-crown hat, which was encircled by a silver band. But the most shocking thing about his appearance was that Houser, who never carried a gun, was wearing one now. And he was wearing it in the way of a man who knew how to use it.

When Houser and the others reached the sheriff's office, they stopped. Deputy Logan was still holding the reward poster in his hand, and he held it up.

"Mr. Houser, are you responsible for this?"

"I am, sir."

"What right do you have to put out such a thing?"

"I'm sure that you know that I hold a special commission from the governor, and as such I am authorized to speak directly for him. My position gives me gubernatorial authority. It has come to my attention that Duff MacCallister, who is a man of some repute in this town, has been guilty of murder and cattle rustling. I owe an apology to the small ranchers, as I have been blaming them for the rustling, when it was MacCallister, all along."

"What makes you think it was Duff?"

"I don't think, sir, I know. We have found the stolen cattle on rangeland belonging to Duff MacCallister."

"Yeah? Well, I'm not going to arrest him," Logan said. "Maybe you can talk the sheriff into it when he gets back from Cheyenne tomorrow, but I'm not going to do it."

"I don't expect you to arrest MacCallister, or anyone else, for that matter," Houser replied. "I am suspending you from duty and asking you to take off your badge. I am declaring a condition of civil emergency, and as such, I, and my deputies, will, henceforth, assume all law enforcement activities. As of now, this town and all activity herein, is under my control."

"What?" Logan's shouted word was so loud that it caused passersby on the other side of the street to look over in curiosity. "The hell you say! There's no way I'm going to let you get away with a thing like that."

Houser drew his pistol and pointed it at Deputy Logan. "I said, take off your badge," he repeated ominously.

Reluctantly, but with no other choice, Logan removed his badge.

"Inside," Houser said, with a waving motion of his pistol. He followed Logan into the office. "Now, release my brother."

Logan took the key ring down from the wall hook, then walked back to the cell to open the door. Shamrock was standing there with a big smile.

"So, big brother," he said. "Have you decided to go back to being Wynton Miller?"

"Wynton Miller?" Logan gasped.

"Get into the cell," Houser ordered.

Sky Meadow Ranch

"Will you be comin' over to the buildin' site today, Mr. Gleason?" Emerson asked.

"I'll be along in a while," Elmer replied. He was watching Emerson and Percy load a wagon of tools and supplies needed at the site where Percy's new house was being built.

"Poke is already over there," Percy said. He chuckled. "He's a good kid, and one hell of a good worker."

"Yeah, he is," Emerson said. "He's better 'n anyone when it comes to climbin' around in the trusses. He can climb like a monkey."

Percy chuckled. "Steve, have you ever actually seen a monkey?"

"Well, no, but I've heard they can climb real good."

"That's a fact," Elmer said, thinking of the ones he had seen in China.

Elmer was about to go back in for another cup of coffee, when he saw someone coming up the long drive that led to the house.

"Here comes someone," he said. "More 'n likely someone wonderin' why you two hadn't got to work yet and . . ." He stopped and looked again as the rider came close enough to be identified.

"Why, that's Ben Turley from over to Houser's place. I wonder what he wants."

"Mornin', Mr. Gleason. Is Mr. MacCallister in?"

"Yeah, he's here. What do you need?"

"He might want to see this," Turley said, holding out the reward poster.

"From what I was able to overhear, they planned to take over the town 'n then just wait for you to come in," Turley said after he told of the stolen cattle that had been moved, during the night, onto Sky Meadow.

"Meagan is there. I will go."

"Mr. MacCallister, how do we know we can trust Turley?" Emerson asked. "Remember what happened to Kirk and Keegan."

"Turley speaks the truth," Wang said of Turley.

"Yeah, he sounds good. But how do we know?" Emerson repeated.

"He speaks the truth," Wang said again.

"If you're going into town, I'm going to go with you," Turley said. "You're worried about Miss Parker, 'n I'm worried about Mary Ellen."

"Yeah, I'll come with you, too," Emerson said, his declaration followed by Percy's own intention to go.

"'Tis good of you lads to volunteer," Duff said. "But I'll need only Elmer and Wang."

"But that will be only three of you, and there are nine of them," Turley said. He counted them off on his fingers. "There's Houser, Harris, Malcolm, Dobbins, Jaco, Wix, Pete, Hawke, and Evans. By the way, I learned that Harris is actually a man named Shamrock. Have you ever heard of him?"

"I cannae say as I have."

"Yeah, well, people don't change their names unless

they're on the dodge. And I haven't liked that son of a bitch since the first time I ever seen 'im."

"Boss, that's a lot of men for just the three of you to go up agin," Emerson said.

"Go and work on your house," Duff said. "They will be needing these things." He pointed to the wagon.

"All right, if you're sure you don't want us."

Chapter Thirty-five

Before they were close enough to be seen from town, Wang and Elmer left the main road so they could circle around and approach town from the opposite side. That left Duff as the only one, and he rode into town leisurely, as if making a normal visit. Dismounting in front of Meagan's Dress Emporium, he tied off his horse and saw in the mirror that was just inside the front window, somebody on the roof of Hart's Bakery, the building just across the street. The man on the roof was aiming his pistol at Duff, thinking that he had an easy shot.

Duff drew his pistol, whirled, and fired. The man on the roof grabbed his stomach, then pitched forward and fell, heavily, to the boardwalk in front of the bakery.

From just up the street Duff heard another shot and, looking toward the sound, saw someone go down. The shooter was Elmer, who smiled and waved at Duff, then stepped in between two buildings.

Catching a motion out of the corner of his eye,

Duff saw Wang, racing along the roofs of the town, leaping from building to building.

"MacCallister!" someone shouted, and three men stepped out into the street, all three with guns already drawn.

Even before the shooting began, one of the men went down, making a futile attempt to stem the flow of blood from around the throwing star in his neck. Duff shot the other two.

Duff started down the street toward the three bodies, when he heard someone behind him call his name.

"MacCallister!"

Turning, he saw someone coming out of Meagan's shop. Meagan was in front of him, and he was holding his pistol to her head.

"Drop your gun," the man called.

"Why should I do that?" Duff replied.

"Are you a fool? Can't you see I have a gun pointed to this woman's head? I heard that she's your woman. Is that true?"

"Aye, 'tis true. Meagan is my woman."

"I ain't goin' to ask you again to drop your gun."

Jaco was the deputy holding Meagan, and he was positioned in such a way that only about two inches of his head was exposed. But two inches was all Duff needed, and in a very swift and smooth action, Duff raised his pistol and fired. The bullet hit Jaco above the eye, killing him before he was even aware of Duff's action.

"Duff, in the livery!" Meagan shouted, even as Jaco was going down, but her warning wasn't necessary, for Evans, the deputy who was aiming a rifle at Duff from the loft of the livery, dropped his rifle and fell, mortally wounded by a shot from Elmer.

"Son of a bitch!" Shamrock said, looking through the front window of the sheriff's office. "All of 'em! MacCallister has kilt ever' damn one of 'em! Me 'n you's all that's left."

"Then the odds are just about right," Houser said with a confident smile. Houser loosened the pistol in his holster, then opened the door and stepped outside.

"Captain MacCallister," he called.

"Mr. Houser," Duff replied.

"It would appear that I have no deputies left, yet the issue remains. You are wanted for murder and rustling, so it is now incumbent upon me to bring you to justice."

"I suppose it makes nae difference to you, that I am innocent of the charges on the poster," Duff replied.

"Most astute of you, sir, you are right. That you are innocent of these charges makes no difference at all. I'm afraid I'm going to have to kill you."

"Are you that sure of yourself, Mr. Houser? It could be that you may be the one getting killed."

"Oh, I'm quite sure. And, by the way, for your edification, sir, before I assumed the *alias dictus* of Brad Houser, I was known as Wynton Miller. Perhaps that name means something to you."

"'Tis nae a name that is familiar to me," Duff replied.

Duff's declaration that he was unfamiliar with the name came as somewhat of a surprise to Houser.

"Well, it has been a while since I was known as such, and you, being a relatively recent immigrant, may not have heard of it. But, in some circles, I say with apologies for my pride, it does elicit a begrudging respect and, dare I say it, fear."

"I'll keep that in mind," Duff said.

"You have been busy this morning. So before we proceed any further, I feel it incumbent upon me to inquire if it is necessary for you to recharge your weapon. Have you sufficient bullets to engage?"

"I have two remaining. I need but one," Duff said.

"Shall we count?" Houser asked.

"Aye. Elmer?"

"Yeah?"

"Would you count to three, please?"

"One, two . . ."

Houser started his draw on two, but Duff was not surprised by his move. The moment Houser suggested that there be a count, Duff suspected that it was but a ploy to give Houser the advantage.

Duff let his "hand think," and even as Houser started his move, Duff's hand was already pulling the pistol from his holster. Houser was fast, faster even than Bodine, because whereas Bodine had barely completed his draw, Houser managed to bring his gun up and fire. The reason he missed was that the bullet that plunged into his chest had pulled his aim off.

Houser got a surprised look on his face, then fell.

As Duff stood there with a smoking gun in his hand, he heard another shot, and turning quickly, he saw Shamrock going down. Looking back to the source of the shot he saw that Meagan was also holding a smoking gun, having shot Shamrock with Jaco's pistol.

Six weeks later Percy and Sara Sue gave a party to celebrate moving into their new house. Everyone who had helped build the house was present, as were all the neighboring ranchers.

Ben Turley was there as well, along with his new bride, Mary Ellen. Turley was still foreman and, for now, sole custodian of Twin Peaks. Turley's first act was to return all the cattle that had been stolen, and illegally confiscated, by Houser. The court had already negated Houser's filing on the open range so that once again every rancher in the valley would have access to the grass and water.

Eventual ownership of Twin Peaks was now being decided by the court. A petition, signed by every other rancher in the valley, large and small, was submitted to the court, recommending that the ranch be owned by hands who had worked there, with Turley owning 51 percent. The preliminary indications were that the court would grant the petition.

"Oh, Sara Sue, your new house is beautiful," Meagan said.

"Yes, it is, thanks to our wonderful neighbors," Sara Sue replied. "And thank you for making this beautiful dress for the occasion."

"Miz Sara Sue, you want me to bring out the cakes now?" Poke asked.

"Yes, Poke, that would be very nice of you, thank you."

"How is it working out with Poke living with you

and Percy?" Meagan asked as Poke went back into the house to get the first of four cakes that had been baked.

"Poke is a wonderful boy," Sara Sue replied. "Percy and I were planning on having a family. Poke is just giving us a head start."

"Yes, having a family is a wonderful thing," Meagan said.

Meagan searched through the crowd until she found Duff, who was engaged in conversation with Webb Dakota, Burt Rowe, and Ben Turley.

"A wonderful thing," she repeated wistfully.

Chapter One

Dewey Mackenzie shivered as he pressed against the wet stone wall and blinked moisture from his eyes. Whether it came from the chilly rain that had fallen in New Orleans earlier this evening or from his own fear-fueled sweat—or both—he didn't know. He supposed it didn't matter.

Right now, he just wanted to avoid the two men standing guard across the street. Both were twice his size, and one had the battered look of a boxer. Even in the dim light cast by the gas lamp far down Royal Street, Mac saw the flattened nose, the cauliflower ears, and the way the man continually ducked and dodged imaginary punches.

At some time in the past, those punches hadn't been imaginary, and there had been a lot of them.

A medium-sized young man with longish dark hair and what had been described by more than one young woman as a roguish smile, Mac rubbed his hands against the sides of his fancy dress trousers and settled his Sunday go-to-meeting coat around his shoulders.

Carrying a gun on an errand like this was out of the question, but he missed the comforting feel of his Smith & Wesson Model 3 resting on his hip. He closed his eyes, licked his lips, and then sidled back along the wall until he reached the cross street. Like a cat, he slid around the corner to safety and heaved a huge sigh.

Getting in to see Evangeline Holdstock was always a chore, but after her pa had threatened him with death—or worse—if he caught him nosing around their mansion again, Mac had come to the only possible conclusion. He had been seeing Evangeline on the sly for more than two months, reveling in the stolen moments they shared. Even, if he cared to admit it to himself, enjoying the risks he was running.

He was little more than a drifter in the eyes of Micah Holdstock, owner of the second biggest bank in New Orleans. Holdstock measured his wealth in millions. The best the twenty-one-year-old could come up with was a bright, shiny silver cartwheel and a sweat-stained wad of Union greenbacks, but he had earned the money honestly at a restaurant in the French Quarter.

Mac held his hands in front of him and balled them into fists. He had worked as a farmhand and a half dozen jobs on riverboats before he washed ashore in the Crescent City three months earlier. Every bit of that work was honest, even if it didn't pay as well as sitting behind a bank desk and denying people loans.

He tried to erase such thoughts from his mind. Holdstock's bank served a purpose, and the man made his money honestly, too. It just wasn't the way

Mac earned his. It wasn't the way anyone else he'd ever known in his young life had earned their money, either.

If he wanted to carry out his mission tonight, he had to concentrate on that. He had gotten himself cleaned up for a simple reason.

Looking his best was a necessity when he asked Evie to marry him.

"Mrs. Dewey Mackenzie," he said softly. He liked the sound of that. "My wife. Mrs. Evangeline Mackenzie."

A quick peek around the corner down Royal Street dampened his spirits a mite. The two guards still stood in front of the door leading into the Holdstock house. Shifting his eyes from the street to the second story revealed a better way to get in without being caught and given a thrashing.

More than likely, Evie's pa had told those bruisers they could toss him into the river if they caught him snooping around. This time of year, the Mississippi River roiled with undertow and mysterious currents known only to the best of the riverboat pilots. It wasn't safe to swim anywhere near the port.

"Besides," he said softly to himself, "I don't want to muddy up my fancy duds." He smoothed wrinkles out of his coat, then boldly walked across the street without so much as a glance in the guards' direction.

He stopped and looked up when he was hidden by the wall. A black iron decoration drooped down from the railing around the second-story veranda just enough for him to grab. He stepped back a couple paces, got a running start, and made a grand leap. His fingers closed on the ornate wrought iron. With a powerful heave, he pulled himself up and got a leg over the railing.

Moving carefully to keep from tearing his trousers or getting his coat dirty, he dropped to the balcony floor and looked down to see if he had drawn any unwanted attention. Mac caught his breath when the guard who must have been a boxer came around the corner, scratched his head, and looked down the street. Moving quickly, Mac leaned back out of sight before the man looked up.

Senses acute with fear, he heard the guard shuffle away, heading back toward the door where his partner waited. Mac sank into a chair and used a handkerchief to wipe sweat from his forehead.

If this had been a couple of months later, he would have been drenched in sweat and for a good reason. Summer in New Orleans wore a man down with stifling heat and oppressive humidity, but now, late April, the sweat came from a different cause.

"Buck up," he whispered to himself. "Her pa can't stop you. You're going to marry the most wonderful girl in all New Orleans, and tonight's the night you ask for her hand."

Mac knew he had things backward, but considering how Mr. Holdstock acted, he wanted to be sure Evie loved him as much as he did her. Best to find out if she would marry him, *then* ask her pa for her hand in marriage. If Evie agreed, then to hell with whatever her pa thought.

He took a deep breath, reflecting on what she would be giving up. She claimed not to like the social whirl of a young debutante, but he had to wonder if some part of her didn't enjoy the endless attention, the fancy clothing, the rush of a cotillion followed by a soirée and whatever else they called a good old hoe-down in New Orleans society.

A quick look over the railing convinced him the guard had returned to his post. Stepping carefully, knowing from prior experience where every creaky board was, he made his way along the balcony to a closed window. The curtains had been pulled. He pressed his hand against the window pane, then peered into Evie's bedroom. Squinting, he tried to make out if she stood in the shadows. The coal-oil lamp had been extinguished, but if she was expecting him, she wouldn't advertise her presence.

He tried the door handle. Locked. Using his knife blade, he slipped it between the French doors and lifted slowly. When he felt resistance, he applied a bit more pressure. The latch opened to him, as it had so many times before. Evie liked to playact that he was a burglar come to rob her of her jewels, then ravish her.

The thought of that made him blush because he enjoyed it as much as she did. More than once, he had sneaked into her room and gone through the elaborate ritual of demanding her jewels, then forcing her to disrobe slowly to prove she had not hidden anything on her body. Both of them got too excited to ever carry on with the charade for more than a few minutes. He went to the bed now and pressed down on it with his fingers, remembering the times they had made love here.

Mac swung around and sat, wondering how long he should wait before he went hunting for her.

For all he knew, her ma and pa were out for the

night. Their social life mingled with Holdstock's banking business and caused them to attend parties and meetings throughout the week to maintain their standing in the community. Mac got antsy after less than a minute and went to the bedroom door. Carefully opening it, he looked down the hallway. Evie's room was at the back of the house, while her parents had the room at the front, at the far end of the hallway lined with fancy paintings and marble sculptures. The Persian rug muffled his footfalls as he made his way to the head of the stairs.

The broad fan of steps swept down to the foyer. He ducked back when he heard Holdstock speaking with someone at the door. From the guest's accent, he was French. That meant little in a town filled with Frenchmen and Acadians. French Creole was almost as widely spoken as English or Spanish.

"I am glad we could meet, Monsieur Leclerc. Come into the study. I have a fine cigar from Cuba that you will find delightful."

"*Bon*, good, Mr. Holdstock. And brandy?"

"Only the finest French brandy."

The two laughed and disappeared from sight. Mac cursed his bad luck. It would have been better if Holdstock were out of the house rather than entertaining—or conducting business, judging by the formality the two showed one another. Some high-powered deal was being struck not fifty feet away. That deal would undoubtedly make the banker rich. Or richer than he already was.

But Mac didn't care about that. His riches were wrapped in crinoline and lace, with flowing blond hair and eyes as green as jade. He stepped back and wondered where she might be.

Then he heard her soft voice below as she greeted Monsieur Leclerc and exchanged a few mumbled pleasantries. The sound of her slippers moving against the foyer floor set his heart racing. He hastily retreated to her bedroom and closed the door behind him. From past times here, he knew the exact spot to stand.

Beside her wardrobe, hidden in shadow when she lit the oil lamp, he could cherish her for a few seconds before she realized she was not alone. Mac pressed into the niche just as the door opened. He closed his eyes and took a deep whiff. Jasmine perfume made his nostrils flare. This was her favorite perfume, but he told her often she did not need it, not with him. Just being around her intoxicated his senses more than enough.

He opened his eyes and squinted as he stared directly into the burning wick of Evie's bedside lamp. She bent over slightly, hands on the bed, her bustle wiggling delightfully.

"I have never seen any woman so lovely," he said. "If I live to be a thousand, I never will forget this moment, this sight, this beautiful—"

She straightened and spun. Her eyes went wide. His heart almost skipped a beat when he realized it wasn't surprise that caused her face to contort. It was fear.

"What's wrong, my dear?" He went to her, but she pushed him back.

"Go, Mac. Get out of here now. Please. Don't slow down. He knows we've been seeing each other."

"I don't care. I love you. Do you love me?"

"Yes, yes," she said, flustered. She brushed back a wayward strand of lustrous, honey blond hair and looked up at him. True fear twisted her face. "I love you with all my heart and soul, Mac. That's why you have to leave."

"Then let's go together. Let's elope. We can find a justice of the peace. We don't have to get married in the St. Louis Basilica."

"Mac, you don't understand. I—"

"I can't give you a fancy house or fine clothing or jewelry like this." He touched the pearl necklace around her slender throat, then moved to caress her cheek. "Not now. Someday I will. Together we can—"

"You have to go before he catches you!"

"I'll go down and beard the old lion in his den. We'll have it out, man to man. I won't let him chase me off from the love of my life." He moved her around so he could go to the door.

Before he could get there, the door slammed open, reverberating as it smashed into the wall. Silhouetted against the light from downstairs, Micah Holdstock filled the frame.

"I should have known you would come, especially on a night like this!"

Mac began, "Mr. Holdstock, I—"

"Papa, please, you can't do this. Don't hurt him." Evie tried to interpose herself between the men, but Mac wouldn't have it. No woman he loved sacrificed herself for him, especially with her father.

"Evie and I love each other, sir. We're getting married!"

Micah Holdstock let out a roar like a charging bull. The attack took Mac by surprise. Strong arms encircled his body and lifted him off his feet. He tried to get his arms free but couldn't with them pinned at his sides. Still roaring, Holdstock went directly for the French doors and smashed through them. Shards of glass sprayed in the air and tumbled to the balcony as he used Mac as a battering ram.

The collision robbed Mac of breath. He went limp in the man's death grip. This saved him from being driven against the iron railing and having his back broken. He dropped to his knees as Holdstock crashed into the wrought-iron railing and fought to keep from tumbling into the street below.

"Papa," he heard Evie pleading, trying to stop the attack.

Mac got to shaky feet to face her pa.

"This is no way for future in-laws to act," he gasped out. "My intentions are honorable."

"She's betrothed. As of this very evening!" Again Holdstock charged.

Mac saw the expression of resignation on Evie's face an instant before her father's hard fist caught him on the side of the head and sent him reeling. He grabbed the iron railing and went over, dangled a moment, then fell heavily to the cobblestone street and sprawled onto his back. He stared up to see Evie sobbing bitterly as her father grabbed her by the arm and pulled her out of sight.

"You can't do this. I won't let you!" He got to his feet in time to see the two guards round the corner.

From the way they were hurrying, he knew what they had been ordered to do.

Shameful though it might be, he turned and ran.

The guards' bulk meant they were slower on their feet than Mac was. Three blocks later, he finally evaded them by ducking into a saloon in Pirate's Alley. He leaned against the wall for a moment, catching his breath. The smoke in the dive formed a fog so thick it wasn't possible to see more than a few feet. He coughed, then went to the bar and collapsed against it. "I say this to damned near ever'body what comes into this place," the barkeep said, "but in your case I mean it. You look like you could use a drink."

Chapter Two

The bartender poured a shot of whiskey.

Mac knocked it back, and it almost knocked him down. He wasn't much of a drinker, but this had to be the most potent popskull he had ever encountered. He choked, swallowed, then said, "Another."

"The first was on the house. The next one you pay for."

"I just had a run-in with my lady friend's pa." He sucked in a breath and endured the pain in his ribs. Micah Holdstock had a grip like a bear. The powerful liquor went a ways toward easing the pain. He fumbled out a greenback for another drink. He needed all the deadening he could pour down his gullet.

The bartender picked up the bill, examined it, and tucked it away. "Don't usually take Yankee bills, but seeing's as how you're in pain, I will this time." He splashed more whiskey into Mac's empty glass.

Mac started to protest at not getting change. As the second shot hit his gut and set his head spinning, he forgot about it. What difference did it make anyway?

He had to find a way to sneak Evie out of the house and get her to a judge for a proper marrying.

"Do tell."

Mac blinked and frowned. He hadn't realized he had been talking out loud, but obviously the bartender knew what he'd been thinking. He ran a shaky finger around the rim of his empty shot glass and captured the last amber drop. He licked it off his fingertip. The astringent burn on his tongue warned him that another drink might make him pass out.

"I'll find a way," he said, with more assurance than he felt. He needed both hands on the bar to support himself.

As he considered a third drink, he noticed how the sound in the saloon went away. All he heard was the pounding of his pulse in his ears. Thinking the drink had turned him deaf, he started to shout out for another, then saw the frightened expression on the barkeep's face. Looking over his shoulder, he saw the reason.

The two guards who had been stationed outside Micah Holdstock's front door now stood just inside the saloon, arms crossed over their chests. Those arms bulged with muscles. The men fixed steely gazes on him. Out of habit—or maybe desperation—Mac patted his right hip but found no revolver hanging there. He had dressed up for the occasion of asking Evie to marry him. There hadn't been any call for him to go armed.

He knew now that was a big mistake. He turned and had to brace himself against the bar with both elbows. He blinked hard, as much from the smoke as the tarantula juice he had swilled. Hoping he saw double and only one guard faced him, he quickly realized how wrong that was. There were two of them, and they had blood in their eyes.

"You gonna stand there all night or you gonna come for me?" He tried to hold back the taunt but failed. The liquor had loosened his tongue and done away with his common sense. Somewhere deep down in his brain, he knew he was inviting them to kill him, but he couldn't stop himself. "Well? Come on!" He balanced precariously, one foot in front of the other, fists balled and raised.

The one who looked like a boxer stirred, but the other held him back.

"Waiting for the bell to ring? Come on. Let's mix it up." He took a couple of tentative punches at thin air.

"Mister, that's Hiram Higgins," the bartender said, reaching across the bar to tug at his sleeve. "He lost to Gypsy Jem Mace over in Kennerville."

"So that just means he can lose to me just east of Jackson Square."

"Mister, Gypsy Jem whupped Tom Allen the next day for the heavyweight championship."

"So? You said this man Higgins lost."

"He lost after eighteen rounds. Ain't nobody stayed with the Gypsy longer 'n that. The man's a killer with those fists."

Mac wasn't drunk enough to tangle with Holdstock's guard, not after hearing that. But the boxer stepped away deferentially when a nattily dressed man stepped into the saloon. The newcomer carefully pulled off gloves and clutched them in his right hand. He took off a tall top hat and disdainfully tossed it to the boxer. Walking slowly, the man advanced on Mac.

"You are the one? *You?*" He stopped two paces away from Mac, slapping the gloves he held in his right hand across his left palm.

"I'm your worst nightmare, mister." Still emboldened by the booze, Mac flipped the frilled front of the man's bleached white shirt. A diamond stud popped free. The man made no effort to retrieve it from the sawdust on the floor. He stared hard at Mac.

"You are drunk. But of course you are. Do you know who I am?"

"Not a clue. Some rich snake in the grass from the cut of your clothes." Mac tried to flip his finger against the man's prominent nose this time. A small turn of the man's head prevented him from delivering the insulting gesture.

"I am Pierre Leclerc, the son of Antoine Leclerc."

"I've heard the name. Somewhere." Mac tried to work out why the name was familiar. His head buzzed with a million bees inside it, and he was definitely seeing double now. Two of the annoying men filled his field of vision. He tried to decide which one to punch.

"He owns the largest shipping company in New Orleans. It is one of the largest in North America."

"So? You're rich. What of it?"

"You will leave Miss Evangeline Holdstock alone. You will never try to see her again. She wants nothing to do with you."

"Why's that, Mister Fancy Pants?"

"Because she and I are to be married. This very night my father arranged for her hand in marriage to unite her father's bank and our shipping company."

"Your pa's gonna marry her?"

"You fool!" Leclerc exploded. "You imbecile. *I* am to marry Miss Holdstock. You have given me the last insult that will ever cross your lips." He reared back and slapped Mac with the gloves. A gunshot would have been quieter as cloth struck flesh.

Mac stumbled and caught himself against the bar. He rubbed his burning cheek.

"Why you—"

"You may choose your weapons. At the Dueling Oaks, tomorrow at sunrise. Be there promptly or show the world—and Miss Holdstock—the true depth of your cowardice." Leclerc slapped his gloves across his left palm for emphasis, spun and walked from the saloon. The two guards followed him.

"What happened?" Mac said into the hollow silence that hung in the air when Leclerc was gone. He was stunned into sobriety.

"You're going to duel for this hussy's favor at sunrise," the bartender said.

"With guns?"

"You'd be wise to choose pistols. Leclerc is a champion fencer. He can cut a man to ribbons with a saber and walk away untouched."

"Heard tell he's a crack shot, too," piped up someone across the saloon.

"Eight men he's kilt in duels," another man said. "The fella's a fightin' machine—a killin' machine. I don't envy you, boy. Not at all."

Mac found himself pushed away from the bar by men rooting around in the sawdust looking for the diamond stud that had popped off Leclerc's shirt. He watched numbly, wondering if he ought to join the hunt. That tiny gemstone could pay for passage up the river.

Then he worked through what that meant. Evie would call him a coward for the rest of her life. And running would show how little her love meant to him. He loved her with all his heart and soul.

If it meant he laid down his life for her, so be it. He would be north of town at the Dueling Oaks at dawn.

After another drink.

Or two.